54x 8/20

# 13½

**Center Point
Large Print**

Also by Nevada Barr
and available from Center Point Large Print:

*Winter Study*
*Borderline*

**This Large Print Book carries the
Seal of Approval of N.A.V.H.**

# 13½

# NEVADA BARR

CENTER POINT PUBLISHING
THORNDIKE, MAINE

For Barbara Peters,
who moves mountains without
breaking a sweat.

---

This Center Point Large Print edition
is published in the year 2009 by arrangement with
Vanguard Press, a division of Perseus Books Group.

The text of this Large Print edition is unabridged.
In other aspects, this book may vary
from the original edition.
Printed in the United States of America.
Set in 16-point Times New Roman type.

ISBN: 978-1-60285-618-9

Library of Congress Cataloging-in-Publication Data

Barr, Nevada.
  13 1/2 / Nevada Barr.
    p. cm.
  ISBN 978-1-60285-618-9 (library binding : alk. paper)
  1. Women college teachers--Fiction. 2. New Orleans (La.)--Fiction.
    3. Large type books. I. Title. II. Title: Thirteen and one-half.
  PS3552.A73184A614 2009b
  813'.54--dc22
2009027274

---

*Butcher Boy. Killed mother, father, sister, and the family cat.*

*"We get to the upstairs hall, and Pat finds a light switch. You're not going to want to print this next part, but by God this is how it was. In the middle of the rug—one of those long narrow hall rugs—was a baby, a little girl no more than two, and she had been cut in half. I about puked, and Pat looked like he was going to.*

*"We hear movement downstairs and think maybe it's the killer. Or somebody hurt. Pat goes first.*

*"In the back bedroom there's two boys. At first we thought both of them had been murdered. The older boy nearly had his leg cut off and had bled so much he was the color of a sheet of paper. The other boy was still in his bed, but at first we didn't even know it was a kid, you know? It just looked like a bucket of red paint poured over some blankets.*

*"Turns out this kid—the one in the bed—has got nothing wrong with him, he's just sleeping like a baby. Or that's what we thought at the time. The ambulance rolls up, so there's paramedics stomping all over everything trying to save the kid with the chopped-up leg when this little bast\*\*rd wakes up from his beauty sleep. He sees his brother being carried out more dead than alive, and he starts laughing like a hyena."*

---

# PROLOGUE

"By the Month or by the Night" read the sign over the entrance to the trailer park.

Wind, cold for April, chased dirt and beer cans up the gravel street. Clutching her geometry book to her chest, Polly stood on the wooden step outside the door of her mother's trailer, her ear pressed against the aluminum. The icy bite of metal against her skin brought on a memory so sharp all she felt was its teeth. She'd been almost nine years old.

*A nightmare* was what she thought. Nightmares had ripped apart her dreams since she could remember. Something heavy pressed on her back, pinning her to the mattress, mashing her face into the pillow so she couldn't breathe. The smell of whiskey and cigarettes came into the dream, and Polly knew it was real life. In her dreams, she never smelled things.

It was Bernie. He'd been looking at her all hot-eyed and smarmy until Hilda got pissed and made her go to bed early. Though Polly's ninth birthday wasn't for a couple weeks, she already knew what it meant when men's eyes went gooey and nasty.

Hot as an iron, his hand pushed down on the middle of her back, burning through her thin pajama top. Like a bug pinned to a board, she thrashed, arms and legs scrabbling against the tangle of sheets.

Easy as shucking an ear of corn, Bernie stripped off her pajama bottoms.

Hilda had told her what would happen if Bernie ever came into her room at night. She'd cut his balls off and make Polly eat them.

With a wrench that made her neck hurt, Polly got her face free of the pillow and screamed.

His hand left her back, grabbed her hair and pulled her head up. His other huge stinking paw slapped over her nose and mouth.

"Shut up. Your mom's so fuckin' drunk, she ain't gonna hear. You stay quiet and we'll have a fine old time. Fun. We'll have us some fun. Bernie knows how to make a little girl sing like a bird. Tweet, tweet. Now, you gonna stay quiet?"

Polly managed a fraction of a nod between the slabs of flesh imprisoning her head.

"Tweet, tweet," he said again. Bernie was such an incredible asshole.

He took his hand away, and Polly screamed with every bit of air left in her lungs. She twisted and bucked. Hair was yanked out, but the pain made her stronger, and she clawed at any part of Bernie she could find.

Her room was never real dark, not like in-the-woods-at-night dark. The trailer park had big security lights everywhere, and the light leaked in around the curtains—when she'd had curtains.

Since the sun had rotted them off, the room's single high window was her own private moon, always full and stupidly square.

Bernie was naked and his thing was poking up like a big old dead stick sticking out of a swamp. It made her scream even louder.

"God damn it!" Bernie hissed and grabbed her face to cover her mouth again. She was yelling and a thick finger went into her mouth. Polly bit down and bit and bit and bit and now Bernie was screaming. He shook her and she felt herself lifted clean off the bed, but she didn't stop biting. Then he threw her so hard her teeth came free; blood and a chunk of flesh came away. The stuff went down her throat. She was a cannibal now.

"I eat people!" she screamed. "I'll kill you and eat you. Momma will cut off your balls, and I'll put them on my Lucky Charms and eat them for breakfast."

The light came on. Hilda was standing in the doorway, still wearing what she'd had on when Polly had gone to bed, but all wrinkled, like she'd been sleeping in her clothes.

"Momma," Polly whispered. Hilda never let her boyfriends mess with Polly.

"Bastard!" Hilda yelled. "You fucking bastard!"

"Momma," Polly cried. Scrambling to her feet, she launched herself at her mother and wrapped her skinny arms around Hilda's waist.

"Cunt," her mother shrieked. "You fucking little

9

cunt." She slapped Polly so hard she saw red things in her eyes.

That was the night Polly realized that what she had taken for caring in Hilda wasn't so much looking after her daughter as having jealous rages.

Bang.

Bang.

Bang.

Polly hit her forehead against the cold aluminum of the trailer door driving the memory out. She was fifteen, not nine—there had to be a statute of limitations on bad memories.

"Nobody's fucking home. Beat it!" was shouted from inside.

Sighing, she turned her back on the racket, put her geometry book on the peeling paint of the step so she wouldn't get her good school skirt dirty, and sat, shoulders against the scarred and dented door. Through the thin aluminum, she listened to the tide of battle ebbing and flowing.

In European history, they had been reading about the Hundred Years' War. England and France had nothing on Polly's mother and stepfathers; they'd been going at it as long as she could remember. The only thing that changed was the stepfathers' names. Used to be, they had married her mother, but the last two or three hadn't bothered.

Why Hilda kept dragging men home was a mystery. It wasn't like they brought money or glamour.

Stinky shoes, hairy backs, and hard fists were more like it. Polly was determined never to get married. "No men," she yelled as somebody crashed against the door.

Except to have kids, she amended silently. More than anything, she wanted kids to protect, love, and teach; to keep safe and happy.

Another spate of profanity scattered her thoughts. It was getting cold. And now she had to go to the bathroom.

A couple times when it looked like somebody was going to kill somebody, she'd called the cops, but they just hauled Hilda or the boyfriend in, and when they came back it was worse than before. "Get over it!" she yelled in the general direction of her left shoulder. "Kill each other or make up. I got to pee! God!" She slumped back against the trailer.

This was the third time this week she'd come home to World War III. When the weather was nice it was easier to deal with. She could go sit in the woods if it wasn't too buggy, or walk down to Prentiss's tiny all-purpose corner store and get a milkshake if she had the money or kill time leafing through the magazines on the rack if she didn't. Mrs. Chandler didn't mind, as long as there were no other kids around.

Mrs. Chandler knew why Polly couldn't go home, but she was too nice to let on. Polly appreciated that. That changed her letting Polly hang around the store from charity to friendship.

"The Farmers don't take charity," her mother would say when she was sober enough to be embarrassed that someone else wanted to do for her daughter what she could not.

*That was a lot of malarkey.*

They'd been on welfare off and on since the third—or maybe the fourth—stepfather had gone north to Chicago, where he was going make a killing in the oil fields and then send for them.

*Truckloads of malarkey.*

Polly's mom had waited by the phone until Polly told her there weren't any oil fields in Chicago.

A fist or a foot or a head slammed into the door. Polly pounded back angrily with the flat of her hand.

"Would you pass out so I can go to the bathroom!" she yelled.

Ma Danko, the old colored woman who lived two trailers down, looked up from the laundry basket she cradled in her stick-thin arms.

"Why don't you come on home with me and have some cookies?" Ma said.

"I better not, but thanks," Polly replied. "You know how it is."

"I do. But you come on anyway if it starts raining."

"I will."

But she wouldn't. Of all charity, Polly's mom hated charity from Negroes the worst. "You just remember you're white," her mother would say. "Niggers got no business feeling sorry for a white girl."

A scudding wind picked up leaves and litter and threw them at Polly in cold mockery. "It's getting downright chilly," Ma said. "It's gonna be a bitter rain. Cookies is still warm from the oven."

"It won't be long now," Polly assured her. The banging inside the trailer was growing sluggish. Nodding, Ma Danko walked on.

Polly pulled up the backside of her full skirt and pinched it around her shoulders to keep warm. Ten minutes passed, fifteen. Finally the noise stopped. She stood and smoothed her skirt back into place. Turning the knob slowly so it wouldn't make noise, she opened the door a couple of inches and peeked in.

Her mom was on the couch crying. Tom, the most recent stepfather, wasn't anywhere in the kitchen-cum-living-room. *American Bandstand* was on the TV. Girls in fringed dresses were twisting in spotlights.

Polly slipped in and closed the door. The kitchen was a mess of dirty dishes. A Miller's can lay on its side weeping beer onto the linoleum, but the lamps were still upright and none of the dishes looked broken.

*All's well that ends well,* Polly thought. It was the title of a play they were reading in sophomore English. She set the geometry book on the kitchen counter and went to the couch to see if her mother was bleeding.

"What're you lookin' at," Hilda Farmer snapped.

"Nothing," Polly said. No blood, no swelling: Tom hadn't hit her. Tom wasn't so bad. He yelled a lot but he kept his hands to himself and never hit unless Hilda stayed in his face too long. Two of Hilda's front teeth were missing, but that wasn't Tom's fault. It was nobody's fault. They'd just rotted and the dentist had to pull them. The bridge with the false teeth was on the counter near the toaster. When Hilda started into fighting mode, she always took them out so they wouldn't get broken.

"What're you doin' home?" Hilda demanded, slurring her words.

Drunker than a skunk. Hilda didn't slur until she'd gone through at least a couple of six-packs.

"School's out. It's nearly four."

"Big deal high school girl," Hilda sneered. "You think you're so damned smart."

Polly's mother never made it to high school. At thirteen, she'd gotten knocked up. When she was on a toot, she'd tell this to whoever would listen, as if Polly had intentionally interfered with the higher education of Miss Hilda Farmer by intruding in a womb that did not want her.

"So damn smart."

"That's right, Momma," Polly said.

"None of your lip."

Hilda forgot she was crying. Reaching out blindly, she felt around until her hand closed on a beer can on the end table.

Drinking deeply, she stared at the television.

"They think that's dancing," she said sullenly. "Wiggling their behinds and shaking their topsides. When I was young we *danced*."

*When I was young.*

Hilda was twenty-eight. When she was Polly's age she'd had a two-year-old daughter.

"Miss High and Mighty Sophomore, just you wait," Hilda said never taking her eyes from the television. "One day it'll be you sitting here, and some snot-nosed kid looking down on you, and there ain't one thing you can do about it, not one damn thing. No high school *dip-low-maaah* is going to get you there." She pointed at the black-and-white figures frugging on the screen. TV-land was akin to heaven in Hilda's mind.

"Dancing!" she snarled. "What a load of crap."

Polly left her to her beer and bellyaching and went to her room. It was so small, if she lay crosswise on the bed, she could put the soles of her feet on one wall and the palms of her hands on the other.

She hung her school clothes carefully in the closet, then pulled on her dungarees and an old sweater left behind by the truck driver her mom had taken up with before Tom. Sitting on the edge of the unmade bed, she stared at the wall between her room and the master bedroom. The wood was so thin she could hear Tom snoring. If she squinted she could imagine the wall sucking and puffing out.

"One day it'll be you . . ."

The wall sucked in.

". . . a snot-nosed kid looking down . . ."

The wall puffed out.

Polly rose, slid open the pocket door, and stepped into the narrow hallway. The door to the master bedroom was open. Flat on his back, spread-eagle on the mess of sheets and blankets, Tom snored, his whole throat collapsing between breaths. His pants were unbuttoned; he'd gotten them half off before he'd passed out.

Polly looked over her shoulder. Hilda was still absorbed in abusing Dick Clark. She tiptoed into the bedroom, though, given Tom's condition, she could probably have roared in on a Harley and he wouldn't have stirred.

Slipping her hand under his half-exposed buttock, she massaged gently until his wallet poked out of the pocket, then lifted it with the dexterity of long practice.

"Baby," Tom muttered, and a fist hit her smack in the eye. Blinded and shocked, Polly fell back. He hadn't struck out at her. He'd been reaching for Hilda in some drunken place they were together. The eye watered copiously. She'd get a shiner out of this for sure. After all the times she'd made up stupid stories at school to explain away bruises, this time the story was so stupid it was true. With the back of her hand, she smeared the tears away and opened his wallet. Twelve bucks. She took all but one. She also took the condom he carried.

Maybe he'd think he spent the eleven dollars on a whore.

Nobody'd bother to use a condom with Hilda. She'd had female troubles. No more kids.

Dropping the wallet on the floor where it might have fallen by accident, Polly stuffed the cash into the pocket of her jeans.

Hilda was still instructing the dance contestants. Her purse was on the counter next to her teeth. Polly felt through Hilda's ratty faux-leather clutch until her fingers closed on the car keys.

"I'm walking down to the little store. Want anything?"

"Shaking their heinies like niggers," Hilda said. The rain had started. Polly ran for the car. She wasn't old enough to have a license but she knew how to drive. It was an important skill to a mother who needed somebody to run to the liquor store when she was "too tired" to go herself. As long as Polly said the beer was for Hilda, Mr. Cranbee had no trouble letting her buy it.

When she'd taken the keys she'd only meant to drive around, air herself off without getting as wet as a drowned rat, listen to the radio—rock and roll out of Jackson if she could get a signal, gospel if she couldn't. There was a gospel station in Natchez that always came in clear. If there was enough gas in the tank she might drive toward Jackson. There was an Arctic Circle in Crystal Springs and, with

Tom's money, she could get a burger or something for dinner.

At the junction with Highway 61 she didn't do either; she just stopped in the middle of the road and turned the ignition off. The windshield wipers froze halfway through their arc. Rain poured down. It was as if the dusk were melting into night. Polly turned off the car's lights. Maybe a semi would smash into her sitting there in the dark.

To her right was the sign for New Orleans: 168 miles. She'd never been to New Orleans. Neither had Hilda. For the good people of Prentiss, New Orleans was the New World's answer to both Sodom and Gomorrah.

Across the highway was a sign reading "Jackson 73 miles." This time of day, in the rain, there wasn't any traffic. Any time of the day, in any weather, there wasn't much. The old Fairlane creaking as the engine cooled, Polly sat, unable to go forward or turn back. There wasn't any place in Mississippi a girl like her could go where a trailer didn't wait.

. . . *and there's not one thing you can do about it. Not one damn thing.*

In the pouring dark of the rain Polly could see the path of her life clearly: a long tunnel growing narrower and narrower until, in the last tiny circle of light, there was a trailer park and, in a line of a dozen or more at the front gate, a mailbox with her name on it. That was death—death after murder is committed and final absolution not obtained. Hell.

*Macbeth*, another play they'd read in English, came to mind. Everybody hated it. Everybody but the teacher and Polly. *If 'twere done, best it 'twere done quickly.*

She turned the ignition key and headed for New Orleans in a stolen car. At La Place, she ran out of gas. Polly didn't want to spend her precious eleven dollars. She put the ignition keys in the glove box and got out of the car. Maybe the cops would find it and take it back to Hilda. Polly liked that idea. If she didn't have the Fairlane Hilda wouldn't try to find her.

She walked to the side of the road and stuck out her thumb.

The man who picked her up was going to Bourbon Street. "Bourbon ain't no place for a kid," was about all he said in the two hours they rode together. The rain had stopped but, with the darkness and the trees, there wasn't anything to look at but the furrow cut by the pickup's headlights. Polly stared at it and felt as if she were falling down a long tunnel, and she wondered if there were worse places to end up than a trailer park in Mississippi.

When the lights of New Orleans lifted the night something akin to hope—but not so grand—lifted Polly's spirits. The man stopped at the corner of St. Ann's and Chartres, or so said the street signs. "Jackson Square," he said. "There's a pay phone on the corner. Call your folks," he said. "Go home."

Polly got out of the truck. "I don't have any folks," she said.

"Suit yourself."

Polly didn't watch him drive away.

Except in a picture book she'd had once of a little girl getting her tonsils out, she'd never seen anything like Jackson Square. The square in the book had been somewhere in England and clean and friendly. Jackson Square was like that place had been stomped until it looked like the fairgrounds after the fair moved on: the dirt full of ground-in sno-cones, cotton candy, and cigarette butts.

She wasn't alone but the people, mostly men, were what her mother would call "white trash." Most of them were smoking and looking around like they were waiting for somebody. There were a few women. Even green from Mississippi, Polly knew they were hookers.

One wasn't. She was sitting at a table with candles on it. She looked as if she'd stepped right out of a storybook: turban, many-colored skirt, hoop earrings. On the rickety table were a crystal ball and a deck of cards. The good churchgoing folks in Prentiss, Mississippi, preached that foretelling the future, playing with the Ouija board, or dressing up as an Indian princess instead of a favorite apostle on the thirty-first of October begged Satan and his minions to stampede in and snatch up the soul. The desperation that had given her the courage to run from Prentiss had dulled. Polly could feel fear trying to break through. On the long drive she'd had to work hard not to think about scary things: food, shelter, money. Now, Satan.

People could tell the future; Polly knew that. Men in the Bible did it all the time. It was okay when they did it, but not okay when a regular person did it. Not that her mom was a big church-goer but a girl didn't grow up in Prentiss without knowing there were about a zillion ways to go to hell and dabbling in black magic was a big one.

The gypsy woman looked up as if she'd felt Polly's eyes on her and smiled. "Come on, honey. Let me read your cards," she called. "I'll tell you your fortune."

If ever somebody needed to know what was going to happen to her, Polly was that somebody.

Satan's hell couldn't be all that much worse than Hilda's.

# MINNESOTA, 1968

---

*John List. Killed wife, mother, and three kids. Sure. I can see killing like this. This List guy had God on his side. That makes it work for him. He wants out of this family thing. He's pussy-whipped, and his mother's a nag, and he doesn't have the balls to leave—that or he thinks a godly guy like him can't leave the kiddies—he figures all these folks he's responsible for are going to go to hell if they keep on sinning the way they have. So, he figures he'll just send them up to heaven quick and save their souls. Like a good daddy. He throws in mom and wife for good measure. It makes sense to me. What kind of louses it up is John takes a powder. If he's Mr. Godly, why doesn't he stay and take the hit? Maybe he thinks, God's got to love me for shipping him five nice angels. Maybe he has other jobs for his good buddy John, so I better keep my ass out of prison.*

*Yeah, I can see doing the List list. Is that what you wanted to hear?*

---

# 1

Richard was hurt bad. He knew it with the awful certainty one feels in that second when he steps back off a cliff and realizes it will be the last mistake he makes on this earth; that eternity of horror before his body smashes on the rocks.

Freakish light filtered through the snowstorm, the bright orange of sodium arc lamps picked up and tossed back by ten billion ice facets: sky, ground, tree limbs, air. Rooms in the house were orange, the whole world the inside of a Halloween pumpkin.

In light the color of fire, Richard couldn't tell how much blood he was losing. A lot. Too much. He could feel it pumping, little squirts against the palm of his hand. For a giddy second he believed the blood flowed into him from the night and out of him from his veins, a pool, a lake, rising.

His little brother lay across the bed where he had fallen. On Dylan's pajamas cowboys and Indians were drenched in red, a war on flannel. Blood ran in a sheet down the right side of Dylan's face.

Dylan looked dead.

"Dyl?" Richard tried to call out but he hadn't strength for more than a whisper. "Dylan, don't you die on me." Richard started to cry, then stopped himself. Taking a deep breath, he tried again. "Dylan, if you're awake, call the operator, the police."

His brother didn't move.

From boy scouts and television, Richard knew if he took his hand away from the gaping wound on his inner thigh, he would bleed out. For a heartbeat or two he considered letting go, lifting his hand, and watching his life pump out of his body. It seemed so eager to leave him, and there'd been so much carnage, why not give in? Drift into the abyss?

Dylan moaned softly. Despite the muffling effect of death dreams, in the absolute stillness of a snowy midnight it grated loud in Richard's ears. He hadn't killed him—his brother was alive.

Dream evaporated; abyss ceased to beckon. Suddenly Rich wanted to live. "Brother," he whispered. Dylan's eyelids twitched. Richard saw a flash of white eyeball, startling in the drying red mask. "Wake up, buddy. Please."

Using one hand and his uninjured leg for propulsion, the other hand clamped tightly over his wound, Richard tried to move across the bedroom floor. Fabric and blood stuck him to the hardwood. By inches—one, three, five—he moved toward Dylan. The effort was so great there wasn't room left for thought. Each tiny movement brought a calamity of pain. The pain had ceased to be localized; his entire being was on fire.

*Don't. Pass. Out.* He forced the words through the clamor of nerve-death in his mind.

Dylan's head lolled off the edge of the mattress at an unnatural angle.

His neck was broken. Dylan would be in a wheelchair, peeing through a tube. A ragged end of strength rippled through Richard. Dylan would be helpless; he would need his brother. More than anything Richard wanted to be there.

*Push your chair, brother. Take you for walks in the park.* An inch. Two. Behind him on the hard-wood was a smeared trail of red. The room was so damn big.

Richard's arm was failing; his uninjured leg cramped. Blinking to stay conscious, he tried to remember why he was bleeding across this waste-land.

The phone. Dial 0, the operator, and ask for the police. The phone on the nightstand looked impossibly far away, as if viewed through the wrong end of a telescope.

"Dylan!" Richard screamed. Dylan didn't move and Richard was out of air.

*Rest.* He would rest a moment. Leaning against the bureau, he watched the orange light pulsate deeper, then paler. It made him sleepy.

*Don't sleep; stay awake,* he warned himself. *Never sleep; your hand will come loose. Sleep is death.* He would just rest a moment or two; then, when he was stronger, he would continue his journey to the telephone, to 0 and rescue.

"Water," he croaked, seeing in his mind the

parched desert crawlers of late-night TV Westerns. He was so thirsty he could have cried. He licked his lips and tasted Vondra. After he'd left her, he'd showered and brushed his teeth, but the taste was still there.

Vondra. He had been with her when he should have been with Dylan. He had not been a good brother. Now Dylan was going to die.

The thought was intolerable, more so than bleeding to death.

Anger gave him strength. By inches and screams, he reached his brother's side. He smoothed back Dylan's hair and kissed him.

Before he passed out he managed to dial the operator.

## 2

Richard woke to white lights and the low constant noise of controlled urgency. The first face he saw was that of a beefy policeman, his skin red and fissured from too many late nights in subzero weather.

The ruddy mask cracked, and from between lips thinner than a snake's came the words, "Hey kid." The tone was fatherly, warm and strong. It brought tears to Richard's eyes. He didn't fight them. If ever there was a time when being seen crying was okay, this was it. Hot and tickling, they trickled from the corners of his eyes and down his temples.

A pair of flat callused thumbs smeared them into his hair. The cop was comforting him, wiping away his tears like he was a small and precious child. This unexpected kindness lent Richard a sense of control. He smiled shakily.

"Hey," he managed.

"You're lucky to be alive," the cop said.

*Alive.* In a rush, Richard remembered everything that had happened. "Where am I?" he asked stupidly. Halfway through the question he realized he was in a hospital, the emergency room. Embarrassed to sound so predictable, he waved a hand at the white privacy curtains surrounding the bed and asked, "Am I in a sheet factory?"

Rather than being annoyed, as his dad used to be when Richard played the fool, Beef Cop gave the appearance of being charmed. His eyes, a glacial shade of blue, warmed. The thick shoulders rounded in to create a less threatening silhouette. Lowering an oversized haunch, he sat on the edge of the hospital bed.

Richard winced.

"Oh, sorry, did I hurt you?" the cop asked anxiously and, to Richard's relief, removed his rear end from the vicinity.

"It's only a flesh wound," Richard said because his brain was foggy and he couldn't think of anything anywhere near witty to say.

The cop seemed to think this was high comedy. A

hearty laugh was followed by a clumsy hair-ruffling.

"No, son, you're not in a sheet factory. You're at the Mayo Clinic. The best there is."

*Son.* He called him son.

With that, he remembered his leg, the wound on his thigh. "My leg." The words came out high-pitched and scared. That bothered him but he didn't try to cover.

"He cut you bad," the cop replied, looking around for a place to sit. Richard was prepared to scream if he put his butt back on the bed. He didn't. Condemned to stand, he went on, "The docs'll tell you more, but the short of it is they got you stitched up, and you'll be good as new pretty near. You don't worry about that leg. You don't worry about a thing. We got you covered."

The policeman liked him. *The belle of the policemen's ball,* Richard thought idiotically.

"You'll be running track in no time," Beef Cop said.

Richard nodded weakly and said, "Good." And "Thanks." He had no idea what he was thanking the cop for, but people liked to be thanked.

"Yep, the Mayo. The best there is," the cop reiterated.

Richard needed to see who else was in the room, but, what with beaming Beef and the sheet factory, he couldn't see more than three feet. The last thing he remembered was Dylan, bleeding, his neck twisted, but still breathing.

Crippled, Richard remembered. His neck looked broken.

"Dylan . . ." he began.

"Your brother's alive. At least for now," the policeman cut in. His eyes reverted to their arctic shade of blue, and his cheeks went from flab to granite. He sounded pissed off, but he wasn't pissed off at Richard. He was pissed off at Dylan.

"Excuse me." Like a leaf on the first winds of winter, a cool voice blew the cop out of Richard's line of sight. A woman in white replaced him, a nurse of forty or so. She, too, smiled at Richard, a real smile, the kind mothers save for favorite sons. "My name is Sara."

Richard liked her voice. It was warm, like she thought he was okay. He tried to smile at her and failed.

"Your brother is fine," she said kindly.

Fine. Going to be fine. Fine meant nothing. Fine was a cover-up, pabulum for kiddies.

The fear that had shortened his patience with the policeman jerked his jaws together and locked them.

"Is he crippled?" Richard demanded, nearly lisping through clenched teeth.

"No, no. Just a concussion," the nurse assured him quickly. "He's going to be just fine." She reached out as if to pat him on the head, then snatched her hand back. Richard was pretty sure his teeth were bared, and he wasn't sure he wouldn't have bitten her if she hadn't pulled away.

Their "fine" was not his "fine."

"Is he crippled?" he yelled, trying to sit up and barely succeeding in lifting his head. "His neck looked broken. Goddamn it, is he going to be a cripple?"

"Shh, shh," the woman hissed, thinking snake sounds would comfort him. "Your brother has a concussion. He's not crippled. I don't know who told you that. Breathe now. You're going to be fine."

Now, he was going to be "fine." She filled a hypodermic needle and squirted liquid out the end just like he'd seen in a hundred TV shows. Inserting the needle in a port of his IV tube, she squeezed the plunger a half an inch or so.

"Just fine," she whispered.

*Warm. Motherly.*

But only for him. The way she'd said "your brother" told him that. Try as she might, she couldn't entirely keep the loathing from her voice.

"You just worry about getting yourself well," the nurse said as she pushed the plunger all the way in. "That brother of yours will be right as rain in a day or so. And don't you worry; we're going to take good care of you."

*Right as rain, white as snow,* Richard thought, and wondered where the words came from. *Drugs?*

"This is going to put you to sleep," the nice, motherly Sara was saying as she pulled out the hypodermic needle. "When you wake up again, we'll have your leg all fixed up."

"I'll be right as rain?" Richard heard himself murmur.

The nurse smiled as if he were the cleverest boy in the world.

In the space of a night, maybe not even a night—he had no idea how much time had elapsed—the world had changed utterly. Richard hadn't. They had. They, them, everybody else had.

Beef Cop edged the nurse out of his range of vision. "Son, was it you who hit your brother?" he asked.

Tears started again. "I hit him," he said. "I had to."

"Good kid." The cop's voice turned flinty. Richard imagined words striking sparks when he talked. "What did you hit him with? That axe? The neighbor girl . . ."

Morphine, or Darvon, or whatever it was furred the edges of Richard's tunneling vision. Through this black fuzzy sleeve he watched the cop pull a notebook from his coat pocket.

"Vondra Werner," the policeman verified. "Vondra Werner said you spent most of the night with her."

At first Richard didn't see the ghost of a grin behind the cop's words. Then he did, and he knew the man thought he was a hero.

Not just a survivor, but a hero.

"That's enough," Nurse Sara said. "Look at him, poor, poor, beautiful boy . . ." was the last thing Richard heard.

## 3

*Nothing was ever going to be right again,* Dylan thought.

Except Rich. Rich didn't die. He almost died, but he didn't.

The first time Dylan saw him again was at the trial. It wasn't held in Rochester because everybody there hated Dylan too much for it to be fair. They were trying him in a little town called Hammond about three hours away. He had to get up at five every morning so they could drive him there in time. The courthouse was small and looked like it was supposed to, with benches and a fence between the audience and the lawyers. Every day it was packed, mostly with newspaper and TV people.

Rich, looking like his old self with color in his skin and everything, his hair a little longer than their mom would have let him wear it and waving in that surfer-boy style he liked, was pushed down the aisle of the courtroom in a wheelchair. His leg was wrapped in so many bandages they'd had to cut open that side of his pants even though it was probably twenty below zero outside. He'd gotten skinnier.

Though he knew Rich would spit on him, or ignore him like he was a bug, or scream he was a psycho, or worse, Dylan didn't look away. He kept watching the rolling chair. When it first came through the double doors, everybody got quiet. Then, as it got closer, flashbulbs started flashing and people started murmuring.

Rich was so cool—Academy Awards, the red carpet. He was smiling for the cameras but kind of sadlike. Dylan loved him more at that moment than he ever had. Nothing Rich had done in the past mattered. This was what mattered. The love hurt Dylan, it was so big.

Since that night the whole inside of him felt black and crusty like the inside of a lightning tree. Mostly, Dylan stayed in the burnt-out hole and didn't think or feel. He didn't know what to be or how to be anymore. No one else seemed to know what he was either. Or what to do with him. Doctors, lawyers, cops asked questions. A newspaper guy got in, and flashed, and questioned 'til the cops chased him out.

Dylan hadn't been able to answer the questions, so he'd coiled up in the black and hid. Until he saw his brother. The pain of loving Rich felt almost good; it made him feel like a person. He didn't look away as the wheelchair rolled down the aisle toward him but steeled himself to take the hit. Maybe it would kill him, but he doubted it. Nothing he wanted to happen had happened for a while now.

Then Rich was opposite him on the other side of the wooden railing. He held up his hand, and the nurse stopped the chair. Dylan felt like crying, his brother was so cool. He'd made the nurse do what he wanted without saying a word, like a cop stopping traffic. Bracing against the armrests, Rich struggled to get up. The nurse, all done up for the trial in her crisp uniform and hat, put her hands on his shoulders to make him stay down, but he shrugged them off.

Dylan stood too. If Rich wanted to hit him, he could. For a weird jag of time, Dylan experienced his brother's fists hammering him, his feet smashing into his ribs and belly, and he welcomed it. He craved being beaten to death like he craved air when he'd been under the water too long.

Getting up must have hurt Rich. His face lost color, and he swayed like he was going to pass out. Holding onto the railing to keep himself up, he made it the two steps to where Dylan stood waiting.

The muttering in the courthouse dried up. Nobody was even breathing. Time stopped, and the people were hanging on the second hand, wondering if the clock was going to work ever again. Dylan wasn't breathing either. He was waiting to die. Not the good kind where everything is over, but to be killed inside.

Rich balanced himself against the rail so he could stand on his bad leg, reached out both arms, and said, "Brother."

The sere, cinder-lined core of Dylan filled with

warm liquid. He was melting from the inside out. Time flowed backward. He hurtled from eleven, to eight, to six. A little boy threw his arms around his big brother's neck and bawled like a baby. Rich didn't have to be so good to him.

Rich was crying too.

People in the courthouse didn't know what kind of noise to make. Their murmuring fattened up with awe and pity, then morphed into white-hot fury. Dylan smeared the tears and snot from his face into the crook of his arm as the sound grew into the feral growl of a mob working up to a lynching. Except he was eleven. So they couldn't even enjoy being mad at him. He was a little kid. They had to pretend to be sad at the same time.

Rich fell back into his wheelchair. Mrs. Eisenhart, Dylan's court-appointed attorney, pulled him from the rail. The judge was pounding his gavel for quiet.

They were all mad for Rich, because he wouldn't be mad for himself. They hated Dylan. They needn't have bothered; he hated himself more than they ever could.

He sat down. Mrs. Eisenhart had brought him the suit and tie his mom got for Lena's baptism. He'd been nine then, and the suit was too small. He squirmed trying to get the crotch to stop crawling up his butt.

Mrs. Eisenhart kicked him under the table. Rich was being sworn in; Dylan forgot about wedgies.

The other lawyer, the one against Dylan, began asking questions. Rich didn't want to answer, but he'd sworn on the Bible and had to. He hadn't seen Dylan do anything. He insisted on that. He'd been next door necking with Vondra Werner. When Rich said that, he looked at Dylan and kind of shrugged.

Dylan turned around with a great big, sheepish grin plastered on his face, looking to see what his mom and dad thought of *that*. Men in the courthouse were smiling; but when they saw his face the smiles whispered out, leaving only the scratching sound of dead leaves in the air. His big old grin brought the undergrowl back into the ambient noise.

The parched silence, the sudden remembering that his parents weren't there, froze Dylan's smile in a creepy kind of way. Like a supervillain had zapped him with an ice ray. Flash bulbs popped. "Butcher Boy," one of the newspaper reporters whispered, and a bunch of them scribbled in their notepads.

Mrs. Eisenhart closed a sharp-nailed hand on his shoulder and turned him back toward the judge.

Rich told the jury, the judge and the lawyers that he'd come home and found Dylan drenched in blood. He'd tried to get the axe away from him, and Dylan had nearly hacked his leg off. Thinking Dylan was possessed, or might hurt himself, or was sick, Rich, even though he was bleeding to death, got the axe away from him and bonked him on the head. Then Rich had passed out and didn't remember anything 'til he woke up at the Mayo. That was it—the whole story.

The prosecutor made Rich tell it different ways. He tried to make him add to it, say he saw things he didn't, but Rich wouldn't do it. Everybody was listening so hard Dylan could feel his brother's words being sucked past his ears into the gallery.

No one listened harder than he did. Mrs. Eisenhart had told him the story when she'd rehearsed him for the trial—it wasn't at all like on television; the lawyers were supposed to tell each other what they were going to say and do and not surprise the other guy; but it was totally different hearing it from his brother. When Rich said it, Dylan finally believed. Until then he thought he didn't remember it because it didn't happen.

*It happened.* This hit him like the axe had—a slam into his head that scrambled his brain. Mrs. Eisenhart kicked him again. She didn't like him any more than anybody else did.

*It had happened. He'd gotten hold of his dad's axe, and it had happened.*

He stared down at the table he and his lawyer were sitting behind. It started to spin and tip like the deck of a boat in a windstorm. Dylan grabbed one edge to keep from smashing his face against the tossing wood surface. With his other hand he took hold of the seat of his chair lest he be pitched onto the floor.

"I tried to kill my brother with Daddy's axe," he whispered. This time Mrs. Eisenhart's kick hurt. He guessed he hadn't spoken loud enough for anyone else to hear because nobody was looking at him. The words hadn't been a confession; he'd said them to see if it would make him remember. Because he didn't. He didn't remember a thing. Not one thing after his mother had put him to bed.

He'd told them that over and over, but even his own lawyer didn't believe him. When she got to talk, she argued that people suffering head injurics from accidents often couldn't remember events that happened immediately before the trauma, that the blow had given Dylan a severe concussion, that he'd been in intensive care, and that, since the incident, he suffered severe headaches.

Nobody felt sorry for him; Dylan didn't even feel sorry for himself. He'd tried to kill his brother.

Rich was on the stand for over an hour. Talking so long cost him. Lines of pain aged his face. During the whole thing, even when the prosecutor pushed, Rich refused to say anything bad about Dylan. Looking straight at the jury the way Mrs. Eisenhart told Dylan he should if she decided to put him on the stand, Rich told them that Dylan never hurt anybody, didn't hit or pinch or call other kids names, minded his mother and father, was kind and protective of Lena, their thirty-month-old sister, and brought home injured animals to take care of. The more good he told them, the less the jury believed it. It didn't even sound like Rich believed it himself.

When the prosecutor was finished, Mrs. Eisenhart didn't ask Rich a single question. As he was being wheeled out, Rich whispered, "Hang in there, brother," and gave Dylan a thumbs-up. Dylan didn't respond; he knew if he so much as nodded he would be six years old again, bawling like a baby.

After Rich testified, things in the courtroom pretty much stopped making sense for Dylan. People came and went without reason. Colors got brighter and brighter until Dylan had to squint to keep them out. Voices were superloud. He could smell things with a dog's nose: traces of his lawyer's perfume would choke him; the stink of an old cigarette on somebody behind them would make him sick to his stomach. The walls crept in, making the room smaller.

This whole-world cacophony made him crazy.

Crazier.

One day the prosecutor called Vondra Werner. Dylan pulled hard on the places where his brain was being sucked out of shape so he could pay attention. Vondra and her family had only lived next door six months or so, but she was always around, snooping and trying to talk to Rich. Dylan didn't think she knew he existed.

"Pink, of course," Mrs. Eisenhart hissed.

Vondra had on a pink dress. She looked pretty,

shy, and nice. Dylan didn't know why that made his lawyer mad. In a low voice, Vondra told everybody how she and Rich had been together. Except she didn't say they were necking; she said they were "making love."

When it was her turn Mrs. Eisenhart made Vondra tell how she was always watching, and following Rich around, and maybe was jealous of his family, and maybe didn't like Dylan. Dylan thought for a minute the lawyer was going to get Vondra to break down like Perry Mason got confessions at the end of the show, and Vondra'd confess she'd done everything.

Then the lawyer said, "Richard didn't like you spying; Mrs. Raines didn't like you watching." Vondra went white like Casper the Friendly Ghost.

"Richard loves me," she said. "Mrs. Raines didn't like *him*." She pointed to where Dylan sat. "I overheard her once saying he did things that scared her."

Panic flooded Dylan, filled his brain until there wasn't room for anything else. People's lips would move but he wouldn't hear anything—or the words made no sense. They could have been speaking Chinese for all he knew.

Except he knew he was *supposed* to understand.

Terror sharpened, began cutting the inside of his skull; he could feel it knife into the bone. Then he could no longer see, not like he should have been seeing. Lights would grow dimmer or brighter, except they didn't. Nobody else saw them do it. Walls, especially pale walls, changed color from white, to pink, to grey. Faces mutated subtly to become frightening.

The fifth or sixth day of the trial, Dylan woke up too scared to look into the mirror. His reflection might melt, become monstrous, and his mind would snap, the kind of crazy snap that showed and got people stuck in rubber rooms with canvas coats that tied in the back. Dylan knew he couldn't be shut up all by himself, all *in* himself. He had to seem okay.

At least, okay for a monster.

He shut down. He moved hardly at all, then carefully, robotically, nothing flapping or wriggling out of control. Food tasted like sawdust. It stuck in his throat halfway down, a glob of paste. He never looked at his plate. If he looked too long, the noodles or whatever might begin to writhe. He ate to stay alive, and he wasn't truly committed even to that. The people who made his meals, the people who served them, they all hated him. They could poison the food or, worse, pee or spit on it.

"I don't know what you think you're proving with this stoic act you've started. You're not doing yourself any good," Mrs. Eisenhart said. "People look at you and see indifference. You won't get the death sentence. I'm a better lawyer than that, and, besides, nobody likes to kill kids, but playing Marble Man is hurting you."

Dylan knew she was right. He was eleven, not stupid. If he let the jury and the judge see his pain, they might take pity on him. Pity might lead to forgiveness. He couldn't hope for the good Bible kind where the Prodigal Son is loved, but there might be a version of "forgiveness lite," where they could tell themselves he was redeemable.

"There's an old Chinese proverb," Mrs. Eisenhart said. "You keep on the way you're going, and eventually you'll get where you're headed. You're a smart boy; you know where that is."

When he didn't respond, she dug newspapers out of her briefcase and spread them on the table between them. On the front pages there were photos of him locked in his panic catatonia. "Butcher Boy Shows No Remorse." That was the headline on the tabloid. The respectable paper was more circumspect but the message was the same.

"Have it your way," Mrs. Eisenhart said abruptly. Leaving the papers for him to enjoy, she snapped her briefcase shut and stalked away, her high-heeled shoes noisy on the linoleum. At the door she turned back and Dylan wondered if she watched that new show *Columbo* and was doing that almost-gone-wait-one-more-zinger move. "You're killing me," she said. She didn't even see why that was funny.

Dylan knew he was killing his chance of any kind of leniency. And he knew he could not show them his pain. Should the least tiny little droplet of it leak out it would breach the dam; the trickle would become a stream, and the stream, a flood. He would be washed away in it.

The last day of the trial a cop took the stand and told the jury Dylan had gone insane and peed in his pants rather than look at what he'd done. He told them how Dylan had laughed. Then two more cops repeated the story. Dylan sort of remembered doing that, but it wasn't the way they said it was.

When the last cop was telling how Rich nearly died from the hack job on his leg and how Dylan had laughed, Dylan shut down his ears. It was too weird. Somebody else did all those things, not Dylan. A monster got in. Maybe Rich was protecting that monster. His *girlfriend.* Vondra was always peeking out the windows at them and making up excuses to come by. Maybe she was psycho.

Maybe he was.

Voices washed around him as he sat straight and stiff and stared at the tabletop and tried to remember stuff—not the bad stuff—just stuff. Searching his mind, looking way back into the dark places where dead-and-over things were stored, he saw only fog, thick and white the way fog was from the machines they used in high school plays. But he wasn't going to go to high school. Even a moron could figure that out.

That afternoon the trial ended. "Dylan, the judge

asked you a question!" Mrs. Eisenhart's voice dragged him out of himself. When she called him, he was seeing a picture in his mind of the butterfly kiss his mom had given him that last night, the tiny gold cross she always wore cool on his cheek. It made him smile.

"Look at him! He's grinning!" a whisper hissed loud in the courtroom.

"Huh?" It took him longer than it should have to make sense of what she'd said. He sounded retarded.

"We are going into the sentencing phase now. Judge Farnsworth wants to know if you want to say anything in your own behalf."

Then he did a stupid thing. He meant to ask if the jury had found him guilty. He meant to say, "I'm guilty?" with the end of the sentence going up, so everybody would know it was a question. What came out was, "I'm guilty."

After that he got so confused he decided not to say anything else.

# 4

Dylan was sentenced to a juvenile detention center in DuWalt, Minnesota, until he was eighteen years of age. On his eighteenth birthday he was to be transferred to the state penitentiary where he would be imprisoned until the age of twenty-seven.

The gavel rapped and the judge rose. Mrs. Eisenhart stood as well, chunked her papers into order on the top of the desk and fed them to her briefcase. Dylan watched as the leather jaws clamped shut on their catch.

"That, as they say, is that," Mrs. Eisenhart said. She found Dylan's dead-fish right hand and shook it perfunctorily. "Call me if you need anything." Clack, clack, clack, and the double doors ate her as neatly as the leather had swallowed the papers.

A quiet man, maybe the bailiff, with a big gut and eyes that were kind even when he looked at Dylan, said: "Come on, boy. Let's get this over with." For a horrible second, Dylan looked around desperately for his mom and dad. The bailiff cuffed him, putting the manacles on carefully so the sliding part wouldn't pinch his wrists, and asked, "That too tight?" This casual kindness was too rich to bear. Dylan couldn't even say thank you and, seeming cold and ungrateful, he walked toward the door.

As before—the before between the night the things happened and the trial—Dylan was put in rooms. Taken out of rooms. People talked over and around him. He held himself tight and still so he wouldn't blast apart and hurt them with the shrapnel of his bones. Finally he was escorted to a big van, the kind church groups use, but with iron mesh and seats where handcuffs could be locked.

For the first part of the four-hour drive to the

detention center the bailiff rode in front with the driver. From what they said Dylan guessed the bailiff was getting a lift home. They pretty much ignored him, and when they did talk to him, they were nice enough. If he could have made their words line up in his brain, he would have answered them; but he couldn't, and trying made the panic so bad he was afraid he was going to vomit. Then they'd think he was carsick, like a little kid.

After the bailiff got out the driver started talking to Dylan. "So you're the famous Butcher Boy, eh." He didn't sound mean, just making conversation, the way somebody might say, "So you're Frank Raines's boy." The thought of not being Frank Raines's boy anymore caught crosswise in Dylan's mind, and he bit down hard to keep from screaming and banging his head against the side of the van.

"Not many little kids in juvie. None as young as eleven as a matter of fact. Lots of half-grown men acting like little kids, if that's any consolation to you. Eleven!" He whistled long and low. For a while, he didn't say anything, and Dylan stared out the window. The snow was deep and silent and blue from the bit of moon. Trees edged the fields like jagged teeth. Every few miles a house showed lights.

No axe boys there. Sleep tight, Dylan thought. Craziness gnawed at him. He forced his mind to make a movie where he could stay sane. He did the television show *The Fugitive,* with the van sliding on ice, crashing, and him getting out. He was going to make it so that he found the one-armed guy, but instead the mind-Dylan who escaped the van lay down in the snow and let the cold freeze him quiet.

Having flicked through a bunch of radio stations and finally gotten bored, the driver started talking again. He told Dylan the juvenile facility wasn't really in DuWalt but on the prairie about twenty miles outside of town. That it looked like an old city hall from the outside but it was for really bad kids. "The place was built in nineteen twenty-nine," he said, sounding like a tour guide. "That was before the crash, but then a whippersnapper like you wouldn't care anything about that. When they built it, it was considered real modern, but it won't look like that to a sharp young town boy like you. The architect . . . You know what an architect is?"

Dylan didn't answer. Maybe he could have put the words together, but he didn't want to. The driver was turning mean. *Must be past his bed-time,* Dylan thought in his mother's voice.

"The architect was an Englishman. He went nuts with all the granite here and built the thing with arches and towers that would have looked right at home in merry olde England." The driver told Dylan the guards were pretty good Joes, but it was thankless work, and he wouldn't do it if wild horses dragged him. "Most are okay, but not all." Then, as if embarrassed that he'd slipped into being nice, he threw in, "You better not try any funny stuff. These old boys won't put up with that kind of thing. You'll find yourself in a box no bigger than a coffin eating nothing but bread and water for a month.

"I don't know where they're going to put you," the driver said. "Little skinny stick of a boy like you, put in with some of them big boys and . . ." He stopped the way Dylan's parents would stop when they realized "little pitchers have big ears."

Dylan went back out the window into the snow where the cold could numb his heart and cool his head.

The next time the driver talked, his voice had changed, the way people's do when they are talking to themselves instead of somebody else. "My gosh. What happened to make you do a thing like that? An axe of all things. I can't imagine what must have been going through your head."

He's scared of me, Dylan realized. A grown-up, frightened of a little kid. They were all scared of him. That's why they called him names. And not just him. He made them scared of all little kids. Dylan wanted to tell him not to be afraid, but he didn't know how to do it without being "impertinent." His mother's word.

"I've heard that rock and roll music works on young people's minds," the driver went on. "That crazy stuff from England about the drugs and whatnot. But it would take a whole lot more than that to get most kids to go off the deep end."

This time Dylan purposely scrambled the words. He didn't want to think about what the driver was saying. He didn't want to think about anything.

They arrived late at night. Snow was falling fit-fully, tiny ice flakes with no substance but only sting to them. The van drove through big gates with a booth just inside. The driver stopped and rolled down the window. Dylan was aware of voices, people deciding what to do with him. Another short drive down a tree-lined road, branches bare and scratchy against floodlights, and the van pulled in front of a stone building that looked like a medieval castle. The front doors had glass windows, which Dylan thought was odd; in movies, prisons never had any glass, only bars. Two men in dark green uniforms—guards, he guessed—came out of the doors and took him from the van. The guards didn't have guns, but they had sticks and handcuffs on their belts.

For a long time he waited in a room with plastic chairs and green walls. The guards stayed with him. Finally Dylan was taken to a room where there was nothing on the walls but a mirror of wavy metal. The one chair was bolted to the floor, and the window had heavy wire mesh over it. There was a tiny eyeball window in the door that led into the hall so people could peek in at him anytime they wanted. Already faces had come and gone.

*A zoo,* he thought, *and I'm the wild animal.*

A while later a lady, maybe forty—older than his mom—came to the room. He guessed she was a doctor by the way she moved and smiled, like she was so powerful everybody would do what she wanted so she could just relax and enjoy it.

Dylan was sitting on one of two hospital beds with white covers and metal roll bars. His back was flat against the wall, and his legs stuck out over the edge into the narrow aisle between the beds.

He would have stood when she came into the room so she wouldn't think he hadn't been brought up right, but he was cuffed to the frame.

The doctor sat on the other bed. She crossed her legs and absently pulled the crease of her trousers straight. Most ladies didn't wear pants, not at work anyway. Maybe lady doctors were different.

Her fingernails were short like a man's. They looked strong. She looked strong all over: iron gray hair and wire-rim glasses, a square face and a chunky body. But she wasn't ugly, just solid.

"I'm Doctor Olson," she said. "I work with the boys two days a week. I'm sure you are aware of the difficulties of finding a place for a boy your age. Most of our juvenile offenders are at least fourteen or fifteen. Some of the bigger boys are . . . Oh, Lord."

When she said "Lord," she took off her glasses and put her thumb on one temple and her fingertips on the other and looked into her hand as if God might be there and she wanted to shut out the light to get a better look at his tiny self.

After she had communed she went on: "I'm one of the on-call psychiatrists. The other, the one you will probably work with, is Dr. Kowalski. You will be housed here for the time being. When you're ready we'll move you in with the other boys. Are there any questions you'd like to ask me?"

Dylan meant to answer, to say no or ask something to be polite, but he didn't.

She waited a moment or two then said, "Okay, then. I guess I'll say goodnight. An orderly will be in to get those cuffs off of you. He'll bring you a pair of pajamas and so forth. The kitchen is closed but, if you're hungry, I've arranged for you to have a snack." Again she waited. Dylan chased after sentence fragments, wanting to say something because she wanted him to, but it was as if he'd forgotten how to speak, how to catch a thought and make it into a sound.

Doctor Olson turned and left. A snick-clunk sound followed—the lock on the door being put into place.

Dylan was home.

# 5

For three days, Dylan stayed in the room with the observation window. Nobody told him but after a while he figured out he was in DuWalt's infirmary. A lot of the time they left the little hatch door on the peep hole open and he could look out. There was a desk with a nurse at it and twice he saw a guard bring a boy there to get bandages or aspirin or something. From what he could see there wasn't any other room for sick people but the one he was in, and since he wasn't sick he didn't know why they were keeping him there. Since he didn't care why, he never asked.

A guard took his clothes. That bothered him. Sitting with the covers over his legs felt weird, like he was sick and should be throwing up. He was afraid he'd have to stay like that and when he got up to pee, people could look in and see him running around in his underpants, but in an hour or so the same guard brought him blue jeans and a denim shirt. They were too big but not as bad as the jockey shorts. Plain, white cotton, they reached to his knees. The slot in the front he was supposed to use was so low it was easier to go over the top. He also got a pair of stiff leather shoes. This last offering was left by an "orderly."

Even in his self-imposed hermitage of the mind, Dylan knew he wasn't a proper orderly like on *Dr.*

*Kildare.* For one thing he was fourteen or fifteen and they didn't make kids orderlies in regular hospitals. For another thing he whispered, "Hey, *blood* brother" and "How ya doin', axe man," and occasionally mimed chopping when none of the real people were around. That was a major tip-off. He also had a tattoo on his arm. A stupid one, just numbers, that looked like a spaz had done it with a ballpoint pen. Dylan guessed he was what in old movies was called a "trustee," another prisoner who has earned certain privileges.

Dylan knew the taunts should bother him but by the time they permeated the blanket of fog he'd swaddled himself in they'd lost any power they might have had when they were still warm. The trustee told Dylan his name was Draco but the staff called him James. Dylan didn't call him anything. Before he'd ended up in DuWalt he would have liked to talk to Draco. Not that his mother would have let them be friends. Draco was what his parents called "a bad crowd" all by himself.

Draco kept up the chopping and saying stuff. Dylan watched without a lot of interest. Even when Draco pinched him once and, one time, held a plastic fork to his throat, Dylan couldn't generate enough energy to speak.

Two days and six meals later, when Dr. Olson came and asked him how he was doing, he found himself answering. Dylan was as surprised as she was.

"Fine," he said, and then laughed because there was no "fine" left in his universe. Dr. Olson looked worried, said some more things and left.

That night when Draco'd come with the supper tray and reached for the pudding cup to eat Dylan's dessert like he always did, smacking his lips and saying how good it was and too bad he didn't get any, Dylan said, "Don't."

The voice that came out wasn't his old voice, his boy's voice; this one was flat and dull and cold, like a knife left out in winter. Draco squeaked like a big fat mouse and jumped a foot in the air. It was funny but Dylan didn't laugh. For some reason he only laughed at sad things now. Then Draco put both hands in the air as if he was a bad guy and Dylan was Marshall Dillon. "Hey, man, no problem," he said. "I've just been kidding around. No hard feelings." He backed out of the room without taking his eyes off Dylan. Dylan was tempted to look in the mirror to see if he had changed into Butcher Boy so completely it showed on his face but he wasn't up to looking in mirrors yet.

When Dr. Olson came again she said, "James says you're taking more of an interest in things than you have been. That's a good sign. That means you're getting stronger." She smiled and fiddled with one of her earrings. It was the kind Dylan's mother used to wear, clipping on tight and leaving a red mark when it was taken off. "If it were a perfect world you would be going to a hospital to live, a place where you could be taken care of better."

Dylan knew what she meant. An insane asylum. He'd never been to one, only seen them in the movies and on television. The thought of being locked up with crazy people jarred him out of his indifference.

"I want to stay here," he said. She blinked at him from behind her glasses and he remembered that what he wanted didn't matter any more. "I'm a danger to others," he quoted the judge. "You have to keep me in jail."

"Unfortunately, you're going to get your wish," the psychiatrist said. "There doesn't seem to be a place for you in the system, so you will stay where you are for the time being. I'm also afraid we can't let you have the sick bay for much longer. There are a hundred and seventy-three boys here at the moment and we have just these two beds that can be secured. You'll be moved to the psychiatric ward, then if all goes well, to Ward C with the other boys."

"You're afraid I'll chop them up into little pieces and flush them down the toilet," Dylan interrupted.

"Not that," she said quickly, but she was lying. That's exactly what she thought. That's what everybody thought. "Most of the boys here are here . . . for different reasons and we want to be able to take better care of you."

59

"What kind of care of me?" he asked.

Dr. Olson sighed. She was tired, maybe tired of monstrous boys or maybe just because she worked other places besides DuWalt. "We have discussed your case a lot," she said.

"The 'Royal We'?" Dylan asked because his mother used to joke, saying, "The Royal We," and though he'd never really understood what she meant, she'd always said it in a way that he knew it was supposed to be funny. In his new voice it didn't sound funny at all.

"Sort of," she said. "The care I'm talking about isn't care for your body but for your mind. I have read your case, and I believe you really can't remember what happened, just that it did happen." She quit talking then and stared at him with that hungry-dog look like she was expecting him to throw her a bone. Dylan had no bones.

"Stop me if I'm chasing down the wrong rat hole," she said and smiled again.

Dylan liked her for talking to him like he was a human being. "No, that's my rat hole," he said seriously. "I know it happened. Mack the Giant showed me."

Dr. Olson's face settled into an older mask; what he said made her think he should be put in the insane asylum and he couldn't find the words to tell her he wasn't seeing things. Mack the Giant was a giant cop named Mack.

She took off her glasses and waved them back

and forth the way his dad used to when he came in from the cold and his lenses steamed over. "Mack the Giant showed you," she said carefully.

A flash memory of blood on the carpet, staining the walls, of Rich's ashen face hit Dylan so hard he doubled over and clutched his middle as if he'd been struck by a baseball bat.

The hit passed. He straightened up.

"Are you alright? Do you want a glass of water?"

"I'm alright," he said and suppressed the urge to laugh like he had at "fine." He was a monster, but he wasn't a *crazy* monster. She had to see that.

"What I think—and Dr. Kowalski, the other psychiatrist, agrees—is that you will not be able to begin healing until you can access those memories. That night, bad as it was, needs to be dealt with if you're ever to be a whole boy again."

A whole boy. Maybe a real boy like Pinocchio wanted to be. All he had to do was remember. That had been what the lawyers, the policemen, and the judge had wanted. They'd hammered at him to remember and gotten mad and mean when he didn't.

Wouldn't, they said. He wouldn't remember.

If they made him remember, then he would go insane; he would be a crazy monster, a crazy-ass, bug-shit Butcher Boy. If he was crazy maybe he'd grab any old axe he found and start hacking people's legs off. When he was sent to jail he'd thought the questioning would be over. He would have prayed for it to be over but that would have been blasphemous.

He started to cry.

"That's a beginning," Dr. Olson said kindly.

The beginning of what terrified him.

# 6

Richard turned fourteen in a private room at the Mayo Clinic. Nothing but the best for Richard Raines. Minnesota could not do enough for her injured children, her orphans, or her celebrities, and Richard was all three. Flowers and balloons from total strangers filled the room, their colors painfully bright in the diamond-hard winter sunlight. Out his second floor window was ice-blue sky, the bare branches of trees spider-webbing against it like cracks in the universe.

In the tradition of gout-ridden kings, Richard reigned propped up on three pillows, his leg swathed in bandages and immobilized. It had hurt like a son of a bitch at first but the drugs took care of that.

*Took care of everything.* The thought drifted through a warm morphine haze.

Kids at Rochester middle school thought they were big deals with a joint or two pinched from their big brothers and here he was mainlining morphine.

Rock star. Dylan would think it was cool.

A whisper of sound pulled his mind from the

morphine summer. The skirt of a highly starched pink-and-white dress poked through the partly opened door like a tongue through lips. Richard leaned his head back and closed his eyes.

From beneath his lashes he watched as a doe-eyed face followed the skirt into his room. This candy striper was new, a girl not much older than he, and so pretty if they'd met in the school lunchroom she probably wouldn't have given him the time of day. Letting herself in silently so as not to disturb the king, she fussed with the covers tented over his wound.

Slowly, he let his eyes drift open. "Could you get me a drink of water?" he whispered.

She refilled his water carafe then poured a glass and held the straw to his lips. The scent she wore was sophisticated. The side of her hand brushed softly against his cheek as she dabbed a drop prettily off his chin, leaning closer than she had to.

"Will you lose your leg?" she asked timidly.

"Maybe." There was a dimming behind her eyes, a darker shadow pooling in the brown irises.

She was shallower than he'd thought. A one-legged boy couldn't ski, skateboard, or whatever she thought was cool.

"Naw," he amended truthfully. "I won't lose it. Might have a limp is all; the doc says I lost a chunk of thigh muscle the size of a softball." The doctor had actually said tennis ball but tennis sounded wimpy.

Her child-woman face softened in pity. It was an act. Since he could remember he had been watching people. His mom thought he was psychic but ESP wasn't necessary to read the minds of ninety-nine percent of people or predict what they were going to do or say. They broadcast their thoughts for anybody paying attention to read.

"Does it hurt?" she asked.

"Bad, real bad," Richard said and grimaced as he remembered how cutting the pain had been in the beginning.

At the moment he felt terrific. Really terrific.

Acutely aware of how much he liked the sweet-dream sleepiness of the morphine dripping into his arm he promised himself he'd start telling the nurses and doctors that the pain was better. When he got out of the Mayo life was going to be hard enough without an addiction.

"Would you like me to rub it for you?" Candy smiled coyly.

The smile had probably been practiced, but Richard wasn't sure. It might have been self-conscious rather than fake. It didn't matter either way. Stupidity turned him off. Rub it? His leg was nearly sliced in half.

"That's awful nice of you but I need to get some rest." He closed his eyes and felt her pat his feet through the thin hospital coverlet before she tip-toed from the room, closing the door with exagger-ated care.

As soon as he heard the latch click he opened his eyes again. His room looked like a florist shop: flowers, cards, stuffed bears, balloons. The outpouring of Minnesotans' inherent kindness had manifested in cash as well as gifts. One of the doctors told him more than two hundred thousand dollars had been sent to the hospital for Richard Raines. The doctor imparted this important fact offhandedly, as if Richard was a child who wouldn't know what to do with more than movie money.

Even if he could get the money, there was no way they were going to let a freshman in high school live on his own, even though he had a home. The Raines house had belonged to his grandparents; it should be paid for by now, or close to it. It wouldn't matter; until he was eighteen he'd have to have a guardian. Social workers were having hushed conversations about where to put him, as if he were a towel they could fold and stick on this or that shelf. Their whispers were about as subtle as theatrical asides meant to be heard in the last row.

No one bothered to include him in these sotto voce chats.

An orphanage had been mentioned, but foster care was in the lead so far. People could dress foster care up any way they wanted but they did it for the money: more kids more money. And kids got shifted around. On the radio he'd heard this whole thing about foster kids being given suitcases as presents because at the drop of a hat they were forced to play musical houses.

Vondra's parents, the Werners, were a possibility. Vondra would try to help, but Mr. Werner didn't like him. Not that he said anything; Richard had read it behind the man's eyes. That he'd been with his daughter in the middle of the night when her parents were out didn't make it any better.

There was a nurse in the ER he remembered. He remembered everything about that night with sur-real vividness. Weeks later it still seemed more immediate than the time he inhabited from moment to moment. He'd liked her. She was smart and quiet and gentle with him. Her name was Lackey, Sara-with-no-*h* Lackey. Nurse Lackey was in her forties and didn't take care of herself: she was underweight, her hair was a mess, and her nails had been bitten down to pseudopods.

Depressed, he guessed.

The next time a nurse came into his room, a hefty woman with an honest face and strong hands, he said, "There was a nurse who was extra nice to me that . . . that night. A Miss Sara something. I'd sure like to thank her."

Hefty beamed approval at him as she deftly set about changing the dressing on his thigh.

"Oh, yes, that's a sad story, that one," she said.

When the nurse finished her bandaging and her story, Richard asked if she thought Sara would come see him sometime. "I liked her voice." Saying it he remembered how good it had felt to hear that warmth, how good it had felt to be the center of her attention when the world was screwed up.

## 7

For nearly three weeks not much happened except that Dylan was moved from the infirmary into the psych ward. It wasn't like he'd imagined, with people thinking they were Napoleon and sneaking around at night smothering each other, but it was pretty bad. There were three other kids. One was always screaming because he saw spiders. After half a day of it Dylan was looking around for the spiders himself. A couple times he thought he felt them on him but he didn't let that show. He didn't want to be stuck in the psych ward forever.

Not that he deserved anything better; he wasn't stupid enough to pray for it or pretend he had a right to get out. Still he didn't want to spend his life with loonies. Another kid was a great big retard, big as a man. There was nothing else wrong with him that Dylan could see. He was stupid but he was nice enough as long as you didn't try to touch his things. The third boy just sat and plucked at his eyebrows and eyelashes, or where they'd used to be; he was bald-eyed as a bunny and blinked rapidly. At first Dylan thought he was staring at him, but Carl didn't stare at anybody; he just stared.

Dylan did his share of staring too. Out the windows mostly. Psych was on the third floor on the backside of the building. Outside nothing but snow-covered fields stretched all the way to the snow-white sky. Dylan put himself in the snow and numbed out as much as he could.

After a while, Dr. Olson decided he could go to classes with the sane kids and eat with them in the dining hall. Given that he shouldn't feel happy or good anymore he felt guilty for being glad to be out of the nut ward. There wasn't enough snow in Minnesota to numb him clear past boredom. It was so bad he was actually excited about going to the school they had for the inmates. He still spent nights with the crazies and had to shower and use the bathroom there.

Being crazy—Dylan supposed he was and it wouldn't have mattered if he was as sane as apple pie, crazy was like cooties, highly contagious, and he was living at cootie central—got him picked on by the sane boys. They didn't beat the crap out of him—not like he'd wanted Rich to that time—but they were always poking and pinching and shoving, making him drop his tray in the dining hall, pushing him so he fell down.

It was still better than doing nothing with the loonies. Being left alone with only his brain to play with was too weird. He'd think about the other kids and what they'd done and he'd think about himself and what he'd done, and then he'd think that they were humans and he wasn't, that he was this other thing, this monster thing, and if he kept on like that he knew he'd be screaming about invisible spiders before long.

At first Draco was the worst. Then, after a while, he got tired of it and decided to be Dylan's friend. "Don't go thinking I like you," he warned. "But, man, you're like Wyatt Earp or Doc Holiday, Jesse James. These sad fucks think they gun you down, they're hot shit. More laughs fucking with them than fucking with you. So you're this big axe murderer. Big deal. My bet is you did them in their sleep. Or somebody else did them and you took the rap. No way a little fart like you could get it up for forty whacks. You know about 'forty whacks?' Lizzie Whatsername slicing and dicing her folks? Worse kids than you been through DuWalt. Me for one."

Draco was always going on like that, like they were all big criminals. Except for Dylan, nobody much was. The other guys were in for stealing cars, or running away from home too many times, or shoplifting. One kid knifed another kid and a couple of older boys were in for armed robbery.

Draco was in for selling marijuana and then stealing the police car when they tried to arrest him. At least that's what he said. Dylan suspected maybe the police car part was just something he liked to think he did.

After he started hanging around with Draco things got better.

Class was good too. Dylan liked school now. Looked forward to it. He pretended not to because crazy cooties got him in enough trouble. If he started doing teacher's pet he'd get the crap beat out of him, Draco or no Draco.

English and history weren't all that great—people could twist them and Dylan was scared of twisty. He'd gotten twisted and twisted and ended up in a psych ward in a jail and didn't remember doing anything wrong. That meant he didn't know when he might do it again. That's why they wouldn't let him sleep in Ward C. Nobody else knew when he was going to start hacking people up again either. DuWalt slept better when Dylan was locked down for the night.

What he really liked was math. Outside, he'd hated it. Now he loved the order of it and that it was always the same. Nobody could twist it. A number stayed the same and if it was added to another number it always, *always* came out the same way.

Phil was the math teacher—he told the boys to call him Phil, not Mr. Maris—and he was part of why Dylan liked math best. For one thing Phil was young. Everybody but the inmates was old at DuWalt, old and musty like the walls. Draco said DuWalt was an elephant graveyard where old prison staffers came to die. Most of them didn't want to be there any more than the boys they guarded did.

Phil wasn't more than twenty-three or -four. He wore his hair long. It was light brown and curled on his collar and over his ears. Draco called him a hippy and laughed at Dylan because he didn't know what that was.

Math and Phil gave Dylan a place to go outside his skull. Dylan's mom would have called that a blessing. He got to thinking maybe monsters were blessed by some kind of monster god.

They weren't.

At half-past ten in the morning a couple months after he'd gotten to DuWalt, Dylan was called out of class by one of the guards, an old man who was scared of the bigger boys and made up for it on the littler ones.

Ten a.m. was math class. Dylan hated being taken out so he didn't move as fast or look as meek as he usually did when the guards told him to do something. The old guy made him pay by herding him down the hall with a bitter monologue: "You really think you're something don't you you little psycho if you'd been a kid of mine by god you'd never have picked up any axe or I'd have shown you what for and don't think I won't do it now you get any kind of idea . . ."

Dylan didn't listen. None of the boys listened. Still the sourness of the man tainted the air. DuWalt smelled old and cold. Under the pervasive odor of the benzene the janitors used was the reek of rancid fat, sweat, sauerkraut, farts and fear. The worst thing was that it didn't smell like home, not like anybody's home. At first the smell had made Dylan lonely and scared. Now he was okay with it. He was okay with DuWalt. Where else could a kid like him be?

On the second floor, above the classrooms and below where the Ward C boys slept, a big hall had been cobbled up into a lot of small rooms with flimsy doors letting off a narrow hallway. Rat maze, the Ward C boys called it. The rooms didn't go all the way to the ceiling, which was built of beams with this cobwebby chandelier made to look like thorny branches.

The guard told Dylan to stop outside the third door then shouldered him aside as if he might be thinking of rushing through and murdering who-ever was inside. Acting like he'd just saved the world from the forces of evil, the guard rapped on the wood. Dylan couldn't help but look at the billy club on the old guy's belt; it was all but sticking in his face. Maybe he wanted Dylan to try to take it so he could beat on him, or spray him with Mace and play the hero.

Maybe he was just a stupid old man.

One day it would get him killed.

"Enter," said a voice. Not "come in" or "just a minute," but "enter," like he was a king and they were his subjects.

The guard pushed open the door and said, "Got

your nutcase for you, Doc." He stood aside and Dylan walked past him into a little office. Two of the walls were plywood, painted white. On one there was a nondescript picture of a foggy landscape, no glass in the frame. Dylan knew it was bolted to the wall; a bunch of similar murky paintings were bolted around DuWalt. The story was they'd been done by a warden's wife and he'd put them up. Maybe they thought it would make the place seem less like what it was.

The other wall was of granite, like a castle from the movies. Against one of the plywood walls was a couch, not fancy leather but a faded cloth couch that had once been turquoise. A wing chair was beside it with a little round table at its arm. A single deep-set window let in a suggestion of the short winter day's light.

A middle-aged man, trim and fit looking, with carefully combed hair and long thin fingers, sat in the room's only chair. He had a short beard and sandy graying hair. His beard was red and looked as if it belonged on somebody else.

"I'm Dr. Kowalski," he said and gestured to the couch.

Lying down would be too weird. Dylan perched on the edge of the sofa. The doctor looked at him for a long time—so long Dylan had to stop himself from fidgeting.

"So you're the Butcher Boy," the doctor said finally.

Butcher Boy.

Dylan had heard it before but for some reason this time the words made his brain skid forward and back. Time warped. For a second he was back in the courtroom in black and white and Chinese. Eleven years outside seemed as if they'd never happened and the months in juvie felt like all of his life. Life before rushed in and then receded and it shook him.

The doctor wanted to shake him; at least Dylan chose to believe that. If it wasn't a trick to get him to respond in a certain way, then Dr. Kowalski was "one mean fuck," as Draco would say. One who wanted to pry Dylan's brain out and look at it under bright lights. Fear shuddered up. He tried not to let it show.

Rich wouldn't let anybody see him scared.

"Yes, sir," Dylan said. The man stared at him. Edges of the fake room wavered slightly like they'd done at the trial. "Butcher Boy," Dylan said, in case that was what the doctor was waiting for him to admit. If the man didn't start talking soon, Dylan was afraid he wouldn't be able to understand him, that his brain would turn on him like it had with the lawyers. Survival instinct told him Dr. Kowalski wouldn't deal well with that.

"And you don't remember anything, that so?" the doctor said.

"No, sir. I mean, yes, sir. I don't remember." He did remember bits here and there but he knew they weren't the bits Kowalski cared about. Besides, he didn't think the doctor really wanted him to answer; he sounded like he had all the answers already and was waiting to spring them.

"I'm here to help you remember that night. I've worked with boys like you—men too. I wrote a book on a case of a woman who had blocked out drowning her infant daughter. Didn't make the *New York Times* Best Seller List, but it sold well enough." Dr. Kowalski smiled and waited.

Having no idea what the *New York Times* list was or whether it was bad or good that the book didn't get on it, Dylan looked at the murky oil painting over the doctor's chair so his eyeballs had some place to be.

"Do you believe that?" the doctor demanded.

Dylan didn't know if he was asking if he believed he was there to help him or that his book had sold well enough. Confusion was growing up thick as brambles in a fairytale.

Tick, and tick, and tick, the doctor let more silence clock by. Dylan knew he should say something, remember something, but since he couldn't he went as far into the murky picture as he could. The painting wasn't laid out very well and it made him slide in his mind toward the trees on the left side. The warden's wife wasn't a very good artist, he decided.

"So, tell me about your dreams," the psychiatrist said. He crossed his legs like a girl and leaned back in his chair.

Dylan came out of the painting with a twitch. The eyes behind the tortoiseshell glasses were boring into him.

"Should I lay down or something?" Dylan asked. The sofa looked clean but it smelled of damp and carbolic.

"Do you want to lie down?"

The way he asked the question made it sound important. Not knowing whether he was supposed to want to lie down or *not* to want to lie down, or if the doctor would think he was going to kill people if he did the wrong thing, Dylan did nothing.

Dr. Kowalski sighed.

*Nothing* was clearly not the right thing to do, Dylan knew then, but it was too late to do anything about it.

"Tell me about your dreams," the doctor repeated.

Usually Dylan dreamed a lot and vividly but as he cast back in his mind he couldn't recall a single dream. It could have been the drugs they gave him at night, but he guessed it was because the doctor was being so screwy he could hardly think.

Kowalski nodded sagely. "You're afraid to dream," he said. "Your unconscious mind is afraid to let you relive the bloodshed." He jotted something down on a little note pad.

Dylan flinched. A dream jerked loose from his brain. He had dreamed. A vivid dream. "I remember," he said excitedly.

The doctor leaned forward, his eyes intense.

"I was outside," Dylan said. "Me and Rich were playing a game or something and Mom called from the backdoor for us to come in. When we went in she was putting supper on the table and a dog was sitting at a chair like a person and we all laughed."

Doctor Kowalski waited, pursed his lips so his whiskers fanned out around his mouth, then leaned back again.

"That's it," Dylan said. "That's all I remember." The doctor didn't believe him; he thought Dylan made up the dream to prove his unconscious mind or whatever wasn't hiding the things that happened.

"Shall I lay down now?" Dylan asked desperately. Dr. Olson had been hinting he might get out of the psych ward soon and he needed to do one right thing before the psychiatrist pushed him down the rabbit hole and his head shut down.

"Do you want to?" the doctor asked disapprovingly. He was just asking; it didn't mean anything now.

For a while longer the psychiatrist asked questions. They weren't the kind of questions anybody should ask. He wanted to know how many bowel movements Dylan had every day and if he liked the way they smelled and if he touched them. When the hour was over, Dylan thought he might actually be glad to get back to the psych ward.

The guard didn't come for him. Draco did.

"You get any cool drugs?" Draco asked.

Dylan didn't know he was supposed to but he didn't want to seem like a dork. "Nothing good," he said.

"You get, you share."

"Sure."

"You're alright," Draco said. They walked down the narrow fake hall where partitions chopped up the once gracious room. "You gotta get out of psych," Draco said suddenly. "You stay in psych you're gonna be crazy as a loon in no time. Seriously. They make you one crazy fuck in there. Get out."

Dylan believed him. He could feel himself becoming one crazy fuck after just an hour with the psychiatrist. "How do I get out?" he asked.

Draco thought for a minute. "What you gotta do is act like you want to stay. You know, like you're sane but you want the easy life, the extra food, the bigger space, like that. You got to ask for drugs, not like you need 'em but like you like 'em for the high. They don't know squat; they don't know those aren't, like, *recreational* drugs, you know. *Catch 22* man. You do that and they'll put you in Ward C before you can say, 'Lithium.'"

"Will I still have to talk to Dr. Kowalski?" Dylan asked.

"Nothing is going to get you loose from Dr. K.

He'll suck your brain out and use it for toilet paper."

Dylan believed it. "I'm already a few squares low," he confided and Draco laughed.

"This candy-assed shrink is going to duh-rug you, fill you so full of pills you aren't going to know whether you're saluting the flag or beating your meat." Draco let out a whoop like this was good news.

"You're so fucking crazy, we're going to end up millionaires."

# Louisiana, 2007

*Charlie Starkweather. Bunch of folks killed. 1958. This one's ancient history. I don't know why I have to do Charlie. But he's easy. He lived in Nebraska. If that's not a good reason to start shooting, what is? It was probably winter, and he just went nuts. Back then, they were all into this bad-boy thing. I mean like Billy the Kid, but modern day. There were those movies and stuff about bad boys and how cool they were; women wanted to sleep with them. They just did what they wanted. Took what they wanted. Then died in a blaze of glory. That looks pretty good from where I sit. Instead of rotting in some little Nebraska berg, you grab a great car and go around the country with your girlfriend, and you live high on the hog, and if anybody tries to stop you, you just shoot them and drive off. I bet Charlie was seeing himself as a Jesse James, Bonnie and Clyde kind of guy, just having a high old time. Putting the baby down the outhouse hole. I couldn't do that. She's crying and all, but there's nobody around for a million miles, so why not let her cry? She was too little to identify them.*

## 8

Booze had never had much of a hold on Marshall. In his teens, he'd smoked a lot of dope. Everybody did. They had to, to get by. Or so they told themselves and each other. He'd never married or fathered a child. In his twenty-odd years as a partner in Stokes, Knight, and Marchand Restoration Architects, he had never taken more than a month or two of vacation all put together.

But lately, he'd sensed a change touching as lightly as an autumn leaf drifting onto the sleeve of his coat, the fringe of a woman's shawl brushing the back of his hand in a crowded restaurant.

*An awakening?*

Marshall pushed the thought aside. He had no patience with self-analysis. It was just that in recent months, after work, he'd stand beneath the wrought iron balcony that shaded his offices on Jackson Square and allow himself a couple of minutes and, in careful measured sips, he'd *enjoy* himself.

He was enjoying himself now, though this would not be evident to even a careful observer. Standing perfectly still Marshall simply breathed. With the breathing came an unfolding, a blossoming which, either by choice or habit, he'd not experienced since he was a child. Perhaps not even then. Or maybe always then. This was how he imagined children feeling all the time: connected, plugged in, the world forming and reforming around them as they moved.

His pulse rate slowed, and a feeling as near to peace as he ever knew ironed the years from his face. The sense of being one of Jackson Square's living statues settled over him.

On the square's southwest corner, where the horse carriages lay in wait for tourists, a silver man, shining from his cropped kinky hair to his tattered running shoes, was frozen in mid stride, an upturned, silver baseball cap by his side to collect coins and dollars. On the northwest corner, where St. Peter's Street elbowed into Chartres, lace skirts cascading artfully down shallow, cement steps, was the golden lady—immobile, beneficent, the Good Witch of the East caught in amber. In front of St. Louis Cathedral, shouldering space between fortune-tellers, a lineman was caught halfway up a pole cleverly self-supported by a camouflaged, steel I beam.

Then there was the Man in a Suit, hair white at the temples, dark blond, and thick where it fell over a heavily lined forehead, suit immaculate, leather briefcase in hand—Marshall Marchand, architect. Becoming one of Jackson Square's living statues suited him. At one with inanimate, yet living, things he indulged in a rare and delicious sense of belonging—to what, Marshall didn't choose to pursue. The sense of connecting was enough.

Maybe he had outlived the demons.

Then again, maybe the demons were immortal. The thought jarred him from his fragile peace and, as his eyes cleared, he saw her.

Framed by ornate arches of ironwork, she was seated on a bench, her head bowed over a book, the spine resting on her neatly trousered knee. Golden and clear as water, spring light poured through the blacksmith arms of a live oak, dripped green-gold off resurrection ferns to warm her cheek and fire the champagne-blonde hair across her forehead. Liquid luminescence curved around the swell of her breasts and set the left half of the book she was reading aglow. Form, function, color, light, and line came together flawlessly.

An inrush of breath kick-started the Man in a Suit to life, heart lurching like the first turnings of a cold engine. Blood pumped noisily past his ears. All at once he was aware of the ten thousand sensations of a new-made being: the pressure of the soles of his feet against the concrete, the pull of the briefcase handle on his fingers, a cinnamon-sugar scent from a nearby bakery, faint skritching of scaled toes on brick as a pigeon strutted by, the balm of the sun's warmth against the back of his hand.

He stepped off the curb—off the edge of the known world—and moved toward her. His brother Danny could have stopped him—would have stopped him—but Danny wasn't there. Watching himself, an awestruck spectator of his own destruction, he crossed the brick lane, drifted up the steps into the garden, and approached the bench where she sat.

A moment passed. Then she looked up to see who had intruded upon her solitude. Her eyes were of moss and lichen, vines over old wood, slow streams in autumn, rich with tannin and fallen leaves.

"Would you join me for tea?" he heard himself say in a level voice. "It's a little past time, I know." He spoke as if he'd been born in the century in which he worked every day—the eighteen hundreds when people had an elevated sense of the importance of human intercourse. It should have struck him as absurd, but it didn't.

In the cool, running depths of her eyes, thoughts flickered near the surface, then retreated again to the shadows. "My name is Polly," she said with a smile and a lilting drawl that could put mint in juleps. "I am a woman of a certain age, divorced, and with two daughters, seven and nine; I am in the middle of a good book, so, if you're a shallow fiddling kind of a fellah, I have no time for you."

"I'm not that kind of fellow," Marshall said gravely.

She laughed, and in his mind, the sound built playgrounds for children, church steeples for bells, and walls with clear, cold, cascading fountains.

"In that case I would simply love to have a cup of tea with you."

## 9

Polly told Marshall Marchand the story of her life—the G-rated version. With the sex and violence edited out, it was a charming fairytale: how a lost child of fifteen had come to Jackson Square, how a gypsy had foreseen a glittering future for her, and how that future had come to pass.

Marshall was captivated as she'd meant him to be. She smiled and leaned in, her head tilted slightly, bangs brushing the thick, dark lashes. "Now tell me," she said sweetly, "how is it that you have come to be a man old enough to have silver at his temples, hold a partnership in a well-regarded firm, and yet are not married?"

Marshall started visibly.

"You don't beat around the bush do you?" He laughed and set his cup back in its saucer.

"Well, I do," Polly drawled, "but only when I have no interest regarding what is in that bush." She was flirting; she could feel the magnetism between them as easily as she could see the sparkle of the candlelight on the wine. It had been a while since she enjoyed such a physical awareness of a man.

"Am I to have no secrets?"

"No, darlin', not a one. If a man wants to keep secrets, he must never let a woman close. We are with secrets the way cats are with curiosity. We simply cannot leave them alone."

He hid the shape of his mouth with his cup. For an unsettling moment, she couldn't tell if he hid a smile or a grimace of fear.

"No secrets," he said, and the warmth of his voice reassured her she was not losing her touch. "Gad, why haven't I ever married? I don't think about it much. My work, maybe? I haven't had a lot of time to find Ms. Right. I like my solitude. I live with my brother. Danny and I were orphaned as kids and have pretty much just each other for family."

He shook his head in confusion, and Polly almost believed he actually hadn't given matrimony a good deal of thought. That, or he was making up the story as he went along and hadn't decided how it was going to end. "Obviously, I'm not the introspective type." He smiled ruefully.

"You live with your brother?" It was not the red flag it would have been had he lived with his mother, but Polly found it mildly off-putting.

A smile deepened one corner of his well-cut lips. "We don't exactly live together. We live in the same building: condos, one on top of the other. Separate beds and everything."

He had a disarming—or alarming—capacity for reading Polly's mind. "And you never married?" She touched the back of his hand and whispered conspiratorially, "First dates are for deciding if we wish to bother with a second."

"Fair enough. I never married. Now you know

the worst: I'm an old maid. I didn't have a date to the prom; never went steady with a cheerleader. I almost got married once—can I get credit for that?"

"All the credit in the world, my dear. I almost stayed married once so we are even."

"Why didn't you? Stay married, I mean?"

Polly eyed him narrowly. "Surely, you do not want to hear about all my husbands?" she said.

"I thought we were clearing the decks for our second date. How many were there?"

Since he sounded more alarmed than amused, Polly chose the truth: "I was married once. He was a kind man, but not a good man; and, in the end that comes to be an oxymoron, doesn't it? One cannot be kind in any meaningful way over any length of time without also being good. We were married for fifteen months."

She picked up her tea and took a slow sip to let any unasked questions pass unanswered. In the brief time between the lowering of her eyes and the lifting of her cup, the last night of her brief marriage played through her mind:

Ten o'clock, and Gracie was standing in her crib, holding onto the bars. Soon, she would be walking. Polly kissed her round face and marveled that such perfection could be built out of such mundane things as milk and pureed carrots.

"It's the love, sweetheart. That's what makes babies grow big and strong," she whispered. "Sleep tight."

Turning out the light, she left the nursery. On her way to bed, she stopped by the small room—a closet really—that Carver called his office. The only light was the glow of the computer screen. Over his shoulder, she could read the words on the screen. Transfixed, she watched, as he exchanged sexually explicit notes simultaneously with three different women, one via e-mail and two through instant messaging. Backing out quietly, Polly went to the bedroom they'd shared for over a year.

She sat on top of the bedcovers in her pajamas and stared at the familiar walls. So little of Carver was represented. Had his clothes not hung in the closet, it would have been as if he'd never existed.

The house was hers; she'd bought it the first year she'd been tenured by the college. The bed was a sleigh bed she had found secondhand and refurbished. Framed photographs she had taken of her favorite places in New Orleans hung to either side of an antique dresser she'd bought on Magazine Street. All of it was from her mind, or from her heart, or from her work.

All of it was clean, and decent, and honestly come by. Sordidness was anathema to her. Lies and foul language, violence—the gods of her mother—nauseated her. To have Carver spinning webs of petty filth in the darkness ten feet from Gracie's nursery gave her that same sense of sickness.

The next morning, she asked him to leave and to give her a divorce. He had refused until she offered him thirty thousand dollars, all of her savings. Three weeks later, she found out she was pregnant with Emma and knew she had everything she had ever wanted.

"You still haven't told me why the marriage ended," Marshall said.

His voice snapped Polly out of her reverie. "It ended, dear heart, because I did not love him," Polly answered truthfully. For a while they sat in comfortable silence, sipping their tea. Like a schoolgirl on a date, Polly laid her hand on the tablecloth and was thrilled when, after rearranging his spoon, Marshall's lingered near it.

What Polly left unsaid was that, except for Emma and Gracie, she had never fallen in love with anyone. She enjoyed the company of men, but she didn't fall in love. Like orgasm or the smell of lilacs, the sensation of falling could not be described, only experienced. She wondered if she were not sensing its first tingles.

The sweet of the evening poured through the open windows on a gentle breeze. Lights in the square were coming on. The glow of the candles warmed Mr. Marchand's liquid-brown eyes, 'til she felt she might immerse herself in them forever. Polly sensed she was being set up by some—possibly malevolent—spirit, the muse of Barbara Cartland or Danielle Steele.

As an English professor and a lover of the classics, a part of her noted with interest how this frisson of emotions flowing through her with the subtlety of velvet-wrapped electricity informed the sonnets she had taught, the romances of Shakespeare and Molière. She reminded herself that the life she had built with her daughters was perfect and precious. A man would scatter dirty undershorts and oversized shoes throughout their orderly universe. The thought of Mr. Marchand's undershorts sent a thrill through her, and she knew she was undoubtedly going to make a fool of herself in the not-too-distant future.

Two teenagers in high-heeled mules, both on cell phones, clattered by the open window. One had the smallest Chihuahua Polly had ever seen. It was pure white, the ghost of dogness, and was being towed on a leash. The little creature stumbled on its two-inch legs, fell, then was dragged up again, as its oblivious mistress chattered on.

"They buy them as accessories, like a purse or a scarf," Marshall said disgustedly. "Miss," he called through the window. "Miss."

The girl turned a blank look in their direction.

"Your dog," Marshall said to her. "Would it like a drink of water? The poor, little guy looks pretty tired."

The girl shook her head and, still talking on the phone, picked the Chihuahua up and tucked it under her arm.

Polly hadn't been raised to respect life or practice kindness. When she'd escaped Prentiss, all

she'd known was she hated cruelty. In the inter-
vening years she'd been both cruel and kind and,
like Sidney Poitier in *A Patch of Blue*, come to
believe compassion was the greatest human virtue.

"You are a good man," she said.

"A virtual god to dogs," Marshall mocked his
good deed. "An old girlfriend of mine—the one I
get credit for almost marrying—used to have a
white Chihuahua, Tippity." His lips closed tightly
on the dog's name as if he wished he'd never mentioned it.

"Did it die?" she asked impulsively.

For a minute, she didn't think he was going to
answer. Before the ease of their camaraderie could
leak away, he began to speak. "I was renovating a
shotgun near Magazine. The place was more or
less just a shell. Danny and I had a falling out, and
I was camping there. Occasionally, Elaine and her
dog would stay over. One Friday Danny brought us
a bottle of champagne as a peace offering. Our
argument had been over Elaine. It wasn't that he
didn't like her, so much as he didn't like the fact of
her, if you know what I mean."

Polly hadn't the foggiest idea what he meant, but
she nodded. She hadn't wanted to know this much
about somebody else's dog, but Marshall seemed
to need to tell the story. Though she'd dragged it
out of him, he now spoke as if he had to tell it
beginning to end, all the words in the proper order.

"So, anyway, the champagne. When we woke up

in the morning Tippity was missing. Elaine flipped out; I flipped out. She finally went to work. To make a long story shorter, I found the dog in the freezer. Evidently, Elaine had gotten up during the night for ice cream, or whatever, and opened it. The freezer was the drawer kind at the bottom of the refrigerator, and Tippity had jumped in. When I got to her, she'd about run out of time."

"Time! Oh, my Lord!" Polly exclaimed. "The time! I forgot my children!" Caught up in Marshall, she had put all thought of Emma and Gracie from her mind. Maternal guilt had her reaching for purse and cell phone before she'd removed the napkin from her lap.

Immediately, Marshall was out of his chair signaling the waitress.

"It's okay," Polly said, as she held the phone to her ear. "I didn't leave them wandering around the Ninth Ward or anything of the kind. A friend is watching them for me. But that dear friend is eighty years old and would probably like to go to bed soon."

"Let me walk you to your car," Marshall said, as he threw enough money on the table to cover the bill and the tip twice over.

Polly had been so absorbed by a handsome man that she had forgotten the children. For a mother, that was terrible; for a woman, it was marvelous.

# 10

Idly, Red shuffled the oversized deck and watched Marshall—Mr. Marchand—talking with the blonde. She knew Marshall Marchand—maybe better than anybody but his brother, Danny, the other Mr. Marchand. Marshall Marchand was why she'd become the Woman in Red: to be near him. And to make a few bucks. Tarot reading on Jackson Square paid pretty well, or had until Katrina. Posthurricane tourists didn't seem as interested in getting their cards read. Maybe they figured if there was anything to it, of the thirty or so fortune-tellers on the square, at least one might have mentioned that the levees were going to break. Nobody'd seen it coming. Red hadn't seen it coming. Though, afterward, she did remember the cards had been running dark most of that August.

Red knew the blonde, too. Not by name and not to talk to. But she knew her by sight. Blondie was a regular. Came about once a month. After getting her cards read, she'd sit in the park with a book or sometimes just watch the people going by. This wasn't the first time a man had come up to her, but this was the first time she'd ever given anybody the time of day.

Jason had done the blonde's reading today. With his phony English accent and swarthy pirate looks, he grabbed up a lot of the business. "Hey Jason," she hissed across the space separating their setups. "What was in the cards for blondie tonight?"

"Her name's Polly. Pollyanna. Good name. Old-fashioned and sweet."

"Yeah, yeah. Anything interesting in the cards?"

Jason cocked an eyebrow as thick and mobile as a caterpillar. Red believed in the tarot. Jason didn't believe in anything. She wondered if he was going to rag her about it. He chose not to, and she was relieved.

"Let's see." He fingered a chin so dark with stubble Red half-imagined she could hear the rasp of his fingernails being filed down. "I did the Celtic Cross. The Knight of Swords was in the sixth."

Daring, brave, handsome, unstable man, Mr. Marchand.

"What else?"

"I don't memorize this crap," Jason said amiably.

"What else? Come on, don't be an asshole."

"The Devil card was in the top of the ninth." Even in the dusky light she could see the twinkle in his eyes. She wondered if he was bullshitting her.

The ninth card represented things that came out of nowhere. The Devil coming out of nowhere was no joke. Not with Mr. Marchand in the mix. "No kidding?" She sounded plaintive, like a beggar. She said it again, better. "No kidding?"

Jason waved a dismissal. "Would I kid about the Devil?" he asked, as he turned to smile on a couple of rubes down from Mississippi or Montana.

Mr. Marchand's blonde, Polly, stood up, and they walked away together. Red whistled softly through her teeth. Ninety-nine point nine percent of the time, watching Mr. Marchand was a major snooze. He didn't do much of anything that she could tell. Just worked, and worked, and went home, and worked some more.

At the gate on the garden's east side, the two of them turned right. Mr. Marchand's head was bent to catch what Polly was saying, a smile—a rare thing with him—playing around his mouth.

Red pushed down on the table to heave herself from her chair. Her hands were pressed flat, fingers, fat at the base, pointed where the acrylic nails had been filed too sharp, splayed out like starfish arms. For an instant, she didn't recognize them. Her hands were slender, the skin smooth and white. These fat, spotty, wrinkled things revolted her.

Mostly, she never thought of who she used to be, but the alien hands made her remember. A wave of self-pity washed over her; if she'd had a cyanide tooth, she'd've bitten down on it. *Second best,* she thought, and fished a silver flask from one of the plastic Wal-Mart bags that served as purse and office.

*Bag lady*, she thought as she took a swig. Two

steps from being a fucking bag lady. The silver flask made her feel a little better, not just the hit of Jack Daniels, but the flask itself. It probably wasn't real silver or even an antique—she'd gotten it for four dollars at the French Market, and there was a dent in it. But if she didn't think about that, she could pretend it was like she was taking a tipple, like an English lady on a foxhunt maybe, a little snort to keep off the chill.

"Hey, Em. Emily," she called, as she delicately wiped the mouth of the flask on her sleeve and screwed the cap back on. "Will you watch my setup for a few minutes? I got to pee."

Emily wasn't a friend exactly, but they'd set up next to each other in the same place for years and got along okay. Maybe that was friendship. Who could tell anymore?

"Go ahead. We're here for the late shift."

"We" meant Emily and her best friend, Bony, an old wiener dog so crippled it had a little cart like a person's wheelchair that carried its rear end around. Bony spent his days on Em's lap. Em lifted Bony's paw and waved bye-bye.

Red took the zippered makeup bag she kept her money in from the sack beneath her chair and stuffed it down the front of her shift until it wedged against the band of her bra. If somebody made off with the rest of the stuff, it was mostly crap anyway.

For a big woman, she moved gracefully. She was proud of that. One time, when she was a lot younger, she'd gotten the bug to take ballet. She'd done real good until she'd run out of money.

Well, what had happened was she'd had a few too many before she went to class, and the bitch who taught it got huffy, and that was that. She'd been going to quit anyway. Too expensive.

Dusk had slid a couple more notches toward night. Hurrying across the garden, she wasn't worried that Mr. Marchand or his lady friend would turn and see her. Most people didn't see her anymore. Sometimes it made her feel bad. More often than not, it came in handy.

They hadn't gone far, just into the River's Edge Restaurant on the corner. They were seated at a candlelit table by one of the windows.

Red settled herself on an iron bench on the brick walkway. It was like she was in a dark theater, and they were the movie on screen, except she couldn't hear what they were saying. She pulled out the silver flask. That never went into the bags unless she was right there with them; it lived in a pocket, and if her gown didn't have a pocket for it, she got that iron-on stuff and made one. A girl needed the essentials.

Red had never seen Mr. Marchand like he was tonight. Narrowing her eyes against the booze, she tried to figure out if it was the candlelight or what. He looked like he'd lost a couple decades. Red took another little snort to help her concentrate and cocked her head to one side.

Not just younger. "Fuck," she whispered. She'd hit on it. Once the thought came to her there was no doubt about it.

Mr. Marchand looked happy. It had taken her so long because she'd never seen him happy before. Not like she'd ever thought about it; she had better things to do than sit around wondering if he was happy or not. But seeing it she knew he hadn't been like that until now. He didn't yuk it up like some guys might, or grin, or anything. It was in his strange, quiet way. He sort of glowed happy, like babies when they're asleep and fed.

Miss Pollyanna was doing it. He glowed at her. Or maybe reflected the light coming off of her because she was a natural glow-er. Red didn't know quite what she meant by that but it was true. The Polly woman had that inner thing going that can't be painted on or faked.

Ms. Polly-the-blonde-charmer didn't know what she was getting into.

Man, was she going to have something to talk about tonight. This was big! Red laughed and tipped the flask again.

"Fuck." It was empty. She tossed it toward the garbage can on the corner, remembered it wasn't a beer can, and hurried to retrieve it before some junky or drunk got it.

Sydney's was down North Peters a couple of blocks. The store carried booze, and chips, and cigarettes. It'd take her probably five minutes, ten at the outside, to go and resupply. For a minute, she stood wondering if she dared. If they got away, it could go bad for her.

Polly laughed, and Mr. Marchand reached out as if he was going to touch her hand. They weren't going anywhere for a while, not unless it was to somebody's room, and Red doubted blondie was the type. She knew for a fact Mr. Marchand wasn't.

Comforted by that thought, she deserted her post in search of refreshments. She wasn't away long, she was sure of that, but when she got back they were gone. A waitress was wiping down the table.

"Fuck me, fuck me, fuck me," she whispered as she turned around in a full circle peering through the gathering darkness, the glittering lights, and the gabbling tourists. A teenager laughed. With instinct born of experience, Red knew it was at her. Once it would have hurt her feelings; now she barely registered it.

If he found out he'd beat the crap out of her. She could lie. No she couldn't. He always knew.

"Shit, shit, shit," she murmured. A mule-drawn carriage pulled away from the curb where they lined up waiting for fares and she saw them on the far side of the North Peters: Polly's hair, the color of the moon under the streetlights; Mr. Marchand's dark suit, a shadow between her and the traffic.

Red trotted to catch up. Years and pounds had built up around her middle, and before she'd made it fifty feet she was gasping for breath, sweat running between her breasts, but she didn't give up. They walked for what seemed like miles but was only five blocks before they finally stopped on Decatur.

There weren't as many tourists here as on the square. Red fought to quiet her breathing. If she kept on huffing like a hyperventilating rhino, everybody was going to look at her. Mr. Marchand took the blonde's keys, opened the driver's door of a silver Volvo, held it as she got in, then handed her keys back. Polly was laughing, and he looked like he didn't know what to do.

He didn't know what to do—that's why he was acting like some asshole out of a Fred Astaire movie. He didn't know people didn't do that crap anymore; they just hooked up, and screwed, and moved on. Mr. Marchand was so stupid he was still doing the whole gentlemen-prefer-blondes routine.

And poor stupid Miss Polly was lapping it up.

*Man, was there ever going to be a shitload of stuff to talk about.*

# 11

A week had passed, and the lovely Mr. Marchand had not called. Polly might have called him but, though the rules in the new millennium had changed, Polly's had not. She was not averse to making the first move; it was the second. A second date set the tone for a relationship. In a man's world, it was necessary that he desire a woman a shade more than she desired him.

Since her marriage to Carver had imploded, Polly had not invested much of herself in the society of men. With the advent of the lovely Mr. Marchand, this had changed. Stifling a sigh, she looked out over the bent heads of her English literature class: Barbara scribbling madly, Tyrell gazing out the window, Bethany staring at the paper the way a bird might stare at a cobra.

After Katrina, New Orleans was a city without children. Schools had been shut down, the students evacuated, enrolled in schools miles—and sometimes states—away. During the last months of 2005, the adults who came back would meet in the rubble-filled streets, mops and shovels in hand, cheering one another with the phrase, "Come January." January was the date the schools were to reopen and, like those left bereft by the Pied Piper, they waited for the children to return and save New Orleans.

Where children were, parents were: living, working, buying, selling, renovating, recreating the cycle of supply and demand the city needed to recover. Images of New Orleanians rebuilding morphed into images of Marshall Marchand recreating the city's historic homes, then to his sudden rare smile. Surreptitiously and undoubtedly with the same sneaky look her students wore when they pulled a similar stunt, Polly eased her cell phone out of her purse and checked to see if she had any calls. Four: one from Marshall Marchand.

Feeling like an idiot, she slipped out of the classroom. In the faculty lounge she checked her messages.

"What are you giggling about?" Mr. Andrews, the eternally sour teacher of American history, had come into the lounge.

"Hot date," Polly drawled and batted her eyes.

He grunted.


"I wanted to show you my neighborhood," Marshall said as they parked on a side street beneath three tall pine trees. "If you'd be more comfortable in a public place, I'd be glad to take you out for dinner."

Polly enjoyed Marshall's old-world manners. She reached across the console and touched his hand lightly. "I'll just keep my cell phone on 911."

A look akin to pain—or fear—flashed in his eyes. It was gone so quickly she scarcely noticed the spark of alarm it triggered in her.

He walked around the car to open her door. It was slightly embarrassing and rather grand to sit quietly and compose one's self while a man did manly things.

Because he was a restoration architect Polly assumed he would live in a monument to old money on St. Charles or in a classic home in an undamaged area of Metairie. But his house was in a pioneer neighborhood. The front yard of the duplex where Marshall and his brother lived contrasted starkly against the weed-filled yard of their neighbor. In the Marchand's yard was a mosaic of brick and moss framed by elephant ears surrounded by a wrought iron fence, the bottom brown with rust from the floodwaters.

They stood on the sidewalk outside the garden gate. Marshall seemed reticent about taking her inside. "I've got the top two floors; Danny lives downstairs. Below him is an aboveground basement. When the levees broke, we got twenty-six inches of water but cleaning out the cellar is a whole lot easier than gutting the front room," Marshall told her.

A man, Danny of course, came out the front door of the lower unit and leaned on the porch rail at the top of the stairs. Though she wasn't touching him, Polly could feel Marshall's aura change. Not that she saw auras, but, had she, she didn't doubt his would have gotten brighter, or darker, or redder. Changed.

There was a strong family resemblance. Danny looked younger and had a less somber cast to his face; the lines of strain that fanned out from the corners of Marshall's eyes were missing from his brother's and, when Danny smiled, there was a playfulness Marshall lacked.

"Who's the lady, Marsh?" he called. Marshall

had not mentioned her to his brother. *Not a good sign,* Polly thought and was annoyed that she was looking for signs.

Marshall made the introductions from where they stood, outside the fence. Only when Danny invited them in for a drink before dinner did Marshall reach for the gate. Because this was New Orleans, and Anne Rice had educated the world on the habits and manners of the undead, it crossed Polly's mind that vampires cannot enter unless invited. A B movie shiver passed down her spine. It wasn't altogether unpleasant.

Danny's home was beautifully appointed in stark, modern blacks and whites and impeccably kept. A framed magazine cover picturing him cutting a ribbon at the opening of the first Le Cure explained his wealth. He owned a chain of high-end boutique drugstores.

"I keep Marsh out of trouble," Danny said, as he handed Polly a glass of white wine without asking what she preferred. He winked, "And you look like trouble to me."

"I have never given anyone a moment's difficulty," she drawled. "Not even as a very small child."

Danny poured a meager whiskey for himself, neat, and sat on the end of the sofa. The leather was soft and matte black, stark to look at, but luxurious to sit on. "So, how did my brother lure you into his clutches?" he said.

108

"He invited me to tea," Polly said and smiled at Marshall.

"Ah, the old tea gambit," Danny said. "Marshall lives on the edge."

The brothers shared an inner communion Polly had occasionally noted in the twins she had taught. Having no family—or, as she said in her archer moments, none to speak of—she held familial ties in high regard. Whoever married one brother would have to be aware that there was sacred ground between them and tread lightly.

*Whoever married.* She was doing it again.

Dinner was as much a surprise as Marshall's home was. While she leaned on the counter in a kitchen better furnished than her own and sipped wine, Marshall made iced asparagus and seasoned sautéed goat cheese on toast. He felt her eyes on him and looked up from his work. "I cook," he said. Again he'd apparently read her mind. "I've also mastered the art of free-range grazing. In this town, a guy can pretty much live on the spread at special events. Kind of like a dog knocking over garbage cans but with a tux and a caterer."

After dinner they walked. Knowledge that another hurricane season was soon to begin lent a sense of preciousness to those who had survived the last. People sat on their front porches or stoops drinking beer and talking with neighbors.

"I came here to invest," Marshall said. "I had a

notion of gentrifying, pocketing the money, and moving to a good neighborhood. Turns out this *is* a good neighborhood."

He took Polly's hand. His was warm, and dry, and callused like a working man's. Marshall was full of surprises. The men she'd dated had hands as manicured as hers.

The neighbors were mostly black or Hispanic, and Polly remembered Ma Danko. She hadn't thought of the old woman in years. Ma had been kind to her. To remember something good about the trailer park startled her and anger she'd not known she harbored eased, loosening the muscles across her back.

Marshall pointed out schools, showed her homes being renovated, told her which businesses were up and running north, south, east, and west and how this ephemeral box of progress would bring the neighborhood up. The talk was dry and serious, and Polly wondered what he was afraid he would say if he didn't talk about urban renewal.

"Did you lure me all the way out here to sell me a house?" she asked to upset whatever applecart he was pushing.

He stopped walking and looked at her. The setting sun dyed his hair red and limned the strong line of his jaw. "In a way," he said quietly.

# 12

Marshall handed Polly out of his vintage truck, highly cognizant of the pressure of her hand, the way she swung her legs, ankles neatly together. He walked with her to the door but did not kiss her goodnight.

She shook his hand—just the ends of her fingers in his—not the hard pumping as of a well handle that women had adopted from their male counterparts. "I had a splendid evening, Mr. Marchand. You are a darling man." With a glance up at him through her lashes, she turned and disappeared inside.

For a moment, long enough to savor the last whisper of her perfume but not so long as to seem a stalker, Marshall remained on the steps. He could not remember when he'd wanted to kiss a woman as much as he did Polly. Never, he expected. The strength of his desire was why he hadn't. He'd been afraid he'd step over the line—or swoon and make a fool of himself.

*Next time,* he promised, and returned to his truck. Thirty years ago when he'd bought it, it was a beat-up, old workhorse, and he'd used it as such. He still had a toolbox in the back full of carpenters' tools, but the truck was no longer a beast of burden. It was mint: a refurbished, spit-shined, cherry-red, 1949 pickup. He didn't take it out as much as he once had but something about Ms. Deschamps had decided him to bring her home in it. She'd loved it.

*And I love her.* The thought sent a stab of terror through him. "Where in the hell did that come from?" he asked aloud. It reminded him of the selling-her-a-house comment he'd made. There wasn't a whole lot of ways a woman could take that. It was a wonder she didn't run screaming down the street.

Marshall buckled his seat belt and resisted the urge to sit in the truck in front of her house just to be near her. He felt as if the day he'd seen her in the square he'd woken up, like Rip Van Winkle; that, until then, he'd been sleepwalking for twenty-five years. This rush of life was heady. With a cold fear that threatened to turn into panic he knew, if Polly were to vanish, he'd fall back into that self-induced coma. Or worse.

Marshall stomped the starter button so hard the old truck virtually leapt to attention. Did he think if he swept her off her feet and up the aisle quickly enough, by the time she found out what membership in the Marchand family entailed, it would be too late?

And how long could he keep lying to her? Lying to Polly was almost physically painful for Marshall, even when done by omission.

Like the first night. In telling the tragic tale of Elaine's dog and the freezer, he had omitted little

112

things, like the dog hadn't actually jumped into the freezer; its paws were taped together and its little muzzle taped shut so it couldn't bark.

Details like that.

Like how he wrenched the freezer drawer off its runners and saw the little dog, jaws rimed with frost, shivering on a bag of frozen peas, eyes big, paws together, silently begging not to be killed.

*That was a long time ago,* Marshall thought. *Things changed.*

In a sudden rage he pounded the steering wheel. "Damn it, things change!" he shouted.

MINNESOTA, 1973

———————

*Ronald "Butch" DeFeo. Killed six family members. 1974. Now this guy is one mean son of a bitch. You look at old Butch, and the rest of us seem like the boys next door. Six! I thought three was bad. Looks like I'm Snow White. Okay, I can sort of see doing it. Here's old Butch kid. Dad is always whaling on him. Mom's a doormat. His dad tells him not to take any shit off the kids at school but heaps shit on him at home. Heaps shit on the mom and the other kids. Yelling all the time. Huge fights. Four brothers and sisters. So Butch turns out to be a chip off the old block. He starts hitting back, and it works great. Gets him all this stuff, this boat, and his own room, and stuff. Dad kind of secretly respects him. I mean, he's been preaching this Butchie's whole life, right? Now, not only is Butch not getting the tar smacked out of him, but his dad is paying him to be cool. Big money, too. I can see where Butch might think he earned that money, what with getting whaled on and listening to screaming matches and whatever. But after he gets used to that for a while, he thinks, Hey, I could get more. These fucks owe me more. Way more. First thing is, he's got to kill the old man. No biggie; he's been hating the bastard forever. Then, probably Mom should bite the dust, too. She watched his dad beat up on him when he was little, so fuck her. The little kids. That's harder. But why not? I mean, who is going to look after them? Not our Butch. Hell, he's doing them a favor. Shoots them in their sleep. I think he's sorry about the little kids. You know, like when Dad had to kill a kitten we had because it got sick, and went blind, and he felt sad about that.*

*But he got over it.*

---

## 13

Dr. Kowalski had grown old treating Dylan. A few years with Butcher Boy, and the psychiatrist's sandy gray hair was thinning, the incongruous red beard flecked with dull white hairs.

Dylan had grown, if not wiser, then more cunning. He figured he'd learned more than Kowalski had. For one thing, he'd learned that Kowalski was not so much treating him—as if there were any treatment for boys who ran with axes—as exploiting him. He also realized that the thinning hair and graying beard had little to do with the fact that Dylan was a murderer, or even a poor tragic boy in juvie, and all to do with the fact that Dylan still wouldn't remember.

As the doctor's decline became more pronounced, he'd taken to looking at Dylan with piercing need. Every boy in DuWalt knew that look. They saw it on the faces of the "girls" who wanted to love them and the users who wanted to fuck them. It was so sharp in the faces of the boys whose folks came to visit that it hurt to look at them. Gangs of kids stared hungry like that when he and Draco peddled the drugs they'd scored. When that kind of naked hunger manifested, Dylan's hackles rose. Either the beast was fed or there was trouble.

In the ward, in the yard, trouble could be met

with fists or knives. Fists and knives wouldn't work with Kowalski.

*They'd work,* Dylan thought with a half smile. *They'd just cost too much.*

Kowalski was still lusting after his *New York Times* best seller. That first day Dylan hadn't known if that was good or bad. Now he knew. It was life and death for Kowalski. Life was when people thought he was a big deal; death was shrinking delinquents in the middle of Piddlesquat, Minnesota.

The "hook," Kowalski had told him in an unguarded moment, was when Dylan, like Kafka's cockroach boy, had metamorphosed into a hideous beast. The climax would be when Dylan remembered his transformation and spewed it forth for the delectation of his brilliant and kindly doctor. Right there in Dylan Raines's brain was fame and fortune. And the little psycho fuck wouldn't fork it over.

Dylan smiled, slumped down until his butt was nearly off the couch and his head at a sharp angle to the backrest, widened his eyes, and stared vacuously at the psychiatrist.

Kowalski knew the Ward C boys called the warren where his office was located the Rat's Maze. What he didn't know was that he was their pet rat. They conducted experiments on him. The result of one such experiment, conducted over a period of six weeks with four Ward C boys, was eye movement. The conclusion was that narrowed eyes excited the doc—not sexual excitement, Dr. K. wasn't AC/DC—but the way a cat gets excited when it sees a bird. The doctor saw a challenge and it goosed up his energy. Avoiding eye contact bored the shrink, and a bored head examiner was a bad thing. He'd start in with the do-you-smell-your-own-shit routine. The way to piss him off most effectively was the idiot stare. All the boys had perfected it.

*Maybe Kowalski's book should be about mental retardation brought on by psychoanalysis*, Dylan thought.

He could have given Kowalski what he wanted, or a facsimile thereof. Under the guise of getting him to remember, he had been forced to study his crimes as assiduously as other boys his age were made to study English, science, and math. He knew exactly what he had done, how he had done it, how long it had taken, where the blood spatters were, and how many steps there were from one body to the next. There probably wasn't a felon in America who knew as much about himself as Dylan did.

But he wouldn't *remember* it.

He would remember his mom and dad, week-ends at the lake cabin. He would remember school and his friends. His last best memory was of his mother's lips pressed like butterfly wings against his forehead the night she died, the tiny gold cross falling from her robe onto his cheek, the fresh-out-of-the-dryer smell of her nightgown, how cool her hand felt when she held his chin and spooned the cherry-flavored flu medicine into his mouth, the tired smile as she said, "Sleep tight, and don't let the bedbugs bite."

Pseudomedical brain battering had reduced those memories to dull, sepia-toned images. Since he wasn't likely to be gathering a whole lot more warm fuzzy memories in the near future, it pissed Dylan off that the mental health professionals had pawed over what he had until they were thread-bare.

Dylan could have told a hell of a good story, complete with adolescent angst and revelations to get Kowalski off his back, but there was no way he'd let the pompous self-serving fuck make a dime off of him. And he'd gotten to where he kind of enjoyed the game.

So Dylan idiot-stared and Kowalski sat, one knee crossed over the other, hands steepled, finger-tips to his lips pretending he could see through Dylan's bones.

Dylan opened his eyes a fraction wider and cocked his head to one side. Kowalski recrossed his legs. There was a moth hole in his right trouser cuff. The left lens of his glasses was badly scratched.

Kowalski was in debt, broke, Dylan realized. Wednesdays and Saturdays the loser parents of loser JDs came to visit. Poverty oozed from their pores, leaked onto their clothes; they stank of it. Kowalski was stinking of it now.

Psychiatrists were rich; they didn't go broke unless they were owned by something—gambling, coke, heroin.

Heroin had been the hot item in Ward C a few years back, but Dylan laid off the stuff. The first time it was offered him, he'd turned it down.

Draco asked, "Saving your virginity for the big house?"

Dylan missed Draco. He'd gotten out when Dylan was thirteen or fourteen, but they still heard from him occasionally. He was doing time in a California state prison for getting caught in a men's room trying to peddle a dime bag to a cop.

Big-time drug dealer, going to "go 'to the coast' and sell coke to the stars." Dylan smiled.

"I'm glad to see you're in such a gay mood," Kowalski snapped from his preshrink silence. He recrossed his legs and checked his watch—the signal that the session was to begin. "I won't be able to come back to DuWalt as often as I'd like," he said in his reserved, we-both-know-I'm-God sort of way. "I have other commitments—a new job, better."

Kowalski was lying.

In DuWalt, lying wasn't a sin; it was an art form. Guys in for more than a six-month vacation got to where they could tell when the shit was being shoveled. There was some natural talent nobody could see through. The retard Dylan had been in psych with was too stupid to know whether he was lying or not. Herman, a big Swede kid, dragged off the family farm for raping a ten-year-old girl— nobody could tell when Herman was lying. He'd learned it young, like a second language. Herman probably dreamed in lies.

Kowalski was an amateur.

"There's no job," Dylan said bluntly. "You screwed the pooch didn't you?" Mostly he didn't call people on their lies. What would be the point? He wasn't sure why he'd done it this time. Maybe because Kowalski was so fucking full of himself. Whatever the reason, the instant it came out of his mouth Dylan knew he'd joined old Kowalski in the pooch-screwing department.

Kowalski hadn't come to DuWalt to bid his favorite psycho boy goodbye; he'd come to do something or not do it. Dylan's mouth had just decided Kowalski to do it.

"We've gotten nowhere with your . . . amnesia," the doctor said. He leaned back and the frayed cuff of his trouser rode up over his sock exposing a white, nearly hairless calf. "Given that our time is limited, we're going to have to take a more aggressive tack."

The last time Kowalski had taken an aggressive tack, about a zillion volts of electricity had been pumped through Dylan's head. Talk about amnesia. After that, he'd had a hell of a time remembering his own name, let alone what happened when he was eleven.

Rich had put a stop to it. Dylan was just a kid; his brother wasn't all that much older. Vondra Werner was still driving him. The Saturday after Kowalski strapped Dylan down and fried his brains, Rich came to see him like he did every Saturday.

Not wanting to be a pussy, Dylan tried to suck it up, not let his brother see what a mess he was. He thought he was pulling it off until Rich started yelling, "What did you do to my brother? What the fuck have you done to my brother?"

Draco said it was the coolest thing he'd ever seen. Dylan sitting flopped over the table, limp as a noodle, drooling and babbling, and Rich standing on his chair doing the avenging angel thing. After that Rich got his adopted mom, Sara, to lean on real doctors, and one leaned on a senator, or judge, or cop, or somebody, and Kowalski had backed down.

Until now.

"There's a new experimental drug we've been having some success with," Kowalski said. "It's called lysergic acid diethylamide." He paused as if to let the momentous cutting edge of his intellect crash into Dylan's consciousness.

Dylan had dropped acid three or four times, once with his algebra teacher, Phil Maris. They'd lain on the floor of the math lab after lights out and watched formulas take wing and mate. The first couple times it made the pictures in his head of the things he built more vivid. The last time, though, numbers came alive—not in a good way, but like people were alive—with emotions, likes and dislikes. Dylan hated the rational world of mathematics infected with the stuff of humanity. After that he'd stuck pretty much to dope.

When a new kid, Purvis Something, was moved permanently to psych after dropping a hit of Window Pane, Dylan swore it off completely. His brain was nothing to fuck with. People learned that the hard way.

"Ell-ess-dee," Kowalski said, playing Timothy Leary's best pal.

"Cool," Dylan said and again thought of Draco: *You get, you share.* If he got a chance, he'd score a few hits for pocket money.

"You seem to be looking forward to it. We shall see . . ." the doctor said with more than a hint of malice. "I have cleared the remainder of the afternoon."

Explaining that the drug had been formulated in a lab at the National Institute for Mental Health to be used for experimental purposes, Kowalski took a vial from his briefcase. There was no label on the glass container. Inside was a square of blue paper with a slight discoloration in the middle. Dylan had been medicated, overmedicated, and eternally messed with; he knew the rituals of medical protocol from the inside. Kowalski was bullshitting him. The hit had been bought on the street. It could be cut with anything—speed, Drano—whatever the cook thought would give more bang and save him a buck.

Kowalski hated him. Dylan read the certainty of it in the set of his mouth, the aggressive jut of the bearded jaw, as he plugged in a tape recorder and arranged the microphone on his desk.

Dylan was unimpressed. Most people hated him. Regular people would have to be crazy not to hate him. He slid down on the couch another six inches, his long legs, strong from ice hockey and DuWalt's stone stairways, taking up more room than Kowalski liked.

"Sit up," the doctor ordered peevishly.

Dylan didn't move. His idiot stare grew more vacuous.

Dr. Kowalski flipped the tape recorder on and held out the blue square of contaminated paper.

# 14

Dylan's last acid trip hadn't been all that great, but it hadn't freaked him out. And though he remembered the look in Purvis Whatshisname's eyes after he'd dropped and hit the wall—like something had reached in through his nose with red-hot tongs and tried to pull out his soul—he'd never been particularly scared of the stuff. Most of the guys did it, and, other than Purv, who was determined to go nuts one way or another, nobody seemed too busted up by it.

He was scared now, though, that was for damn sure. All gloved-up like he was handling nuclear waste, Kowalski was poking the blue square of paper at him on the end of a pair of tweezers he'd probably used to pull his nose hairs out that morning.

Street shit. Even that didn't put the fear into him. It was Kowalski's eyes. The doctor looked crazy, bug-shit, a kind of hungry, desperate crazy. The monkey on his back—the addiction, the need, the lust, the whatever—had been working the doctor over.

For half a second Dylan thought of refusing the acid, of getting up and running out. He was bigger than the doctor. Kowalski couldn't stop him.

He couldn't stop Kowalski. Doctors were gods at DuWalt. They did what they wanted with the kids, whatever they wanted. Dylan pinched the paper from the tweezers and popped it in his mouth. What the hell? It had to be better than elec-troshock.

He dry-swallowed, smiled slowly, and said, "Thanks, Doc. The warden know you're my drug dealer now?"

Kowalski sat down on the edge of his chair, hitched it a couple of inches closer to the couch, and leaned forward.

The doctor was *out*; the man on the chair was not

a psychiatrist or a medical professional. He was scarcely even a man. He was a big fat zero waiting for something to come make him count, fill up the hole.

*Welcome to monster world, Doc.*

"You are going to fucking remember," Kowalski said, the obscenity jarring not only because it was the first time Dylan had heard him use anything stronger than "heck" or "darn" but because the word was uttered with the same smooth, pseudo-caring voice Kowalski used when he was shrinking kids in front of visitors.

"You are going to fucking remember every whack," he said, then leaned back and waited.

"Eighty-one," Dylan said.

"Is the LSD taking effect?" Kowalski checked his watch, as if he genuinely thought he could time street-drug reactions.

"Forty, done. Father, forty-one," Dylan said to remind Kowalski of the Lizzie Borden poem.

"It's starting," the doctor said.

*What a stupid fuck.* Dylan could say or do anything he damn well pleased, and the fool would write it off to the acid. "Your beard's on fire."

"Ahh," said Kowalski with satisfaction.

"You ever drop acid, Doc?"

"I . . . I have taken it experimentally."

Kowalski was lying again. He wanted to seem cool for some reason, wanted to impress a teenage axe murderer. How pathetic was that?

"Good thing you got lab stuff. That street shit's got some kinky side effects. A kid in detention over in St. Paul got hold of some. His brother said it was pure angel dust. This kid, he's like Superman all of a sudden. Ripped the door off its hinges. Then ripped the face off a guard."

Kowalski's skin paled.

*Be scared, you piece of shit,* Dylan thought, and enjoyed his petty victory. Meanness and fear were the only kind of power left to DuWalt's inmates.

The doctor pushed his chair back the three inches he'd infringed upon.

"Okay, Dylan, we've got work to do. Today, we're going to go back year by year until we get to the night of the murders. Are you ready to start?"

He was talking in the voice of a TV hypnotist, dreamy and smarmy. It didn't strike Dylan as funny. It creeped him out. The whole thing, saying fuck, threatening—and there was no way it wasn't a threat; people on the outside might mistake it but a kid in juvie, never—then acting like everything was normal, was majorly creeping Dylan out. Anxiety, the scalp-crawling, bone-breaking kind he'd learned in the courtroom, started pouring into him, freezing his blood.

*Shit. Not on acid,* he begged the cosmos. This crap on acid, and a guy could live in la-la land for good.

"You don't fuck with me, I don't fuck with you," Dylan said desperately.

The doctor had no idea what he was talking about. "That's right," he said soothingly, doing Dr. Kildare now instead of a hypnotist on Ed Sullivan.

Kowalski's left eye snapped from gray to green, then flashed red. It was happening. "Jesus," Dylan breathed and wondered how many hits were on that scrap of blue.

"Close your eyes," the doctor crooned.

Dylan did, not because he was told to but to shut out the red eye and whatever else was to come. It didn't help. The colors were in his mind.

"Go back." Papers rustled like snakes uncoiling. One began to uncoil in Dylan's skull. He didn't see it; he felt it. Great scaling scales sliding over one another. Then he saw it: blue sparks in the black, sparks struck from the snake's back as the huge metallic sheets of its skin slid over each other. He opened his eyes.

"Close," Kowalski murmured.

"Fuck you." The last letters of the word "you" trailed out of Dylan's mouth in smoke rings and broke apart around the doctor's face. Around the still-red left eye. Dylan closed his eyes. Better the snake within than the one without. Panic was growing inside him along with the snake. Eventually it would be too big for his cranium and the bones would shatter, splatter out.

"Good boy," Kowalski said. More rustling. Then the doctor began to read from his notes. "You remember going to trial. Go there now. Go back to your trial. Are you there?"

"No." Dylan forced his eyes open. Stared at the doctor's eye. It cooled to gray. He was going to be alright.

Before the thought could stop the rising storm of panic, the psychiatrist's face melted and reformed into that of the judge but wrong, pulpy; bits of it could fall off and drip onto the floor. "Shit," Dylan whispered, then said, "I'm guilty," because that was what he'd said when he was eleven.

Judge Kowalski smiled. The snake rustled and sparked. "Gooooooooood," the judge said with the *o*'s flowing out of his mouth in pinks and greens. "Go back to the night it happened."

"Murder," Dylan said. The word was red, blood red. It was such a cliché, he laughed. The wall behind Judge Kowalski, the one with the bad painting Dylan had grown familiar with during years on the couch, leaned in until it was almost touching Kowalski's head. "Duck," Dylan said.

"You're seeing ducks?"

"I wasn't." But now two of them flitted past the corner of his eye.

"Forget the ducks." The judge was annoyed. He looked around, maybe for a gavel. Grabbed up snake pages instead. They slithered through his hands, making blue sparks.

Spawn of the snake coiling in Dylan's brain. The wall came closer. The door on the adjacent wall leaned in to meet it. Dylan put out his hands to hold them back.

"You had the flu the night before. Remember?" The judge sounded peevish, and the peeve scoured the judginess from Kowalski's face. He was just Kowalski again.

"Gooooooooood," Dylan said and watched his own *o*'s flutter out and break like bubbles against the wall.

"Go back," Kowalski intoned, remembering he was on television.

Dylan sank into the couch. The worn cushions rose up to embrace him, pushing his outstretched arms forward into the position of a man about to do a half gainer. "Diving in," Dylan said and looked down. The floor rippled wetly. He wasn't far gone enough to jump. "I don't think I can fly yet," he said seriously. To him this was a good sign.

"Go back," the judge ordered. "Your mom put you to bed. She put you to bed. Can you see the bed?"

"It doesn't work like that," Dylan tried to explain. Acid wasn't like that. It did what it did. "I'm just along for the ride."

"Your mom put you to bed," Judge Kowalski went on inexorably. "You had on"—rustle, spark, slither—"flannel pajamas with cowboys and Indians on them."

Dylan remembered those pajamas. Really *remembered* them. He hadn't thought about them, not ever, and now they were on him, soft, and warm, and smelling like home. Like soap and fresh air. Cowboys on horseback, little and perfect, galloped across his thighs and his chest. He didn't so much see as feel them. Flannel and soft and purring. Ginger the cat, purring. She was on the bed. A ginger-colored cat, she purred like a machine gun rattling. He reached out and put his hand on her. No cat. Couch.

Rich started to laugh and Dylan turned, expecting to see him in the doorway pretending to die a million ways. The door pushed closer. The laughter was there, bubbling and going farther away. "Rich!" he shouted, wanting him to come back.

"Rich was there. Good."

Dylan focused on the doctor. Colors were rampant, raging; he squinted through them. The doctor's lips were moving as if he chewed the air. Words fell out in chunks. They didn't make sense. Panic rushed into Dylan until he was so cold, he shook with it, his teeth banging together.

"Yergall ley wink ang deader mom."

"Mom." Dylan recognized that word. "Mom," he said again with relief. "Momma." The room filled with butterflies. Kowalski's words turned from chunks to butterflies; the colors stopped attacking him and painted their wings. The cubical was filled with them. Dylan looked up. The stone ceiling thirty feet above was a swirl of beautiful butterflies; they lined the blackened rafters. Their wings left trails of faint color in the air.

Dylan laughed. "Momma," he said again, and the word broke into more butterflies, and they smelled of warm cotton and cherries. "Momma!" he cried, and the butterflies came down and lit on his arms and his hands, his shoulders, his hair. Their wings brushed his forehead, warm butterfly kisses.

"What are you seeing?" The doctor's words cut through the butterflies, killing those in their path.

"Butterflies. Don't talk—killing them," Dylan said.

"Killing? You are killing. Killing Mom?" the doctor demanded.

Dylan closed his eyes so he wouldn't see the saw-toothed words hack through the bloom of butterfly wings.

"The baby, you killed her first, didn't you? She was trying to get to her mom, and you killed her. That was first, wasn't it? That was it."

Even with his eyes closed Dylan could see jaws of words chewing the lovely creatures from the air, spitting their still bodies onto the floor and the walls. He raised his hands to his eyes. He had forgotten he was covered with butterflies. They turned to paste under his palms, squished between his fingers. Their bodies ran warm and thick over his face and hands. "No!" he screamed and opened his eyes. His hands were red with blood. Blood covered his thighs and arms; his face was sticky with it, his hair stiff with blood. "It's me! It's me, I'm killing them," he said, aghast.

"Killing your parents, your sister." Kowalski's words came into Dylan's ears sharply, cutting their way in past eardrum to brain.

"No," Dylan protested.

The last butterfly, saved because it had hidden in Dylan's mouth, flew out on the word and lit on his cheek, and he was home, little and in bed, a kiss like a butterfly warm from the sun, brushing across his cheek. A gold cross on a fine chain caught the light. The sweet cherry taste of syrup was on his lips, but wrong, the kind of wrong that lets you know there's medicine under it and the cherry is supposed to fool you.

Dylan wasn't fooled. It's hard to fool an eleven-year-old boy, but he'd taken the medicine with good humor to please his mother, and because he knew if he didn't get over "the dread blue mocus" as his dad called the colds and flu that tormented Rochester's citizens from October until April, he wouldn't be allowed to skate in Saturday's hockey game.

The medicine made him sleepy. His mom sat on the edge of his bed and sang to him like she had when he was little. He let her, so as not to hurt her feelings. Her voice was okay, kind of deep and skritchy, but she couldn't carry a tune for sour apples and just sort of made it up as she went along. It reminded him of the Japanese singer they had to listen to in class to prove nobody was still mad over a long-ago war. For some stupid reason, she decided to sing a second song, "Hush Little Baby."

Singing it to Lena, who was two, was one thing, but his mom was slaughtering it and he was eleven for cripe's sake. What was he supposed to do? Start sucking his thumb and stroking his blankie? He was about to tell her to go sing to Lena, or pester the dog, or do some other mom thing, when Rich stepped into the doorway and started "dying" all sorts of ways that cracked Dylan up: pulling up a noose and lolling out his tongue, shooting himself in the head and sliding down the door frame.

Every time Dylan laughed, his mother turned, but there Rich would be looking innocent, like he was just enjoying the music. Finally, she gave up, kissed him, and left.

That kiss was the last normal thing that happened to him. The last good thing. A warm butterfly on his cheek, someone who didn't think he was a monster.

Next, there was yelling and bright lights, men with radios—cops. Sirens screamed from outside and more of them screamed in his head. His head was huge and broken, a piece of jagged glass slicing through his brain. Rich, limp and dead looking, his face the color of the zombies they laughed at in the old movies; but it wasn't funny.

Rich wasn't goofing around. He was dying. One of the cops, a huge cop, like a giant with hands bigger than Dylan's face, had Dylan by the back of the neck. He felt warm and wet and wondered if he'd wet the bed.

*He'd pissed the bed and his parents had called the cops. Rich had fainted because he'd peed in the bed.* He laughed because it was too weird to be real. When he did, the cop's hand tightened until he thought his head would pop like a ripe pimple, his brains squirting out like pus. "You fuck bastard," the cop shouted.

"Take it easy, Mack," said somebody.

"You crazy fuck bastard," the giant shouted, his face so close Dylan could smell the stale coffee on his breath and see the bristly hairs on his cheeks.

He raised his hands to push the man away, and they were red. Red-red and sticky. He was covered in the cherry medicine. Too red. Blood, he was covered in blood. His chest was smeared with it. The covers on his bed were soaking in blood. It was on his face and his arms. Vomit choked off the laugh.

"Let's go take a peek at your handiwork, you sick little prick."

"Mack, back off!"

But Mack didn't. Dylan felt himself being pulled from the bed by the scruff of his neck like a cat. The pain in his head brought down black around the edges of his eyes, and his legs didn't work right. The cop, Mack the Giant, was dragging him from the room. Two men had taken Rich into the hall and were doing things to his crotch, or that's what it looked like.

"Is he dead?" Dylan managed.

"Not yet, you fuck," said Mack, and Dylan wondered if they were going to kill him, if maybe they weren't real cops but men dressed as cops who'd come to kill them. They'd killed Rich, and now Mack was going to take him someplace and kill him too. They must already have killed his parents, or his dad would have gotten his double-barreled shotgun from behind the dresser and blown them into tiny pieces.

"They're dead," he screamed to Rich, to get him to wake up and run or fight, to let him know there was no help coming. "Momma and daddy are dead!"

"Aren't you a proud piece of shit," the cop said and hauled him out of the bedroom and into the upstairs hallway. All the lights were on, glaring and cold, and there was a man with a camera that flashed and burned the back of Dylan's eyes. "Look, you lousy fuck." The cop pushed him to his hands and knees in the hallway.

Lena, little Lena, lay face down in the middle of the skinny rug that ran down the hall to protect the hardwood. Her head was in two pieces, like in the cartoons when somebody unzipped somebody else and they fell into halves.

"Happy?" Mack yelled and shook him. "Lots more to see."

He was lifted by the neck again. His feet tried to keep up so the cop wouldn't pull his head off. Mack, the cop giant, was taking him to his parents' room. Dylan didn't want to see what they'd done to his mom and dad. With a strength born of sheer terror, he began to kick, and bite, and scream. He did wet himself then and didn't even care. The world had gone insane.

But it hadn't. Dylan had.

"No!" he screamed.

"Look," Kowalski insisted. "Look. I found it for you."

Dylan looked hard through the falling colors, through the blood in his eyes, through the dark from the walls leaning too close. Kowalski had something across his knees. He was holding it in his lap like a child.

"Look what I brought for you," the doctor said. "I brought this to help you remember. This is the axe. The one you used to hack your family to pieces. Look at it. Look at the axe. Remember the axe? Here it is. See the axe. I brought it for you."

Dylan looked. The axe. Blood poured from his eyes; he could feel it hot on his face. Panic clanged in his ears so loud he couldn't hear anything else. The axe lay there, alive, waiting. Dylan looked at Kowalski's face. It changed again. No judge. A cop. Mack, the giant cop, the fake cop, the bastard cop who had dragged him from his bed. This time he wouldn't be afraid. This time he wouldn't stop. This time he would get them all.

With the power of the snake in his brain he rose from the couch on a clear, cold wave of revenge, rose like a god, shooting up. His hands caught the axe from Mack the Giant's grasp. It weighed nothing. He was a man now, not a little boy. He was strong. The axe swung high over his head, the blade glittered. The butterflies were coming back. He could save them.

With an exultant cry he brought the blade down onto Mack the Giant's skull.

## 15

Again and again Dylan chopped. The axe blade sang; the butterflies flashed brighter and faster. Dylan could feel the muscles working beneath his skin. If he looked, he could see them, see through them to the bones, hard and long, wielding the axe.

Mack, the giant cop, the fake, bastard, fuck cop, fell from the chair but wouldn't die. Dylan swung harder, driving the blade through the crawling back, hacking where arm met shoulder, down again through spine and base of skull.

Still, the man crawled, scuttling crablike, making for imagined safety beneath the desk. Dylan followed, his legs strong now, not the skinny pins of a little boy. The floor shuddered with each mighty step, and Dylan laughed. This time Mack wouldn't do it; he wouldn't drag Dylan down the hall and show off his grisly work. With Mack dead, the butterflies would be safe. Everybody would be safe.

The last of the cop disappeared beneath the old battered metal desk, his feet tucking up inside like a kid hiding from his brother, like the Wicked Witch's toes curling under Dorothy's house. Axe held loosely in his right hand, Dylan grabbed the edge of the desk with his left and heaved. His strength was a hundredfold. The heavy metal desk rose up and smashed against the wall. The murky painting broke loose and fell.

Again, Dylan raised the blade.

"There is no axe! There is no axe! The axe was a joke. There is nothing in your hands! Guard! Guard! Help! There is no axe. Your hands are empty. Jesus! Help me—somebody help me. Guard!"

The curled thing on the floor, the cowering coil of flesh, screamed these words, had been screaming these words. Noise became language; language became English and began to make sense.

"Your hands are empty, you fucking psycho. There is no axe!"

Dylan brought his hands down from over his head. He held nothing. Nothing. His fingers curled around empty air. He stared down through where the axe handle had been to the man at his feet. The cop was gone. Mack the Giant was Kowalski.

Nobody was dead. Nobody but his family. And the butterflies.

Dylan shut down so hard and fast he never even felt himself falling.

He came to slowly, nausea rising out of the depths to meet a shrieking headache. His mouth was sour with bile and the faint taste of decay heavy sedatives leave behind. He twitched, wanting to raise his hand to scrub the cobwebs from his face. His arms were strapped down. Dylan knew the feel of them; leather cuffs lined with sheepskin and chained to the bed. Kowalski favored them for shock therapy.

For a hellish heartbeat, Dylan thought he was there for that purpose, that any minute the volts would rage through his brain, ripping thoughts and memories out by the roots.

If it hadn't already happened.

Then he remembered the acid: the acid, and the axe, and the butterflies. He couldn't remember if he'd killed Kowalski or not.

But then he wouldn't remember, would he?

"Fuck," he groaned. Whether Kowalski still breathed or not didn't change the fact that *he* was still alive. His throat was so dry he could scarcely swallow, and his bladder felt full to bursting.

"Hey," he croaked. He started to turn his head but it hurt too much to move. "Hey!" he shouted again after a moment. "I gotta take a piss."

That brought an orderly running. They hated like hell to clean up piss.

They hated like hell to do anything for the inmates.

Dylan listened to the shuffle of rubber-soled shoes on the linoleum. He was in the psych ward. It was the only place other than the infirmary where they used the leather and sheepskin cuffs. After Kowalski had fried his brain, he'd woken up here. Even without the cuffs Dylan would have known where he was without bothering to open his eyes. The psych ward had a distinctive odor. The usual smells of bodily effluvia and pungent cleansers were there, as was the stink of stale food and medicines, but added to that familiar brew was a scent Dylan had identified in his mind as hopelessness. The odor, slightly like that of rank earth, came into the brain as a low note into the ears—dust dropping into a place where there was no wind to blow it away. Breathing the mixture made it hard to believe the sun shone anywhere on Earth, that all cats did not eat their kittens, and that there passed a single parade unrained on.

"Hey!" Dylan called again.

"Keep your pants on," came a bored voice. "I'm coming." It was Clyde.

That was good. Clyde was okay. He was old, slow and stupid, but he wasn't full of hate. In Dylan's world that qualified a person for near sainthood.

"You going to go chopping me up with an invisible axe if I take you to the toilet?" Clyde asked, as he undid the cuffs. Dylan guessed the orderly was under orders to have him use the bedpan. But that would mean Clyde would have to wash it. Grateful for the old man's laziness and the shred of salvaged dignity, Dylan assured him he would not chop him to pieces but, indeed, would give him an invisible twenty-dollar bill if he could close the bathroom door.

"No dice."

Dylan had only asked to be asking for something. Since he'd been put away he'd done nothing in private, including dream. Sometimes he wondered if, when he got out, he'd need an audience to get himself to take a dump.

Clyde held open the door to the little toilet off the recovery room and Dylan brushed by him to step inside. Contact with the old man was alarming. The sensation of life that close was too much stimulus. Inside, Dylan had the burnt-out-hole feeling a bad trip left.

Clyde had to steady him so he could hit the john. As they'd done when he was tripping, the walls wavered and leaned—the acid was still in his system—but now, added to it, was whatever they'd given him to bring him down, so the wavering and leaning was in slow motion. He kept jerking as if he were toppling over, only to find that he was still on the level; it was the walls that were sneaking out.

"That was some bad shit," Dylan said in hopes his own voice would make him seem more like himself to himself.

"*Bad* as in *baaaaad*, meaning *good*, or *bad* as in *bad* meaning *bad*?" Clyde asked seriously. The inmates ragged him because of his desire to keep abreast of the current slang.

"*Bad*, as in *shit*," Dylan said and dropped the skirt of his hospital gown.

"Ah," Clyde said.

Through the skin on Clyde's bald head, Dylan could see the gears in his brain working that one over. An impulse close to kindness—a sensation pretty much alien to Dylan—hit, and he wanted to explain but couldn't; he'd forgotten whatever the hell they were talking about.

As Clyde helped him get back into the bed without toppling onto it face first, Dylan chanced the question he'd been avoiding since resuming this twisted brand of consciousness: "Did I kill anybody?"

"Nobody that matters," Clyde said.

A stab of fear so visceral it caused him to clutch at his gut flashed through him. Clyde saw it. "No, kid, you didn't kill anybody. You didn't kill anybody at all."

Relieved, but still shaking, Dylan lay back on the pillows. "You have to cuff me again?"

"I got to."

Dylan put his arms in the leather cuffs, palm up

so Clyde could find the buckles more easily. "Is Dr. Kowalski okay?"

The orderly chuckled, a whispery winter leaf sound. "Nope. The warden threw his scrawny ass out in the snow. Fired him. Warden Cole doesn't hold with that kind of thing, not without the proper whatnot. Like he's always saying."

Clyde didn't have to voice it; Dylan had heard the warden on the subject a number of times. In juvie, it was surprising how many experts wanted to use the inmates—all in the name of helping them, of course.

"These are not guinea pigs," the warden was fond of saying. "They are *boys*. Real live *boys*."

*If Pinocchio had known what it was like, he wouldn't have been so hot to trot on the real-live-boy thing,* Dylan thought as he drifted back into the black drug place that sufficed for sleep.

When he woke again, he wasn't alone. It was full dark outside, and a single lamp burned on the little table bolted to the floor by the hall door. Two hands held onto his right wrist. He opened his eyes the barest slit. Phil Maris, his algebra teacher, was holding his wrist; his head was bowed as if in prayer. Phil was slender and short, maybe five-eight. His long hair was tied back in a ponytail. The warden let him get by with it because, under the radical trappings, Phil was a good, solid, Midwestern boy and an excellent teacher. Dylan closed his eyes and let himself enjoy the comfort of the man's touch. Phil was nearly thirty and still unmarried, but he wasn't queer. You didn't spend four years in DuWalt without figuring out who wanted to jump your bones. Phil was as straight as they came.

"I am so sorry, man." Phil had sensed Dylan was awake.

"He mind-fucked me bad," Dylan said, and was shamed by the nearness of tears in his voice.

"Hey, man, you know better than that."

Phil never let the kids use that kind of language in his presence. He said four-letter words only served to let others know you were too stupid to come up with something better suited to human discourse.

"I'm sorry about the acid," Phil went on. "I never should have dropped with you. I don't do that stuff anymore. I've seen too many burnouts."

"If I hadn't dropped with you, I would never have found my way back from this trip," Dylan said truthfully. "Kowalski, *Doctor* Kowalski, was taking me some bad places. *Real* bad places."

"He said you flipped out and tried to kill him."

"I guess." Kowalski would have told them what he thought would get him off the hook. Dylan didn't bother to defend himself. Matricide, patricide, killer of little girls versus The Doctor; nobody would believe him.

"Promise me you won't do it again."

"Flip out?"

"Drop acid."

Phil asked Dylan for the promise as if he thought Dylan would keep it. Dylan promised. He would keep it. Not only because he'd been offered the chance but because the acid had pushed him too close to the edge.

"Jesus," Phil said, and dropped his head as if talking to the man himself. "I've got to get you out of here." Dylan said nothing. Nobody could get him out of DuWalt. From here, he went to the state pen. Still, he appreciated the sentiment.

For a long moment neither of them said anything. Dylan was watching the walls. For the most part they were staying upright. There were things at the rim of his consciousness, nasty acid things, but they were not coming forward at the moment.

There'd be flashbacks from this one. He could feel them like storms building just over the mountains of his mind.

"Dylan, you're a good kid. A smart kid. In here, you'll end up garbage. No kidding. Garbage. If you don't fight like a panther the doctors will make you crazy, or the crazies will make you like them. These boys—most of these boys—never had a chance. They lie because they have no idea what the truth is. They steal because they can't picture tomorrow, so what the heck, take what you want today. You could be different, but you've got to get out. You've got to have a place to go that's sane.

"A safe place," Phil said. "Are you up to building?" Phil taught all the math sciences: algebra, trig, geometry, calculus. Trigonometry was his favorite, and he often set Dylan to building something in his mind. That skill had been the foundation of the walls he'd made to contain his evil.

"I've got a safe place," Dylan said. Phil was the only one he'd told about the fortress in his head where the beast was caged.

"No, man, a beautiful place, a good place. A garden maybe. Yeah, a garden."

Dylan had never considered a place of peace, of beauty. The idea warmed him and, in DuWalt, in January, the cold bones of winter broke brittle in the soul.

"I don't know how to . . ." he began and faltered because the tears wanted to come back into his voice. When he'd frozen them, he went on. "I mean, shit, man, what do I know about gardens?" What did he know about beauty, was what he'd been going to say, but it sounded like such bullshit in his brain he didn't.

"We'll do it from pictures. How hard is that? Come on, man. Do it. You got to do it or you'll die here," Phil pleaded. "We start with dirt. Jeez, man, you know dirt, don't you?"

"Dirt." Dylan closed his eyes to please his friend and teacher. He and Phil picked a place with gentle rolling hills, like those that could be seen from the third-floor windows. They laid out a wandering path. That was enough; it was a start.

The door opened, and a guard stuck his head in. "Got a visitor." Dylan returned from the survey of his interior garden. Visitors were never allowed in any deeper than the reception area.

Surprises in DuWalt were not a good thing.

This one was. Rich pushed in behind the guard. Time was screwed by acid, but it seemed to Dylan as if he stood too long staring at him and Phil. He felt the warmth of Phil's hands leave his wrist and, in the drug residue, he saw the warmth flit away, gold and fragile.

"You two look cozy," Rich said with a smile.

"Hey, brother," Dylan said. "This is Phil, my math teacher. I've told you about him."

"Yeah." Rich shook hands with Phil Maris and took his place by Dylan's bedside.

The math teacher stood awkwardly for a second, then left with a "Later, Dylan."

"Phil's a good guy," Dylan said. "He's about all that keeps this place from being hell."

"I'm glad you have somebody you can talk to," Rich said, but he didn't seem all that thrilled. "How you doing, brother? One of the guys bribed a guard and called me. I had to raise holy hell to get in. Sara pulled some serious strings. They manage to completely fry what little brain you've got?"

"'Fraid so," Dylan said. "Goddamn fucking

weird. Kowalski's crazier than the kids he works on."

"No shit. The warden said he's history."

Acid residue was turning the stain patterns old leaks had left on the ceiling into ugly things. Dylan closed his eyes. The garden he and Phil had been planning appeared, rolling hills, the serpentine path they'd laid out, marked with stakes, each tied with orange surveyor's tape. *Dirt.*

"I love old Phil," he said, the sedatives over-laying the LSD slurring his words.

"Yeah?"

Rich, the room, the cuffs slid away. Dylan held out his hand, a shovel came into it, and he began to dig. He'd plant butterfly bushes so they would come back.

# 16

"I love Phil."

Dylan passed out after that. Richard watched his eyes. He was dreaming, the eyeballs twitching under the lids. "Brother," Richard said, then louder, "Dyl!" but got no response. Richard had never dropped acid, didn't touch pot, and drank sparingly; drugs weren't what got him high.

"You got to clean up your act," he said affection-ately to his brother's inert form. "What kind of creep gives a sixteen-year-old kid LSD? I should have gotten the bastard fired when he tried to electrocute you. Fuck." Richard turned from where his brother lay in uneasy sleep and crossed to the window. It was dark out, the heavy wire mesh dulling even the searchlights around DuWalt.

"What kind of creeps give an eleven-year-old kid seventeen years in prison?" he whispered. Dylan could be locked up until he was twenty-eight. He looked back at his brother, pale and sweating under the room's single light. What kind of a man would Dylan be by then?

"You going to be a drug addict, brother? Go with the gangs when you get to the big house? You can't do that to me." If juvie had changed Dylan, Richard did not want to see what the state pen would do to him.

Dylan's hands were moving spasmodically in the padded cuffs and there was a slight smile on his face.

*Dreaming of old Phil?*

The thought soured Richard's already dark mood.

It was a hell of a long drive to DuWalt from Rochester, and he'd had to cut school to do it. Not that he gave a damn about school. He'd surpassed those morons when he was in eighth grade. And that was just the teachers. He'd been born smarter than the pimply fools he sat in homeroom with. He maintained a 4.0 average just to let them know he could.

"Brother," he tried again, but Dylan was still in Never Never Land. "I drive four hours, and you

153

pass out on me. What a deal." Dylan's hand, palm up where it threaded through the restraints, convulsed, the fingers grasping. Richard took it between his own. Flesh on flesh was not a sensation he usually enjoyed, but he did with Dylan. Maybe because he was family.

His brother's hand was rich with life. Richard felt it coursing under the skin, touching up against his own life with such force the two flowed together. He could feel the acid burn leaking into his blood, the dulling of the sedatives blanketing his thoughts. He didn't remember being this close to his brother when they were kids. The whole power thing between parents and children worked against it. The night of the killings something had happened. Their blood had mixed on the blade of the axe and they'd become more than brothers—they'd become blood.

Richard took back his hand. "Got to quit the drugs, brother. They're killing me." He laughed, then said, "I'm not kidding." He leaned back and stretched his legs. He was six feet even in his stocking feet, taller than Dylan by two inches, though he doubted that would last. Dylan had a couple years to catch up.

Richard had fought against sending Dylan to DuWalt, but, fourteen and wounded, no way was he effective. In hindsight, DuWalt was probably the right choice. He'd been too naïve to realize after the killings that Dylan would probably have been beaten to death by the good citizens of Rochester if he hadn't been locked up. They paid lip service to the tragedy of his extreme youth, but they were scared to death of him. Scared their own little boys and girls would flip out some night and start butchering the family.

DuWalt was giving Dylan a better education than he would have gotten at the jail in Rochester—as good as he would have gotten in public school. The warden was a cutting-edge kind of guy. Until he'd let a berserk psychiatrist mess with Dylan's brain a second time, Richard had been cool with him.

The state penitentiary was going to be a different ballgame. Richard heard stories of what happened to guys in the pen. Dylan said it wasn't a problem in juvie, that there were "girls"—boys who were into it—and they took the pressure off. In the penitentiary, rape wasn't about sex. Sex wasn't about sex; it was about dominance. Richard knew that instinctually. The thought of anybody touching his brother made his skin clammy. For a miserable heartbeat he could feel the rape inside of himself.

"Shit," he said to banish the visceral image. "Dylan! Wake up, man. Talk to me!"

Dreaming his dreams, Dylan slept on.

Richard settled back into his slouch. Four and a half years had passed since his brother was locked up. Richard was old enough to get custody of him as a minor, if he was free and if Sara would vouch for him. Sara was a nurse. That was about as solid as a citizen could get. She wouldn't like it; Dylan frightened her.

I would be my brother's keeper, he thought.

The door behind him creaked open. "Hey, man, give us a few more..." Richard stopped. It wasn't the guard; it was the math teacher.

Good old Phil.

"Sorry," Phil said. "I didn't know you were still here."

"Where else would I be?"

Phil didn't answer that. He pulled up a second chair and sat too close, studying Dylan's face. "Rest will do him good," he said.

"Yeah."

For a minute they sat in silence. Richard waited for the fool to go and got the feeling Phil was waiting for the same thing. It pissed him off. Good old Phil could wait until hell froze over.

"Dylan ever talk to you about that night?" Phil asked.

"He doesn't remember it," Richard said coldly. "I nearly bashed his brains out with an axe."

"So they tell me."

Richard didn't like the tone the math teacher was taking.

"I've seen your brother nearly every day for four years. Dylan's a good kid."

"For a killer," Richard said.

Phil looked at him hard.

Richard said nothing.

Phil kept staring at him. "You don't live with a kid for four years without getting to know him."

Phil, good old Phil, was heading toward something. Richard watched him warily.

The hippy hair, the I'm-your-best-friend note he took with Dylan, what kind of teacher was that? "What are you getting at?" he asked.

"Long drive isn't it? Four hours or something?"

"Something like that."

"Never miss a visit, do you?"

"You have a problem with that?" This guy was getting on his nerves in a big way. "I've got a good barber I can recommend," Richard said.

Phil ignored the cheap shot. *Rose above it,* Richard thought acidly.

"Eight hours round-trip twice a week. Lot of time and energy. Most kids your age wouldn't do that." Phil's pupils widened slightly as if he wanted to look past Richard's eye sockets and into his mind. "Why do you?"

"Because he's my brother," he snapped. "What are you getting at?"

"Nothing, man, just talking is all." He stood up. "Take it easy," he said. "We'll look after your brother."

He left.

Goddamn stupid fuck, who did he think he was talking to? "Fucking cunt," Richard whispered. "Guard!"

An old man in a gray uniform stuck his head in the door. "We're counselors now, didn't you know that boy?" The old guy grinned, but Richard wasn't in the mood.

"I have to see the warden."

"Warden's gone home. Having his supper about now, I expect."

"I don't care if he's having his goddamn hair done, I need to see him. Now."

The guard looked uncertain, deciding whether Richard's rage or tearing the warden away from his dinner would go hardest on him.

"The warden will want to hear what I have to tell him," Richard said. "Trust me on that. And trust me, if you're the one makes him hear it later rather than sooner, you're going to be out of a job."

The guard blinked then. "Okay, kid. You win. Come with me."

Richard left without saying good-bye to his brother.

# Louisiana, 2007

*James Ruppert. Kills eleven family members at Easter dinner. 1975. This guy was nuts. I guess we're all nuts though, so I'll do him. I don't see myself killing family the way Ruppert did and, before you ask, no, I didn't crave this sort of action back when I was at home. But you've got to admit his family was shitty to him. And here he is, forty-one and still living at Mommy's house. That had to say "failure" in a big way, proving what his dad was always saying he was. Big brother's over to dinner with his eight kids—Eight! You'd think the brother would have shot his own self—and his wife who used to be James's girlfriend, and while she's cooking up the Easter ham, he knows Mom's thinking about throwing him out on his ear; and he hasn't got a job, so he's broke. Then you factor in that he stands to get a lot of dough from insurance. Shooting the family starts to look pretty good. Sane even. Until you get to the kids. Maybe he figures they aren't quite people; with eight of them, they wouldn't seem like an endangered species exactly, just a housecleaning issue. What I don't get is why go to all that trouble then wait for the cops? Did he think he would get off on a thing like that? If he did, then he really was nuts. Hey, maybe he should have gotten off on the insanity plea. Catch 22. We're all nuts, but if we tell you that, then we're not. I feel sorry for James; he was fucked from the start.*

## 17

Marshall was scared. Polly could see it behind the
sparkle in his eyes, behind the sparkle of the two-
and-a-half-carat diamond ring on the table
between them. Whether he was scared she would
say yes or refuse, she didn't know.

Despite the cynicism she cultivated in her deal-
ings with the opposite sex, Polly was a romantic.
*Ivanhoe* was a favorite of hers, *Sense and Sen-
sibility, Sleepless in Seattle.* As a girl, she'd read
Costain's *The Black Rose* so many times the cover
began to look like third base at the Little League
park. She had taught True Love, as seen by poets,
playwrights, and novelists most of her adult life.
As she would point out to her students, not only
did true love not necessarily run smooth, it was
often fatal.

They were in the courtyard of the Court of Two
Sisters in the Quarter. A canopy of ancient oaks
sequestered the garden, each tree strung with a
thousand tiny lights, and each light refracting in
the facets of the diamond engagement ring. It surprised her that she wasn't surprised. It also surprised her that she wanted to pick it up, slip it on
her finger, and scamper down the aisle in a cloud
of white taffeta. Perhaps love was like the mumps.
If a woman came down with it after forty, it could
kill her.

Staring at the black velvet box with its glittering promise so lusciously displayed, she heard herself saying, "We've only been together for a month."

"But what a month," Marshall replied and, with the long-fingered hand she loved to hold and watch when he drew pictures for Emma and Gracie, nudged the box a few inches closer.

She wondered if she eyed it as the mouse eyes the bit of cheese in the trap, not knowing it will soon make literal the notion that it was dying for a nibble.

"Cliché or not, I feel like I've known you my whole life," Marshall said softly.

Polly felt that way as well. They had re-created a timeline she had skipped over: They played as children with her daughters, they giggled on the phone for hours like teenagers, they sat up late over wine arguing politics and saving the world like college sweethearts, they went to openings and museums like upwardly mobile thirty-somethings, they sat on his balcony in rocking chairs the way old folks were said to do. A lifetime together.

"The girls . . ." Polly said lamely.

"I aced the interview," he reminded her with his wonderful smile, slightly crooked, as if a part of him mocked the hope of his own happiness.

Polly worked hard at treading the thin line between being completely open and honest with her daughters and burdening them with adult concerns. She had kept her so-called love life—the sporadic dates she'd enjoyed over the years—separate from her home life and her children. That hadn't been true with Marshall. Knowing Gracie and Emma noticed the interplay between them, she told them they might be getting serious.

The next afternoon, as she walked across campus to her car, her cell phone rang. Fishing it from her purse, she checked the screen. Gracie. Cold spiked in Polly's chest. Their cell was only to be used for emergencies.

"Are you okay? Is Emma okay?" Polly demanded. "Aren't you supposed to be in school?"

"Momma, take a breath," Gracie returned. The annoyance in her tone reassured Polly. "We are at school. It's recess. Momma . . ." The quality of the sound dwindled. From the use of "we," Polly guessed Gracie was conferring with her sister. In a couple of seconds she was back. "Momma, remember last night you said you and Marshall were like serious boyfriend-girlfriend? Do you think he wants to marry us?"

The fear that had gripped her when the cell phone rang returned. If the girls rejected Marshall, then he was out of their lives. It was as simple as that. Except this time it wasn't. Polly was in love. Being in love, though as grand as the poets had promised, brought with it a terrifying helplessness.

"I remember, sugar," she said carefully. She beeped the Volvo open and slid behind the wheel, her briefcase and purse on her lap. She put the key in the ignition and started the car so the air would run, but made no move to go.

"Well . . ." There was another brief conference at the other end of the ether.

Realizing she was clutching her phone so tightly she was in danger of breaking it, Polly forced herself to relax.

"Momma?"

"I'm here. Tell me."

"Me and Emma want to interview him."

"Emma and I," Polly corrected automatically.

When Gracie hung up, Polly called Marshall and invited him for dinner. "Come early, around five," she told him. "The girls want to talk to you."

After school, Emma and Gracie went into their room and closed the door. Polly could hear them murmuring and laughing; sounds that usually filled her with joy grated on her nerves.

They didn't come out until Marshall rang the doorbell at four-forty-five.

Gracie emerged as Polly let him in. "You're early. We're not ready yet," she said and disappeared back into the bedroom.

Polly laughed nervously. "I have no idea what they're planning, Marshall, only that it's important to them. Can I offer you a strong drink?"

"Later, maybe," he replied. "Later, definitely," he amended. "I'm afraid it might not make a good impression on my inquisitors."

He was not joking.

Sitting in the living room, he on the couch and she in the chair, they tried to make small talk. When that failed, they stared at one another and waited.

At five o'clock the bedroom door again opened and the girls came out. Both had on their best dresses. Both wore shoes. It should have been endearing, comical, even, but Polly saw the alarm she felt reflected in Marshall's eyes.

Gracie carried a yellow legal pad and a pencil. "Mr. Marchand," she said politely. "Would you like a glass of water or to go to the bathroom or anything before we get started?"

"*Mr. Marchand?*" he said, with a half-smile and a cocked eyebrow.

"It's formal," Emma explained gravely. "You'll be Marshall again after. Okay?"

"Okay. As long as I get to be Marshall again."

Gracie sat on the coffee table facing him. Emma, just as serious but still Emma, bounded up onto the sofa next to him.

"Ready?" Gracie asked.

Marshall nodded. Polly imagined his palms were starting to sweat.

"First question: Why do you like Momma so much?" Gracie read from the legal pad.

It was a good question. Polly had to make an effort not to beam at her offspring.

Marshall thought for a while, his hands folded

neatly on his crossed knees. Finally he said, "I think it's because, even though the world can be a scary place, she makes me feel like it's full of wonderful things and that we will find them and be happy. Not all the time, of course, but a lot more than we are ever sad."

Gracie looked at Emma. Emma nodded, her blonde hair, as fine as it was when she was a baby, swinging over her pixie ears. Gracie drew a neat line through the question.

Marshall shot a glance at Polly. She shrugged. He was on his own.

"Do you like children?" Gracie read off the next question on their list.

"I don't know any children but you guys. If all children are like you, then I like children. My guess is that children are like everybody else. I'll like some and won't like others."

Again the exchange of nods and the line through the asked-and-answered question.

"This is the last one," Gracie said encouragingly. "If we let you be Momma's boyfriend, how would our lives be better?"

No wonder the list had taken them all afternoon, Polly thought. They must have been Googling advice columnists and picking out the hard questions.

"Gosh," Marshall said. Then, "Gosh, that's a tough one."

"Take your time," Emma said kindly.

168

"How about that drink now?" he said to Polly. She laughed but didn't move. She had no intention of missing a minute of this.

"Okay. Let me think. I have some money," he said slowly. "But your mom makes enough to buy everything you need, so that wouldn't make it better." He seemed to be floundering. Polly worried that he would choke. "It's easier to fold sheets with two people. There would be two cars, so it would be easier to get to all the places we want to go. I could take care of the lawn and fix things if they got broken. I could help build things—I'm a trained architect and builder, you know. I could kill cockroaches for you."

"We don't kill them. We put them out," Gracie said repressively. Neither she nor Emma was looking impressed and Polly felt oddly hollow.

Marshall looked at his hands for a minute or more. When he looked up, his face was as open as a child's. "The only thing I could bring to make your lives better would be more love," he said. "I have a lifetime's worth saved up. That should count for something."

Gracie looked to Emma. Emma nodded. Gracie drew a line through the question. "That will be all," she said formally. "Thank you, Mr. Marchand, Momma."

"Thank you," Emma echoed, and, Gracie leading, they filed back into the bedroom and closed the door.

Simultaneously Polly and Marshall expelled their breath, then laughed.

"What happens now?" Marshall asked. "Do I go home and wait by the phone? Give the names and addresses of my former employers?"

He stood and Polly rose to put her arms around him and lay her head on his chest. They stayed like that without speaking until the bedroom door flew open and Emma, dressed again in shorts and a T-shirt, exploded from the room and launched herself in Marshall's general direction.

"You passed!" she shouted as he caught her. "You aced it!"

Gracie followed her sister. She'd changed out of her tribunal clothes as well and wore blue cropped pants and a matching tank top with a giant pink paw print in glitter on the front.

"Does this mean you'll marry me?" Marshall asked her. Had Polly not been seated, her knees would have buckled. Marriage had not yet been discussed.

"No," Gracie replied. "It means we won't *not* marry you."

Polly smiled at the memory. "Yes, you did ace the interview," she admitted and took a sip of champagne, giving herself time to settle.

"I love you," he said simply. "Finding you was like finding I was not deaf, dumb, and blind, though I had learned to live that way. I wish you'd been in the square when I was thirty, but you weren't. Now my biggest concern is that, even if we both live to a hundred, we won't have enough time together."

Polly arched an eyebrow. "I do not have one foot in the grave. The women in my family live to a great old age. Well, our bodies do; it's our minds that tend to go when we're in our seventies," she teased. All of it was a tease. Polly had no idea how long the women in her family lived. Her mother had died at forty-three. According to the neighbors Hilda passed out drunk and fell face down outside. It rained heavily that night and Hilda, like the apocryphal turkey, drowned in two inches of water.

Marshall pushed the hair back from his forehead. His fingers didn't merely comb through the hair, they raked.

Removing a crown of thorns was the image that flashed in Polly's mind, and for a heartbeat, she waited for the drops of blood to seep from his flesh. The thought was sacrilegious. Though she no longer believed in heaven, the concept of hell had never truly left her.

He reached across the table and rested his hand over hers on the white cloth. "I suppose, if it weren't for the girls, we could just move in together, but even that wouldn't be enough for me. It wouldn't pay you the honor you deserve, and it wouldn't honor the love I have for you." He smiled. "Quite a speech. Believe it or not, before I met you, I was the strong silent type."

Proposals of marriage were not alien to Polly. Something about her put men in a marrying frame of mind. There were a couple of reasons that prevented her from indulging in gestures of mad passion: Emma and Gracie. No less carefully than Marshall built his houses had Polly built hers: her daughters and her teaching, friends, quiet moments with a book, ballet lessons, soccer, the theater, flower-arranging classes, evenings with Martha. She owned her own home and did as she pleased.

American mythology would have it that divorced or widowed women in their middle years were desperate to remarry. That had not been Polly's experience. Most had made lives they enjoyed and would only compromise for a very shiny white knight with a particularly breathtaking steed.

*And a very long lance*, Polly thought, and smiled at the turn her thoughts took.

"A smile. Is that a yes?" Marshall was trying for lightness and failing. The shadows in his eyes suggested her answer was a matter of life or death.

Both flattering and unsettling.

"We have known one another for four weeks," she reminded him gently.

"The time doesn't mean anything," Marshall insisted. "You can live with someone for years and have the marriage fall apart two weeks after the wedding. You know that's true. Polly, since the night we had tea, I have never had a second thought. Never. About the logistics, sure. But not about how I feel about you."

Polly had been carried away on the same whirlwind. On their third date—the night following their second, two nights after their first, she'd brought Marshall home to meet the girls. Very few of the men she had dated had been privileged to meet Emma and Gracie. Because they were good girls, they had been polite but maintained a sense of reserve. Not with Marshall. He fit into the family as if there had always been a place waiting for him.

His quiet gravity, the way he addressed them as adults and listened with genuine interest to what they had to say, the easy concern he showed when they were worried, the kindness when they were peevish or tired had won them over with a stunning rapidity. Another reason to proceed with caution: should she and Marshall separate, hers would not be the only heart broken. She pushed the glittering diamond back toward him. "Much as I would like to, I cannot," she said simply. "This is too much, too soon."

"Keep the ring. Think about it. Please. These chances don't come often. For most people they never come." His urgency had the quality of a man who knows he's dying—and wants to collect the brass ring before the Grim Reaper collects him.

"Maybe we should take a breath," she said. "Take a little time apart. I need to collect my thoughts." He looked so devastated, she softened her decision by saying, "A girl cannot think clearly around you, my darling."

"Don't reject it." He nudged the ring back toward her. "Think about it."

"Despite the wisdom of song and tradition, diamonds are not a girl's best friend. Though I must admit, most women take better care of their diamonds than men do of their dogs." Polly was trying to lighten a mood that had suddenly become fraught with storms she couldn't see but only feel as a pressure behind her eyes.

"I will think about it," she promised.

"Don't think too long."

## 18

The phone had been ringing for some time before the sound worked its way through Polly's dreams and dragged her into the waking world. "Yes?" she said into the receiver as she felt around for her glasses.

"That's what I was hoping you'd say."

Marshall. They'd not spoken in the week since he'd proposed. She switched on the bedside lamp and squinted at the clock. One-fifteen a.m. She had missed him. His intensity had scared her. The girls asked after him. She enjoyed her freedom. Her thoughts were only of him. Emotions hard to quantify during the day batted inside her head like birds in a chimney. "It's late," was all she could manage.

"I'm sorry. I woke up. I guess I heard a noise or something and . . . and I needed to hear your voice." He sounded like a man who had awakened from a nightmare of hell fire and brimstone. He laughed ironically. "If you can't stay awake, just put the phone on the pillow and let me listen to you breathing."

A nightmare of fire and brimstone—Polly smelled smoke. Gray-white tentacles were reaching under her bedroom door, curling up the dark wood of the door.

"Oh, my Lord!" she whispered.

"What, what is it?"

"Smoke."

"Is the smoke alarm going off?"

Phone to her ear, Polly swung her legs from the bed and took two steps toward the door.

Like a blind hungry ghost, the smoke reached for her feet. The peach-colored paint on the door began to crack, black fissures snapping through, blistering like burned skin. She opened her mouth to scream for the girls but stopped herself. If Gracie and Emma heard her voice, they would wake and try to come to her.

"Don't open the door. Don't hang up. I'm coming," Marshall was saying. Polly disconnected and pushed 911.

"Please, please, please," she murmured to whatever gods listened as she ran for the bedroom window, the phone pressed hard to her ear. "There's a fire," she said when the emergency dispatcher answered and gave her address.

"Get out of the house immediately," the dispatcher said. "The fire station nearest you was flooded after Katrina and has not been reopened. The closest trucks are fifteen to twenty minutes away. Stay calm."

The bedroom's one window was the only way out and it had been painted shut when Polly bought the house. Without hesitation, she picked up her dressing chair and smashed the glass.

The 911 dispatcher was still talking as she threw the phone out onto the grass. Shards of glass the size and viciousness of shark's teeth razored out from scarred frame and broken mullions. She'd be gutted like a fish. Using the legs of the chair, she broke out as much glass as she could. Behind her, all around her, she could hear the fire snickering, licking, devouring, a thinking beast that roasted and ate human flesh. Again and again she banged at the old window, its many layers of paint holding onto daggers of glass like stubborn old gums to the few remaining teeth. Screaming an obscenity she'd grounded Gracie two weeks for using she threw the chair against the wall. Spinning from the wreckage she dragged the bedspread off the bed and shoved it through the opening. Belly on the sill, Polly began pushing her body through the ruined window.

Pain raked her left shoulder. The first hot pierce of glass then the rip as it clawed into her. All Polly felt was fury that it slowed her down. Grasping fistfuls of a rhododendron bush, she wrenched herself free from the jaws of the window and fell. Stiff branches caught at her clothes and grabbed at her hair until, screaming with rage, she made it onto the lawn. Staggering to her feet, she began to run. The house was small: two bedrooms separated by a short hall, with a bathroom on one side and the living room and kitchen on the other. It was no more than forty feet from her bedroom window to that of her daughters. In true nightmare fashion, the distance lengthened. Polly felt as if she forged her way through waist-deep mud, yet when she reached the corner of the house, her speed snatched her feet from under her on the dew-wet grass and she fell.

Two feet, hands and feet, it was all one to Polly. She clawed her way through the dense wall of sharp-spiked holly she'd planted beneath the girls' window as a natural security fence. Cupping her hands around her eyes to shut out the streetlight's glare, she peered through the burglar bars she'd had installed on this one window so she could sleep nights, unafraid of someone creeping into her children's room and taking them, as those girls in California and Utah had been taken.

Billowing smoke pushed down from the ceiling like alien clouds in an old science fiction movie.

Wraithlike and malevolent, it poured upward in a sheet from underneath the door. Emma's Tinkerbell nightlight flickered in and out of focus. Inanely Polly thought, *Clap if you believe in fairies.*

The girls were asleep, each in her own little bed. *Or dead.*

The thought hit Polly's brain with the force of a wrecking ball, and she cried out, grabbing the ornate cast iron as if she could rip the bars from their moorings. "Gracie!" she shouted. The window was open a few inches, enough to let in the breeze. Polly pressed her lips to the crack, "Emma, Gracie, wake up!"

"Momma?" came Gracie's sleepy reply.

"Wake up, honey. We've got a fire in the house and we have to go outside." Polly's voice was higher than usual, but she sounded reassuring. "No need to panic," she said as much to herself as her daughter.

"Momma? Where are you?" Gracie was sitting up in the bed now, staring at the smoke crawling up the far wall.

"At the window, honey. Here. That's right. I'm going to get you out. Wake up your sister, but don't scare her, okay?"

Polly pulled on the bars. They were iron and screwed into the side of the house. She tried to shake them. They didn't even rattle.

"Firemen will be here in a minute," she promised. The little house was old: shingled roof, oak floors, walls of wood and plaster. A two-hundred-thousand-dollar tinderbox.

"Gracie, stop," Emma whined.

"Wake up, Momma said. The house is on fire." Gracie's voice quavered, but she was pretending not to be scared. She was being brave for her sister. Polly thought she would die of love for her. With a guttural cry that brought both children to the window, she wrenched on the bars. They didn't so much as creak.

"Stay by the window, my darlings. You hear me? Put your mouths up to the crack and breathe this good air. Don't open it any wider, okay? It will make the fire want to come in faster. You just sit tight. Don't open the door. I'm going to get you out."

Breaking this tenuous connection with them hurt so deeply, pain knifed through her chest. Praying she wasn't having a heart attack, Polly tore free of the holly and ran to the front of the house. Orange light danced in waves of heat. Gouts of flame cut through smoke billowing from the windows. Paint on the front door bubbled. Great heat blisters popped and breathed white vapor.

There was no way in. She wouldn't live long enough to reach her children. The girls would die alone.

Polly howled and heard Gracie scream. Then white light blindsided her. She fell to her knees, images of the house exploding burning behind her scorched eyeballs.

Engine roaring, a truck pounded over the curb and smashed through the azaleas to lurch to a stop on the lawn. The door flew open and Marshall leapt from behind the wheel.

"Where's the fire department?" he yelled as he ran across the lawn. "My God, you're bleeding."

"They haven't come." Polly grabbed his wrist and dragged him toward the side of the house.

"Where are Emma and Gracie?"

"Inside," Polly cried. "Emma and Gracie are still inside. Marshall, I had security bars put in!" The words tore her throat. "I don't know how to get them out." Polly's fingernails clawed into the flesh of his wrist as she pulled him through the slash of leaves to the window.

"Momma!" Gracie screamed. Polly could scarcely see her for the smoke. It was coming out the window now. Behind the glass Gracie's pale face shone like a ghost.

Marshall tore free of Polly's grasp and ran. "No!" Polly shrieked, but he was gone.

Gracie was crying. Polly squeezed her face tightly against the bars trying to see her child. The iron was hot.

"Momma, Emma wouldn't stay. I tried to make her, but she got away. Momma, she opened the door, and I can't see her. I can't see her."

"Emma!" Polly shouted. Smoke burned her eyes.

"Emma, you come back! Come to my voice, baby."

"I couldn't stop her, Momma. She pulled away so hard, and she's so fast." Tears streaked white as they cut through the grime coating Gracie's face.

"I know, honey. Emma is as quick as a bunny. Stay at the window, baby. You stay right here."

*Emma was dead, and Gracie was going to die*

"Give me your hand. That's a girl." Polly pushed her fingers through the narrow opening, raking the skin from her knuckles. "The fire trucks are on their way. Emma!"

"Don't move!" came a command, then a crash so loud Polly and Gracie shrieked.

Marshall raised the sledge hammer and drove it into the siding a second time and the house shook. A hole was opening through the siding of. Smoke trickled out. He struck again, and the hole was big enough for a small person to crawl through. Two more quick blows, wood shattering inward, plaster dust swirling into the smoke, and a narrow door half the height of a man was made between two upright two-by-four studs. To Polly it was a miracle. She'd not known a hammer could so easily knock a hole in a house.

In a heartbeat, Marshall was through the breach. "Gracie," she heard him call.

"Go to him, baby. Quick as a wink." Polly said urgently. She let go of her daughter's hands. "Go to Marshall, baby." Gracie's ghostly face slid into the smoke. Polly fought the need to call her back to the window. Within seconds she was through the hole, coughing and clinging to her mother.

"Get away from the house," Marshall shouted. "I'll get Emma."

Knowing there was nothing else she could do, Polly wrapped her arms around Gracie and led her to the sidewalk across the street. Even fifty feet away, the heat was palpable. The roof over Polly's bedroom was intact, but the side of the house up under the eaves was burned away, and flame licked at the shingles.

On her knees on the concrete, Gracie held against her, Polly imagined Emma, small pink feet on floorboards hot as a griddle, ruffled nightie ablaze, her silky hair crackling like lightning. Had Gracie not been between her and the fire, she would have walked into it to stop the pain of the vision.

Smoke ceased to trickle from the hole Marshall had made and began to pour.

Faintly in the distance Polly heard sirens, fire trucks racing from whichever functioning station-house had taken them in, the ranks of firefighters depleted by those who'd evacuated and never come back. Gracie's crying became a slow, steady keen. Polly rocked back and forth trying to soothe them both.

A firefighter came up to them as his fellows rolled out the hose. A second engine arrived, lights and horns blaring.

"Anybody inside?"

"Yes," Polly heard herself saying as if from a great distance. "My daughter."

The fireman's face hardened, and she supposed he was trying not to telegraph his thoughts. Because the loss of Emma was not to be borne, Polly looked away from him.

A gout of black smoke burst from the hole Marshall had knocked in the wall of the girls' room.

Gracie started to struggle, trying to get free of Polly's arms. No!" Polly cried and held her more tightly as if Gracie, too, would run into the flames to be with Emma.

"Momma, let go. Look!"

At first Polly saw nothing; it was as if the fire had burned her retinas. Then from the smoke, a shape emerged.

"Momma, it's them!" Gracie cried.

Black as a chimney sweep, Emma clinging to his neck, Marshall fell through the jagged gap in the side of the house, staggered to his feet, and fell a second time. Polly started to run to them. A fireman stopped her. She fought him until he shook her, yelling, "Ma'am, ma'am, it's not safe." Two others ran to help Marshall. The first took Emma; the second lifted Marshall from the ground. Keeping a firm grip on Polly's upper arm, her fireman got on his radio, asking for the status of the ambulance.

"Anybody else inside?" he asked Polly.

"No."

"Just your husband and the kid?"

"My fiancé," Polly said. Then with a vehemence that surprised her, she repeated, "He is my fiancé."

19

The day Marsh met Polly, he had gone mad. Or gone somewhere. Danny felt him leave—a sucking sensation that left a vacuum behind, a north wind snatching away a coat, the dentist drawing a living tooth. Now, three months later, he and Marsh were standing shoulder to shoulder in the Methodist church on St. Charles waiting for the bride. If Polly had been younger, it would have looked suspiciously like a shotgun affair.

The church's steeple was missing, smashed by Katrina.

The guests had to enter under scaffolding.

And it was too fucking hot for a wedding.

Though the church was air-conditioned, Danny could see the beads of sweat at his brother's hairline. Marsh was getting what he wanted, and it scared him.

*It should scare him. It should scare everybody,* Danny thought.

It was the fire.

Marsh appearing on scene in the nick of time and playing hero. Just as the fire was getting started, Marsh had phoned Polly and awakened her.

184

*Such perfect timing.* From the beginning Danny wondered if Marsh knew more about how the fire started than he should have.

Danny wasn't worried about trouble with the law. Wind and flooding had damaged electrical wiring. Debris had piled under and around buildings. Police and fire departments were desperately understaffed. The loss of Polly's house was one of many in the months following the storm. Whispering at the far end of the room cut into his thoughts. He felt Marsh tense. They were not touching but a connection had been forged between them as kids; Danny knew his brother, felt his brother, as another part of himself. In more ways than most people realized they were the same man.

At the end of the room, the doors opened a few inches, giggles trickled out like water over rough stone, then they clicked closed again. The judge smiled. Marshall smiled back. There was an expectant murmur from the guests: partners from Marsh's firm, Tulane people on Polly's side. All seemed delighted these two were joining together in holy matrimony.

None of them knew Marsh—or Danny for that matter. All they saw was the shiny careers the two men had built around themselves. Polly was marrying a man no one but his brother could see.

The door reopened and Emma and Gracie, in identical high-waisted dresses of lavender, silk sashes a shade darker, and neat white Mary Janes, marched solemnly into the church. Danny winked at Emma, making her laugh. Her older sister quelled her with a look, and the two of them finished their dignified walk up the aisle, then retired, one to each side, like small pastel soldiers on parade.

Emma and Gracie were the only children Danny had ever bothered to get to know. To his surprise, he rather liked them. Before Emma and Gracie, he'd tended to think of children as much like animals, only stickier. Children were as unlike animals as they were unlike adult humans. There was a basic fiendishness in them, a primal distrust of the rules, that he found fascinating.

Fluttering like purple butterflies, Emma and Gracie settled.

Marshall's attention remained fixed on the empty doorway. Danny amused himself by imagining his brother's eyes *sproinging* from their sockets, his tongue rolling out in a long red carpet, and his still-beating heart zooming out on extension tongs in the tradition of moonstruck cartoon characters.

*True love.* Hallmark made a fortune off the concept, as did more self-help authors than should ever see publication.

Danny had a sneaking suspicion it was the American version of bread and circuses. As long as the masses could be kept entertained pursuing the holy—and expensive—grail of True Love they didn't tend to pay much attention to the systems that were bilking them.

A moment of dramatic tension, and then the recipient of Marshall's lost heart stepped into the doorway: Polly Deschamps née Farmer, divorcée, mother of two. She wore a dress of pewter with daffodil piping, colors that set off her silver-blonde hair. The collar was mandarin and closed with a frog that matched the piping. The style was pure fifties, from the years when fashion worshipped Marilyn Monroe and Sophia Loren.

Ms. Deschamps was nobody's fool.

Seldom had Danny met anyone, man or woman, around whom he felt so unpleasantly transparent. Marshall's intended would never be so déclassé as to pry, but Danny knew she *saw*. There was a rich undercurrent in her eyes. He'd seen hints and shadows that suggested she took very little for granted. Not the person one would want to try to keep secrets from.

Polly turned and there was a tantalizing susurration. Few fabrics moved the way silk did.

Danny admired her taste. Polly did not conform to the trivial. She defined her own beauty. Earlier in her and Marsh's courtship, Danny flirted briefly with the idea of winning her away from his brother. It wasn't that he wanted Ms. Deschamps; he just wanted to remove her from his brother's life before somebody got hurt. He had discarded the notion as soon as he realized it would be an either/or thing: he could either have Ms. Polly or he could have his brother. He chose Marsh. A no-brainer, as the vernacular would have it.

Polly stepped from the apse. With an innate—or, this being the Deep South, more likely a learned—sense of feminine theatricality, she twitched the full skirt clear of the door frame, looked up from beneath bangs that seemed windswept even in the still, warm air of the chapel, and smiled.

Danny felt the push under Marsh's sternum, the ache across his shoulders, and knew the effort it cost his brother not to dash down the aisle and take her into his arms.

Polly knew it, too. Danny read it in her face. Then he felt it, felt *her,* inside Marsh, inside his brother. He tried to breathe, but his lungs wouldn't fill with air. She was in Marsh's head and spine, reaching out through his hands, looking out through his eyes. She was inside and all over him. All over them. And Marsh opened himself to it like he had never opened himself to anyone since he was a little boy.

A white-hot point lacerated the back of Danny's left eye. A central core of him shook. He was having a heart attack or a stroke. An aneurism, a fall of black, killing blood, trembling and pulsing, was breaking, bringing down eternal night behind his eyes.

"Danny? Danny? Hey man, you okay? Danny boy? Should we call a doctor or something?"

Marsh's voice brought him back to the world, the room. It was over, done. The ceremony concluded, the bride kissed, and all the while Danny had been dying. He looked from Polly, to Emma and Gracie, to the pastor. They looked back, their faces ludicrous with concern.

"Brother, are you okay?" Marsh said. He laid his hand on Danny's shoulder and Danny began to breathe again.

"Overcome is all," he said. "I've missed having a sister." He smiled and opened his arms to Polly.

MINNESOTA, 1975

*Susan Smith. Killed two little kids. Drowning. See, this I can understand. People look at what she did and say, "Oh, my God, how could anyone be so cold and heartless?" I can see doing it. Who knows what she was thinking, but maybe it went like this. Here she is, this down-and-outer. Maybe not much money and no hope of getting any. She's lonely all the time, and she's got these two little kids. The kids are stressed out, crying all the time and fussing, and she's worn out with taking care of them and herself. Then, here comes this boyfriend, and she sees maybe a way out. So she falls hard. He has only one problem with taking her out of her misery. He doesn't want the kids. In my movie, she's torn up by this, miserable, but she sees no life for her or the kids without this boyfriend. She doesn't want them in a foster home with all that shit. So she thinks the only way to save herself and keep her boys from being passed around is to quietly end their little lives. Blaming a black man, I can't go there. That's pure cowardice. But the murders. Sure.*

# 20

People changed. *People,* not Richard. Watching his reflection in the mirror as he knotted his tie perfectly, he knew that at twenty he was better looking than he had been at fourteen, or fifteen, or seventeen. His shoulders had broadened, and his chest filled out his suit coat nicely. The baby-fine, wavy, brown hair had grown darker, but not by much, and his jaw had firmed up. Richard paid only cursory attention to the physical changes. He could not remember a time he had not felt precisely like he did now, like himself.

Others were children, then adolescents, then adults. Their loves and hates traded places over the years, religion turned to cynicism, and cynicism to a desperate belief in God. Richard was as he had always been.

"Rich, honey, are you about ready? I'm so sorry to rush you . . ." The words were accompanied by a head of tight gray curls sprayed stiffly in a coronet, peeking around the door frame.

"You're not rushing me, Ellen," Richard said, smiling for her. Ellen was Sara's oldest friend. She'd cheerfully taken Sara's shifts when his guardian had needed time off to work out the adoption and when she had come to watch him in debate tournaments. "I just want to look my best is all."

"I know you do, honey. You take your time. We'll tell the driver to wait."

The head disappeared and he heard the clacking of her heels on the hardwood of the upstairs hallway. Sara had moved like a ghost in rubber-soled shoes. A lifetime of nursing left her with a bad back, a penchant for soft-soles, and a sense that she was constantly disturbing someone. Most of Sara's friends were nurses. They would all be there today if they weren't on shift at the Mayo. A few doctors might come, but not many. Unless the nurses were young and beautiful or total screwups, the doctors didn't much notice them.

Shrugging into his jacket, Richard looked around at what had once been his parents' bedroom. Now it was his; he'd taken it against Sara's wishes when they'd moved into the Raines house. That, too, had been against her wishes, and though it was twice the size of hers and immeasurably grander, she'd never been comfortable in it.

"Why don't we sell it?" she'd say. "Buy something more modern?" He knew she wanted the move more for his sake than hers, at least in the first year they'd lived there.

When getting him to sell failed, she tried to change the house from within. "Why don't we knock this wall out, make this room into one big space? It would be much lighter in winter." Or, "Let's get rid of all this dark old paneling and put up cheery wallpaper!"

Richard didn't change anything. Dylan might need to come back here, might need to see it again, and he wanted the house to be as his brother had left it.

Richard turned back to the mirror. He looked like a million bucks, which, with the inheritance his parents had left, the little nest egg from Sara, and the gifts of cash from kind-hearted Minnesotans back when he was an injured child, was very close to what he was worth. Richard knew the value of money. Money bought time and influence; that it also bought cars, and books, and meals out was a side issue. People who focused on that didn't keep their money long.

Dylan was looking like a good candidate for early parole. If it came through, Richard was determined to give the court no excuse not to release his brother into his custody. Money would do that for him. What made bellboys and chief justices alike was that they respected money, believed the rich were more deserving than the poor.

With luck, Dylan could be out in a couple of years.

*Good old Phil.*

Richard's mouth tightened. He wished he could be the one to help his brother, but Phil Maris must have moved up the food chain since he'd been fired. He evidently had connections in high places now. Maybe he'd had some even then. The whole incident of the firing from DuWalt had been swept under the rug. Nobody but Richard, DuWalt's warden, and maybe Dylan knew he'd gotten canned. The official story was that he got a better position in St. Cloud.

Richard dismissed Phil from his mind.

In the mirror, the image of his face softened, saddened. "Sara was good to me; we were good for each other. I shall miss her," he whispered. Shrugging into his new coat, he took a last look in the glass. Satisfied, he headed downstairs to the waiting limousine.

Valhalla Cemetery was outside of town, situated on gentle rolling hills, wooded at the crests, with the headstones filling the valleys. There wasn't a nicer place to be dead than Valhalla. The plot had cost a bundle, but it came with perpetual care, and Richard knew it would please Sara's friends. They would believe her to be resting easier there than in a more crowded, less scenic graveyard in the old part of town.

It was January; the trees were black and wiry and the hillsides dun colored. An early thaw warmed the temperature to near fifty. Muddy remnants of snow were shrinking, filling the narrow lanes with running water. Richard winced as it ran over his new dress shoes but held steady to help Ellen and Sara's other best friend, Opal, from of the back of the limousine.

Across the dead grass a clot of people waited at the gravesite, standing on three sides of the hole, staring expectantly into it as if it were giving instead of receiving today. On the fourth side of the grave, incongruously kelly green under a covering of fake grass, was the soil that had been removed. It was oozing back into the earth in dribs and drabs as the ice melted.

Dr. Ravi, not yet American enough to know he didn't have to show his respect for the dead if they didn't have an MD, stood alone and to one side. In a tight group at the opposite end stood Dylan and two "counselors." Discounting the psychiatrists and high school teachers, Richard doubted if there were half a dozen college degrees in all of DuWalt.

"Brother," he said and left Sara's friends looking daggers after him, past him, toward Dylan. Richard hugged his brother and was startled to feel hard muscle where a boy should have been.

Dylan leaned awkwardly into him and Richard realized they had him in handcuffs. Anger flashed through him like klieg lights coming on in a dimly lit theater; suddenly every corner was thrown into stark relief. Illusion was destroyed, stark reality exposed.

The men who had brought his brother to his adopted mother's funeral in shackles had no more original thought than dumb animals. Far from stirring compassion in his breast, it made him want to bludgeon them with a sledgehammer the way they felled cattle at slaughter houses. For a brief moment, time enough for the guards to see the darkness behind his gaze and shift uncomfortably without knowing why they did, he considered them as dead meat. With the barest of nods, he released them. It would be inappropriate to make a scene at a funeral.

Dylan smiled, shrugging off the embarrassment of the manacles. Clumsily, he clasped Richard's arm in lieu of a hug. "Whoa," Dylan said and banged gently on his brother's arm, pretending to listen as if to ringing steel. "Been working out, huh?"

Richard was inordinately pleased by the compliment. Though he courted admiration, he didn't really care much about it. But when Dylan thought he was cool, Richard basked in it. He was Dylan's best friend. And Dylan was his.

"You, too, buddy," he returned the compliment sincerely. "Pumping iron? Don't go cliché on me. I don't want you coming out looking like Bluto."

For a moment they grinned at each other, foolish as puppies. Then, "Hey, man, I'm sorry about Sara," Dylan said quietly.

Remembering where they were, Richard sobered up as well. "Sara was good to me; we were good for each other. I'm going to miss her. It's my fault . . ." he began and was surprised to feel tears welling up.

"You can't take that on yourself. You took care of her as well as she took care of you," Dylan said. "You remember that. You carry the weight of the world, brother. Put some of it down. This one isn't yours."

The minister made come-to-order noises. Richard stepped away from his brother to share himself with Opal and Ellen. Ellen, the closer of the two, took his arm possessively and glared at Dylan as if he was going to murder them all.

After the service was read and Richard had dropped a clump of mud onto the casket's lid—there wasn't a dry handful of dirt to be had in all of Valhalla at that moment—the two brothers, two elderly ladies and two prison guards watched the pastor leave, hurrying over the wet sod, picking and hopping like a water bird trying to scare up lunch.

"I wish we could have had Father Probst," Ellen said sadly.

Richard groaned softly. Opal hissed, "Ellen!"

Ellen, looking older than she had on the drive out to the cemetery, her nose reddened with the chill, her eyes with crying, grabbed the breast over her heart as if stricken. "Honey, I am so sorry. I just meant . . ."

"I know what you meant," Richard said kindly and tucked her strong, chapped fingers under his arm. "I wish she could have had her priest as well. Mass was a comfort to her. I just wish I could have helped. I knew she didn't want to move back into that house. Being there preyed on her mind. Jesus." Tears had come again. Richard dropped

Ellen's hand to fumble under his coat for a hand-kerchief.

Opal snatched his arm. "There was nothing you could do, honey," she insisted. "Sara'd been depressed for so long. Since her divorce really and then, well, you know, her son and all. You gave her more happiness than she would ever have had. Don't you think different. Sara wouldn't allow it," she said trying for cheer.

"Sara spoiled me rotten," Richard admitted. "Whatever I wanted, she let me have."

"She couldn't say no to you, could she?" Ellen said, and then she started to cry again.

"I think she was spoiled herself!" Opal said in sudden startling anger. "This was a rotten, selfish thing if you ask me. Doing like that! What did she think it was going to do to her friends? To you? I don't think I'll ever forgive her for letting you find her like she did."

"Rich?"

Dylan's voice cut through the outpouring of emotion that was choking Richard. He was glad of an excuse to move away from the women. Opal's hand pulled out from the crook of his arm, catching and dragging at him like a strangling vine. It was all he could do not to jerk free.

"Bad day, brother," he said smiling sheepishly at Dylan.

"No shit. Look, I've got to go. Sorry. You know I'd stay if I could. Those biddies are liable to feed you to death on casseroles and cake without some-body to back you up."

"Let my brother come home for a bite," Richard said winningly to the smartest-looking guard.

"Sorry. The service is all," the man replied stoutly.

His nose was redder than the fifty-degree tem-perature and pleasant breeze could account for. This guy liked his booze.

"Come on," Richard urged. "You and your partner could use a little stiffener, a little some-thing to take off the chill. What do you say? I get the comfort of family; you get a break from rou-tine." Richard's smile was a beauty. When it came to dentistry, Sara made sure he spent money on himself.

Rudolph the Red-nosed looked at his cohort. "Whaddyasay?" He could already taste the booze, Richard could tell. The other guard probably had his own addictions but Richard guessed they had nothing to do with drugs and all to do with the boys he "counseled."

"Just the service. Orders."

"Come on, man." Richard tried to put the smile back on. "Just for a few minutes. Nobody has to know. What can it hurt?"

"No can do," the priggish little man said stiffly.

"Don't be such a jerk," Richard snapped and knew he'd pushed too far. Even Rudolph suddenly got a spine.

"That'll be enough out of you, kid. I'm sorry your aunt or whatever—"

"You morons get your AA degree at community college and a job bullying kids in juvie, and you have the nerve to come to my aunt or whatever's graveside, my mother's funeral, for God's sake—"

"Rich, stop. Be cool. Come on, brother." Dylan took his arm in both hands, the cuffs making it awkward. He shouldered in between Richard and the guards.

"It's okay, Rich. Thanks. But they can make it worse back at juvie." To the guards he said, "Give my brother a break. The guy just lost somebody. Don't be such pricks. Back off, why don't you?"

The two men backed off a couple of paces. Rudolph lit a cigarette.

"It's no biggie, Rich. I'm out of there in a couple years anyway. Eighteen and I go to the big house. What a trip, huh? Come on, brother, you grieve for Sara. I'll be okay. It's okay." Dylan leaned close, his forehead nearly touching Richard's, his manacled hands still firm around Richard's arm. "They're not worth it, Rich. Take it from me. They aren't worth the sweat."

Richard breathed in slowly and deeply and tried to blow out some of the ice rime that had formed around his heart. "I'm okay."

"You sure?"

"Yeah. I'm sure."

Dylan was wearing a cheap suit coat DuWalt had

given him—or more likely lent all the boys—for formal outings. Richard put his hand on his brother's wrist causing the jacket's sleeve to slide up exposing Dylan's forearm.

"Tell me this is a joke," he said, pulling Dylan's arm out straight, staring at the ink marks on the white flesh.

Dylan said nothing. "Shit," Richard said. "Why don't you just have your *bros* write 'lowlife ex con' across your forehead and be done with it? You know what this does? This brands you as a piece of shit. When you get out, everybody will see this and think you're a scumbag. Shit."

Richard turned away and stared into the sun, trying to burn out the cold that was coming back into him. "Pumping iron and getting prison tats. You proud of yourself?" he asked without turning back.

"Let it go, Rich. It was stupid. I was high. Let it go."

"High."

"Let it go, man."

There was something in Dylan's voice that turned Richard around to face him. Dylan felt dangerous.

"Sure," Richard said. He smiled and clapped Dylan on the shoulder. "Sure." He walked with his brother and his brother's keepers to the paddy wagon, an old station wagon tricked out with a screen and bolts in the floor to anchor chains and manacles.

"The big house," Dylan had said. Richard thought he'd heard a hint of pride or boasting in the words. Like a baseball player in the minor leagues talking about going to "the show."

Pumping iron and tattoos.

He had to get Dylan out while he was still Dylan, still his brother. If it meant kissing Phil Maris's well-connected ass, so be it.

# 21

"Screw Phil Maris. He was nobody," Rich said. "His aunt wasn't even anybody; she just happened to be the governor's secretary. The bastard should have done it years ago. You were eleven for Christ's sake."

"He's right, Dylan. I'm glad Mr. Maris worked this out but you don't owe him anything." This from the backseat of the car, where a man in a heavy wool suit was sitting. The man who'd come with Rich. Mr. Leonard from the Minnesota Department of Corrections.

Dylan tuned them both out and watched the fields pass by through the car's window. He wasn't shackled, he wasn't behind a heavy mesh security screen, and there was a handle on the inside so he could open and close his door. He could get out any time he wanted.

He was free.

A sick sort of guilt lay in the pit of his stomach

like a piece of rotten food. Why wasn't he brimming over with gratitude toward Phil? No big house, no state pen. Freedom. Anybody else would be high, back slaps all around, telling stories of what they would do when they got to the nearest bar, or restaurant, or woman.

Dylan just felt scared. He wouldn't admit it to Rich or the guy in the backseat—he wasn't really even admitting it to himself, not in words—but mostly he wanted to go home, back to DuWalt. Not really. He didn't really want to be there. But in DuWalt he knew the rules; he knew who he was, how to act. What would happen outside when people found out he was the infamous Butcher Boy? Inside he had his pals; they watched each other's back. Dylan had status; an old-timer in a short-time facility.

Outside would they beat the crap out of him? Keep their kids inside when he walked by? Set their dogs on him? His mom and dad had a lot of friends. Would they try to get him put back inside? There was no place for the likes of him in the real world. He belonged behind bars. Rapists, thieves, wife beaters, murderers—they were his people.

"Rochester's out," he said suddenly. "Minnesota is out." He had no idea where he meant to go. Other than visiting California when he was four to see some cousin, he'd never been anywhere more exotic than Iowa.

Silence followed his announcement. The feeling

of guilt spread like poison up Dylan's esophagus. Maybe he was carsick, but he didn't think so. The silence stretched. Miles slid by, fields green with summer air so clear and sweet the birds sang with it. Dylan was going to cry if he didn't watch it. Like a little kid.

"I kept the house like it was," Rich said finally. "I thought you'd want to come home."

Why would anybody think he wanted to go home? *Home is where the heart is.*

Dylan pictured his heart, out of his body, lying in the bloody hallway beside the mutilated corpse of his sister. The vision was as brief as it was toxic. He shoved the picture back into the recesses of his mind. These were things he'd worked at not seeing for years, worked to keep Kowalski from dragging up. He'd gotten good at it.

He said nothing, just kept looking out of the window. Cows were grazing by the road. If he could choose a life, that would be the one he picked, the life of a cow munching grass never knowing one day it would be hamburger.

"I can see why you might not want to go back to Rochester, son," the man in the backseat said carefully.

The "son" grated on Dylan. He was nobody's son.

"Reentering life on the outside is hard. Lots of boys don't acclimatize. Maybe even most boys. They end up back inside. I hope that's not the case with you, but it could be."

Dylan thought about that for a while. It wasn't news. In his seven years in DuWalt he'd seen the revolving door spinning, kids in, and out, and in again. Mostly, they came back boasting about the time they'd had outside, like they were sailors back on the ship bragging about their conquests during shore leave. He could do that—boost a car or get in a fist fight and get himself thrown back in jail. The state or federal pen this time. He was eighteen.

"Guaranteed," Dylan said.

"Why? You've got no more family to do in but me," Rich said. He laughed, but the words were sharp as knives. Dylan had hurt his feelings; he'd not appreciated what his brother had done for him, continued to do for him.

"Fistfights," he said succinctly. "In Rochester I'll be fighting all the time. Eventually, I'll kill somebody." There was no boast there; it was just fact. Dylan was big and he was strong. Hit somebody wrong, and they were dead.

Nobody argued with that.

After a time Rich said, "I got you enrolled in the junior college where I went. You don't want to sling hash all your life do you?"

"You have to go to college, son," said the brown suit from the backseat. "Phil Maris said you were one of the smartest kids he'd ever taught. You don't want to waste that on fistfights and the like."

*College.* The word rang through Dylan, reverberating like the morning bell at DuWalt. Guys in DuWalt didn't go to college; guys bound for the pen at eighteen didn't think about it any more than they thought about flying out the window on a magic carpet.

The one true, clean, linear joy he'd had in DuWalt was Phil and math class.

Phil hadn't bothered to say good-bye. He'd never even written.

For Dylan the peaceful order of planes, dimensions, numbers doing precisely what they should eventually returned. Phil Maris never did. Until now, Dylan figured he'd forgotten about him. "College?" He said it so softly Mr. Leonard, in the backseat, didn't hear him.

"Why not?" Rich said. "I can afford it."

"They let guys like me do that?"

Mr. Leonard caught up with the flow of ideas. "It could be done," he said slowly. "Not in Rochester. Not in Minnesota," Dylan insisted. Richard laughed. It wasn't the bitter laugh he often had; it was a good, fat laugh, like he'd thought of some grand scheme, something cool to do.

"Hey, the winters are too damned cold up here anyway," he said.

LOUISIANA, 2007

*Andrea Yates. Drowns five kids. I can't condemn the woman. I can't even get up a good steam of outrage. How can anybody blame her? She's young, alone, depressed; her husband is off at his job but micromanages her life. She can't send the kids to school. There's no money for help. She's supposed to be teaching them lessons. The whole religion thing is coming down on her.*

*Then a voice tells her there's a way out.*

*You've got to hand it to Andrea. She fought the voice. Tried to get help. Told her husband she had thoughts of killing her kids. That must have taken courage. Jesus, is there any worse thing that a woman can admit? Nobody helped her, or not enough, and she landed back with that killing pressure.*

*And the voice, telling her there's a way out.*

*Poor woman must have been so desperate by that point, I doubt she could tell what was real and what wasn't. Her reality was insane, so insanity looked logical.*

*The voice gets pushier. The kids get wilder. She thinks she's a lousy mother, and anything's got to be better for the kids than a lousy mother.*

*Then, one day, the voice wins. She drowns them because there is no other choice left.*

*I admire Andrea Yates. Not for the killings, but for the heroism and strength she showed in fighting insanity in an attempt to save them. Had anyone stepped in and helped her with this battle the kids would have survived. And so would Ms. Yates's mind.*

———————

## 22

*Married.* Standing on the cathedral steps at twilight, watching the lights come on around the square, Polly resisted the urge to look at the rings on her left hand. A breeze filtered through the cooling bodies of the tourists ruffling her hair. Letting the magic take her as she always did when she came for a reading, she closed her eyes and breathed deeply. The French Quarter smelled like a traveling carnival: cotton candy with a whiff of naughty sex and stale beer, urine dressed up with French perfume, and running through it like a current of unstoppable life, a mother on a rampage, a teenaged girl on a tear, the smell of the river.

On such a fine evening the tarot card readers were out in force, lined up umbrella to umbrella in a postpsychedelic mushroom patch, facing off against the gleaming white stone of St. Louis, the forces of the old magic in tawdry defiance of the Christian interloper. While debating which reader to patronize, Polly wondered what the cards would say. For years they'd hinted at a mystery man waiting in her future to sweep her off her feet. There'd been men and there'd been mystery but only with Marshall had she been swept away. Surely the Lovers would be in her reading, and the World, and the Moon. Polly smiled. Love had made her such a fool.

Two girls—children in Polly's eyes but of the age she'd been the first time she'd come to Jackson Square—rose from a table tucked between the benches opposite the cathedral doors. They were tricked out in the unfortunate fashion that decreed female children dress as prostitutes in a world full of predators.

The girls looked around like actors searching for an audience, then, catching her eye, the bolder of the two—at least that was what Polly surmised from the acreage of skin exposed—called, "If you're going to get a reading, you should go to the Woman in Red."

"The fat-fat one," the second girl said rudely, but at least quietly.

"The Woman in Red," the first girl repeated insistently, "is truly awesome." Stretching out an arm displaying half a dozen bracelets, she pointed to the table they had just vacated. There a voluminous woman—the very air around her swelling and rippling along with her layers of scarves—beckoned. Palms up, her screaming scarlet nails waggled as if she tickled a trout from midair.

"The Woman in Red it shall be," Polly said and smiled as ghosts of her past walked away giggling. She'd noticed the reader on previous pilgrimages to the square in search of her future. It was hard not to. Shades of shrieking sunset, roses, and hearts of fire, cherries, apples, blood and wine were thrown together. If one shade of red was loud, this woman's ensemble was cacophonous.

Before time and sunlight had taken its toll, her khaki-colored setup had evidently been as red as the rest of her. As she shifted her considerable weight, her chair's wooden frame moved and flashed thin ribbons of the canvas's original color, that of freshly butchered meat. Polly descended the cathedral steps and the fortune-teller leaned forward, reaching out with a beggar's aspect—or that of a drowning woman bent on pulling her rescuer down. "For zee lady, zee reading eez free," she said in a voice both ruined and childlike, the worn-out voice tape of a Chatty Cathy doll with a fake French accent.

Hucksters and harlots never honestly meant anything was free. Having been a little of both in her time, Polly knew "free" just opened the bargaining. She settled into a rickety captain's chair.

Crimson fluttered, cheap jewelry jangled, and the woman shuffled the oversized cards with the ease of long practice. Grubby things, told through her fingers many times, the corners were dog-eared and the edges worn soft. Polly cut the deck. With a theatrical flourish, the reader began dealing.

Tarot cards depicted hanged men, hearts pierced by swords, priestesses, forts, golden goblets, astrological signs, wands, Jungian archetypes, numbers, and a thousand other symbols cobbled together in a mishmash of the world's myths and religions, a dim sum of the spiritual, psychic and psychological worlds.

Candle flames igniting the colors, the cards kaleidoscoped down with hypnotic speed. Fabric, paper, dye, paint, and uncertain light confused the eye. The familiar pattern of staff and cross seemed to rise up from the designs on the tablecloth.

"The Celtic Cross," the reader said. Her voice was no longer accented. France had been replaced by the echo of someplace cold, the northern Midwest or upstate New York. Fingers flying over the filthy bits of cardboard, long acrylic nails creating colorful exclamation points, words began to pour out flat and fast. Like a third grader terrified of forgetting her lines, Polly thought.

But these weren't the words of a child. Repelled and fascinated, Polly moved closer to hear the hushed rapid-fire monologue. An errant thought sparked: in his sleep, had Hamlet's father leaned just so, anxious to receive the poison in his ear?

Paralyzed, she listened as the reader told her of real things, secret things: the abortion Polly had seven hours before the high school prom, one of her stepfathers watching her through a hole he'd drilled in the bathroom wall, the student-aid counselor she'd seduced to get a full scholarship her freshman year at Tulane, Gracie at eight months rolling off the bed and Polly living in terror she'd grow up brain damaged.

As suddenly as it had begun, the outpouring

stopped. The woman pursed her lips, the lipstick so heavy it ran in bloody feathers up wrinkles and studied the cards lying between them on the table.

Around the edges of Polly's consciousness, like dancers around a fire, thoughts came in and out of the light: of knocking the cards to the ground, of rising and running, calling the police.

The reader pushed her face nearer to the cards, and Polly saw the white roots under the Lady Clairol–red hair. Without relaxing her lipsticked mouth, she began to speak in a Halloween-like moan. "You are mired in deceit. Lies grow up around you in choking vines. Your children are threatened. Your life hangs by a frayed rope. Old evil has taken root and begun to grow."

Her eyes, heavy with mascara, narrowed in the fleshy face. She pressed her bulk across the small table, so close Polly could smell cigarettes and alcohol. A hand bearing a burden of dime store rings shot out; acrylic nails dug hard into the skin of Polly's forearm.

"Your husband is not who you think he is," the woman hissed. "You will kill him."

Polly tried to jerk free. Acrylic talons dug deeper. The woman shoved her nose within inches of Polly's.

"Your husband will die at your hands."

For a short eternity, Polly stared into the reader's face. Drugstore foundation, showing orange in the strange light of dusk, caked in the wrinkles. The black-rimmed eyes were rheumy, the whites yellowed with age and abuse. The cloying stench of despair rolled off her, a mental levee breached, poison waters flooding out.

"No," Polly managed finally. Finding strength in the sound of her own voice, she yanked her arm free, leaving pieces of her flesh beneath the Woman in Red's fingernails. Standing so fast her chair toppled over, she backed from the table.

"Open your eyes," the beast was saying. "Open your eyes."

Polly fumbled in her purse, pulled out three twenties, and threw them on the table.

"The reading is free," said the beast, but she eyed the money greedily.

"Nothing is free," Polly whispered. She ran to the corner, turned, and walked rapidly down the shadowed lane between the park and a row of shops.

She would have cut through the garden, but it was locked at sundown. At a side gate a young woman, hands clutching the wrought iron bars, gazed into the garden. As Polly neared, she turned and looked at her. "Cats," she said. "Everywhere."

Polly saw only the cockroaches. They lived like kings on the crowds' droppings. A nauseating clot of the insects fled from around the girl's sandal-clad feet. She didn't seem to notice.

Or she didn't mind.

"What are all the cats doing?" she demanded of Polly.

Polly stepped up beside her and looked into the fenced garden. A spangling of tiny white lights on the trees deepened rather than illuminated the shadows beneath. Pale concrete paths caught the lights and glowed. Into this almost colorless dreamscape had come at least a dozen cats: grey tigers with long legs, short fur, and languid attitudes. They bathed. They stretched. They napped with half-open eyes. They stared without blinking. Safe behind the wrought iron fence, they preened with studied indifference.

Polly looked at them, and they looked back through her. "I don't know," she said to the girl. "I don't know what they are doing."

"Probably waiting to kill something," the girl said darkly.

Polly fled.

## 23

The story of the tarot reading, as Polly told it over dinner was funny and silly, the scary parts exaggerated for comic effect. Emma and Gracie took up the tale and predicted even direr events.

Their laughter was torture, eating was torture. Peas, bread, even the mashed potatoes stuck in Marshall's throat. He worked to get them down. A snake swallowing, swallowing, swallowing a rat down the length of its body. A rat in his throat, not clawing, not fighting, but alive; he could feel it swell against his esophagus as if it struggled to breathe.

"Don't."

Marshall had spoken aloud. Conversation around the table stopped. Three sets of eyes looked at him: Emma, Gracie, Polly. They'd been a family for only a few months. It had started after they got back from Venice. It had come into the house. Now it was reaching out, touching Polly. "Jesus, no," he murmured.

"Talking to yourself is the first sign of insanity," Gracie said. "I read that somewhere."

"Uh oh," Emma joined in. "Tell us if you start hearing voices."

"*Especially* in dog language. Who was that guy whose dog told him to kill people?"

"Sam," Emma said.

"Son of Sam," Marshall corrected. Too abrupt. Too loud. Startled into silence, Emma, Gracie and Polly stared at him.

"Neither Sam, nor his son, nor his son's dog are welcome at our dinner table," Polly said, shooing away the unpleasant silence with the ease of a born hostess. With the tip of the serving spoon, she scooped up three peas and put them on her younger daughter's plate. "I am so sorry, darlin', but I believe I inflicted more of these on your sister, and one does strive to be fair with one's offspring."

Normalcy reinstated for at least the three of them, she asked Marshall, "Don't what, sugar?"

"Don't mind me," he said and tried for a smile. It must have passed muster. The girls looked relieved. "I've got a little indigestion is all."

"If it was my cookin', I'll make it up to you. The kitchen isn't my best room." Polly batted her eyes at him, a fluttering of the lashes that was both sexy and satiric.

Caught in the universe of her eyes, Marshall pushed at the darkness in his mind hard enough that it brought jagged lightning to his peripheral vision. First harbinger of a migraine.

It was happening again.

*Nothing happened,* Marshall silently shouted down the voice in his head. *A slip. A bad dream.*

He loved the girls nearly as much as he did their mother, and he had planned to adopt them. They were so beautiful. Emma was lithe and olive skinned; Gracie was blonder, broader of smile and wider of eyes. She'd be twelve in two weeks.

Polly wanted to get her a kitten.

A flash of memory showed him Tippity, the Chihuahua, with ice around its tiny jaws.

Did people outgrow that kind of thing? Was there a statute of limitations on human misery? BTK, Bind, Torture, Kill. Wichita. Coming forward after so long. But Dennis Rader wasn't repentant. He wanted credit for his work.

"I've got some work to do," Marshall said abruptly and stood up. Memory lightning-flashed again. This time it brought a faint ghostly virga. He

223

needed an Imitrex and quickly. Polly looked concerned but said nothing. Gracie and Emma were still young enough to accept that all stepdaddies came and went with sudden sweats on their foreheads, rocky clenches in the muscle of their jaws. One day they would realize they'd been cheated out of a normal papa.

If they lived long enough.

Fear—or a migraine—clawed the back of his neck so sharp and mean he half-thought if he looked in a mirror, he'd see a monster with scales and talons attached to his back, its fangs buried in the base of his skull. Walking straight, keeping errant words and sighs tight within him, he left the dining room and made his way up the stairs toward his office.

A spectral hand pressed hard on the back of his neck. Marshall squeezed his eyes tightly closed, his face scrunching up like a child's.

Like it was yesterday. Like it was now. Like it had never stopped happening. Pressing one palm to his forehead and the other to the back of his head to keep his brain from smashing out through his skull, he stopped on the landing.

He could smell the past, shit-sharp in his nostrils. The odor gagged him, and the spasm tore through his head with the force of a band saw.

His wife, the girls—he saw them superimposed over the images in his mind, and cried out.

"Sweetheart, are you okay?" Polly called from

the room below in the voice he so loved he sometimes pretended he didn't hear so she would say
things a second time. He who, with the exception
of his brother, had never loved at all since he was
a kid now loved too much.

Danny knew that would trigger it. He'd done
everything to stop the marriage but stand up during
the does-anyone-know-why-this-couple part of the
service and volunteer the truth.

"Sweetheart?"

"I'm okay," Marshall managed to call back.
Forcing his eyes open, he again started up the
stairs. Faintly, from the depths of the dark places in
his mind, he heard sirens, felt the hands of police
and EMTs, still cold from the outside, lifting as he
writhed and twisted in fear and pain.

He was going crazy.

No. He'd always been crazy; he just thought
he'd left it behind. Now, crazy was coming back to
get him.

Concentrating on moving and not thinking and the
pain, he succeeded in muting the movie in his head,
but he couldn't stop it. Black and white and blood-
red, the familiar frames clicked behind his eyes.

In the upstairs bathroom, he fumbled a pill bottle
from the medicine cabinet. Feminine clutter
avalanched into the sink, razor and blades making
a noise that cut as sharp as tempered steel. He
stopped and stared at Polly's Lady Schick and the
packet of blades.

Death held an allure; he'd admitted that to himself a long time ago. But suicide was death without honor, a way for a coward to avoid his debts. Before Marshall had become an architect, he didn't have much to be proud of in his life, but he had taken pride in the fact that he took what was dealt him without whining or shirking.

The razor in the sink, pink and thick handled, Polly's razor, made him think that maybe death was the better part of valor. He pushed the thought away, opened the envelope Danny had given him, shook two pills into his hand, added an Imitrex, and washed them all down with water from the tooth glass.

Thank God for Danny and drugs.

He replaced the bottle, closed the door of the medicine cabinet, and stared into the sink to avoid the face in the mirror.

A kitten. Why in God's name did she want to get Gracie a kitten? If he'd stuck a Chihuahua in the freezer what would he do with a cat? Deep-fry it?

*Jesus.*

Vertigo caught him on the crest of a wave, and he held onto the sink to keep from falling. The razor was between his hands, the mirror waiting for him to look into it. Turning, he half fell into the upstairs hall.

Seventeen more steps and he'd be at his office. Despite what he'd told Polly, he hadn't come upstairs to work; he'd not come for the drugs, though he wished he'd dared to take twice as many.

Marshall had to come upstairs because he had to see.

Leaning into the psychic wind, he pushed forward two more staggering steps. Outside the master bedroom the mental storm reached gale force. Holding onto the door frame, he tried to overcome the need to go in. Three times this evening he'd made the pilgrimage through the stairwell's nightmares to this room to see if it had reappeared. He didn't know whether this time would be a relief or further proof that he should get to know his wife's razor more intimately.

Maybe he'd imagined it in the first place; maybe it had never been there at all. A fourth time was killing him; his head was imploding behind his right eye. A fourth time was beyond careful, beyond compulsion. It was not normal.

Normal was something he knew about. His life had been a case study in normal. Normal didn't live in a garbage heap; nor did it obsess about minutia. Normal wore clean clothes but did not panic if a stain or a spill marred the fabric. Normal shook hands for one point seven seconds.

Normal did not look repeatedly for something that wasn't there because he, himself, had taken it away. That was the hitch. He'd taken it back to the basement and hung it on the two nails driven into a beam for that purpose.

As if from a distance, he watched himself cross the carpet to the bed, saw himself staring down at the coverlet. His doppelganger fell to its knees, reached down, and folded the bed skirt neatly up onto the mattress. With a suddenness that snatched the breath from his lungs, Marshall slammed back into his body, a body kneeling in prayer to a dead or indifferent God.

Taking a lungful of air as if he was about to free-dive forty feet, he bent double and looked under the bed.

Nothing.

Shoe boxes, hat boxes.

Nothing.

With exaggerated care, he folded the bed skirt back into place and smoothed the bedspread. Then he laid his head on his fists, thumbs hard in the corners of his eyes to keep the tears from beginning.

## 24

*The Woman in Red*, she thought as she leaned across the tiny bathroom sink to get closer to the mirror. The sink was black with use, and the mirror hazy from years of accumulated dust, hairspray, bath powder, and other bathroom effluvia. In a way, the filth was her friend; as footage shot through gauze, it softened the less pleasing aspects of her face. Blubber drowned the ravages of age, lard filling out wrinkles and rounding what would have been a sagging jaw line. Close in, just eyes and lips in focus, she occasionally even felt attractive.

Her left eye crossing slightly to accommodate close vision, she concentrated on her lipstick. Red. Always red. Tired of it after so many years and tubes, she'd tried other colors, but they'd looked wrong, as if her mouth belonged to some other woman.

"Fuck," she whispered as the shaking of her hand smeared a red line nearly to her nose. "Darn," she amended firmly. Mr. Marchand did not like the *F* word. He used to like it just fine, but a year, or two, or twenty ago, he had slapped her silly for using it in front of him. After that she never heard him say the word. It was like he'd gotten religion or culture or something. He didn't have to slap her like he did. All he had to do was ask. Saying no to him had never been an option.

Not since that first night.

Remembering then was better than remembering now. Snow was drifting down from a low dark sky. The world was cold and quiet, not hot and hungry like Louisiana. Her mom and dad were at a prayer vigil for a deacon who had passed. Stillness, snow, and darkness swaddled the house. She was at the window on the second-floor landing looking into the next-door neighbor's house.

Through snowflakes half as big as her fist falling

through the halo of the street light, she watched his mother, wearing a flannel nightgown with matching robe and slippers, just like June Cleaver, kiss his brother on the cheek, then sit on the edge of the bed and sing to him.

He came into the doorway and watched them. She loved the way his hair waved, long in front and short over the ears. She loved his dark eyes, the four-square way he stood, feet shoulder-width apart, like he could take on the world. He was what her grandmother used to call an "old soul."

Leaning against the window to be closer, she'd fallen asleep. Then, for no reason she could think of, she opened her eyes. It wasn't like waking up; it was like already being awake, and suddenly, in a pitch-black theatre, the movie comes on.

He was right in front of her, walking down his dimly lit hallway toward her window. He stopped, looked right into her eyes, and smiled that slightly crooked smile that made her weak at the knees.

"Sssshh," she heard herself hissing. The sound dragged her back to the mirror and the lipstick running up to her nose.

She needed a little something. A stiffener.

A glass of bourbon sat on the back of the commode in a space carved out by repetition. The rest of the toilet tank was obscured by a broken eye shadow container, hair pulled from brushes, two bottles of hairspray, a dirty washcloth, and assorted hair pins and tissues. The overflow hadn't far to go. A pile had built up over time until the space between the side of the tank and the sink cabinet was full. Where the glass rested was an almost perfect circle in the mess delineated by old rings from the bottom of the tumbler.

Lifting it carefully, she pushed out her lips to do the least amount of damage to her makeup and took a sip. "Cocktail," she said to chase away the word "booze" that clicked into her mind.

The bourbon was just to steady her hand; she didn't want to get tipsy tonight. Fortified, she tried applying the lipstick again. Better. Not perfect, but better. At least most of the color was within shouting distance of her lip line. Since her lips were naturally thin, she colored outside of it anyway to make them look fuller. Admiring the effect, she shook a cigarette from a partially crushed pack of Dorals and lit it. "Shit." The lipstick was okay, but she had another cigarette burning on the edge of the sink, adding its burn-and-nicotine footprint to half a dozen others. Pinching it up, she dropped it in the toilet and set the new one down in its place.

Another hit of bourbon and she began on her eyes. Most days she just ringed them with black shadow and piled on the mascara. Back when she was boring, before she'd come to New Orleans and become the Woman in Red, she would never have dared wear so much makeup. If she had, either her mother would make her wash her face or some nosey parker would say, "And just who are you supposed to be?" and then that biddy would tell her mother. New Orleans loved masks, and makeup was a mask of sorts. Paint to cover youthful extravagances and sins, to let a woman be who she should be instead of who she had to be. When she'd first caked it on, she'd been putting on a character, the Woman in Red. Now heavy base, white powder, carmine lipstick, charcoal eye shadow and gobs of black mascara were part of the persona she'd worn for so long it ceased to be an act.

Tonight, she wanted to look nice, have the charcoal shadows neat and the mascara without clumps. Squinting through the fog of bourbon, smoke, and dirt, she carefully combed out her lashes with an old toothbrush. At least she hoped it was the old one.

At eight o'clock she was going to meet Mr. Marchand, and she wasn't going to shame herself. Not this time. She wasn't going to be too tipsy. She was going to have it together: nice dress, face on straight, hair done. This meeting was a big deal. Mr. Marchand was like family, but better—closer—and meeting him wasn't a casual thing.

"It's him moving forward in our relationship," she said solemnly to the face in the mirror. In her heart she knew that wasn't the way it was. He did things for his own reasons and hadn't bothered to tell her what they were for years. No, he'd never bothered to tell her why he did things or had her do things. "This is like Mr. Marchand taking me home to meet his mother," she said and took a long drag on the cigarette. Her heart put in its place, she picked up the hairbrush.

Before moving to New Orleans she'd never heard of tarot. Because she needed to stay close to Mr. Marchand, she'd had to find something to do that would let her hang around Jackson Square where she could keep an eye on his office door. Since she couldn't paint or draw caricatures, and there was no way she could stand still like the statues, not even when she was thinner, tarot reading seemed easiest.

Turned out she was good at it. Too big, and too red, and too much of most things, and too little of everything else, she didn't think she'd ever be good at anything, but she saw things in the cards that were true. People liked to mock her when she said that, especially Mr. Marchand, so she didn't brag about it—but she didn't stop believing it either. There wasn't anything else she could say good about herself except for that. It was true and right and she would not think it wasn't.

Privately she believed she was a good reader because she'd spent her life being not enough—not pretty enough, smart enough, rich enough, lucky enough—and that gave her a special insight into people.

Ego didn't get between her and the deck. She

could see where the clients who came to her table were broken, and the cards told her how to help them. Of course, lots of times it was an act. Tourists paid for the act as much as for the reading. But not always. Once in a while there was a true "seeing." Like when she'd warned Mr. Marchand's wife. That had blown her mind. The act was mirrored in the cards so exactly she knew it wasn't an act at all. A window between now and the future had opened for just that few minutes. She'd looked right through it, right into the awful place that woman was headed. The words weren't hers, at least not all of them, but the seeing, that was all her.

Her hand twitched and she jammed the mascara wand into her eye. Pain shot through her and she knocked the lit cigarette to the floor. Not the floor, the floor was no longer visible; a crust of garbage an inch or two deep at its thinnest covered the hardwood. The smoldering butt fell into a stack of magazines and rolled behind the toilet. Bourbon got her as she bent down, and she fell into the toilet, banging her hand against the bowl.

She'd accidentally gotten tipsy.

Grunting, she dug the cigarette out and pounded the place it had landed in case anything had ignited. Dropping the butt in the toilet, she saw the acrylic nail of her right index finger had snapped off exposing a scabby stub where the real nail had been filed down to take the epoxy.

"God damn it!" she hissed as she levered herself back to her feet. Her nails were fake, but they were pretty, the prettiest thing about her. Upright, her finger in her mouth, she turned to the mirror once again. Sucking had smudged her lipstick and black tears poured down through her makeup leaving gray runnels that would be a bitch to cover up.

"Fuck!" She threw the mascara wand at the mirror. Leaving a black smear, it bounced off the glass and fell into her half-empty bourbon glass. "God damn it!" she shouted and started to slam her fist into the mirror.

Bad luck, seven years of it. That was all she needed!

Sucking in her breath, she closed her eyes and began to mutter. "Seventy-eight cards, twenty-two major arcana, trumps, cannot be changed, fifty-six minor arcana divided into four suits . . ."

When she'd gone to read in Jackson Square, she'd memorized the paragraph marketers put on the card boxes for the tourists. That was the extent of her knowledge when her first customer sat down. The oft-repeated litany calmed her. As a little girl she'd used the Lord's Prayer. It had never paid off in nearness to Mr. Marchand, let alone twenty-dollar bills like the tarot did.

"Okay. Okay." She opened her eyes but didn't let them veer to the mirror. "We're moving slowly, carefully," she coached herself, as she picked up the bourbon, fished out the mascara wand, and let it fall to the floor. "Both hands, that's my girl." Holding the tumbler as a believer might hold the grail, she took a long sip. Later, when her hands were steadier, she'd fix her makeup. That way it would be fresher for her date.

*Date.*

That cheered a smile from her. He would laugh if he heard her use that word. That, or he'd get mad. Lately, since Mr. Marchand's wife had come into the picture, he'd been on edge. Before she'd come along, he'd made fun of her but he didn't get so mad so much. He didn't pace and hit. Polly Marchand and those little girls kept him upset. He was going to do it again. Mr. Marchand had told her that.

A shame. Ms. Pollyanna seemed nice, but it was hard to tell; the cards told a lot, but they had their secrets.

Tonight she didn't want to think about Polly Marchand. There was another thought she'd liked. For a moment she couldn't remember what it was. The grail made another trip to her mouth, and it came back to her.

*A date. The Woman in Red has a date*, she thought and laughed. Nobody had to know she used that word. If he could keep secrets, so could she.

All night she'd think of it as a date, a real date. He thought he could read her mind but she didn't think he could, not most of the time.

"Date, date, a date, I have a date. So there to you,

Mr. Marchand. We are on a date," she sang as she threaded her way through the crap on the floors to the cupboard in the next room. She was running low on bourbon.

Mr. Marchand paid for her to have air-conditioning, and she kept it turned up high so the apartment didn't smell too bad. He'd promised he'd get her a nicer place if she'd clean this one up. She was going to do it soon. Lots of valuable things, she thought. It would be crazy to just throw them out. She'd make time to go through it. Things kind of kept getting away from her these last few years.

Two bottles left of the cheapest stuff. "Neat, straight up," she said to an imaginary bartender as she poured three fingers. A swallow soothed the pain in her eye and her disappointment over breaking a nail. Refill clasped to her chest, she returned to the bedroom.

"I'm late, I'm late, for a very important date," she sang as she rifled through red in her cramped closet, and more red, each garment more tired than the last. Over half of them no longer fit, but she kept them. As soon as the weight came off she'd be wanting them. Finally, she settled on a red polyester caftan. The fabric didn't breathe in the heat, and there were tiny irons and coffee pots and mixing bowls in black on it but it fit and, if she wore it backwards, it didn't look too stained. Back or front, what did it matter? The thing was shapeless.

Dragging it from the pile, she wondered when

the clothes had migrated from the hangers to the floor.

Two winters before there'd been ice and she'd twisted her knee. Healing took a long time. The place had gotten out of hand while she was injured. The closet was one of the places she would start on first. There were probably some nice outfits in there, new shoes. As soon as she got squared away, she would organize the closet, she decided. Could be there was a whole new wardrobe just waiting for her.

The caftan had been squished, so she spread it over the stuff on the bed and ironed the wrinkles out with her hands as best she could. A small slop of the bourbon got on it but that would dry fast. Alcohol dried fast. Congratulating herself for remembering to mash her lips together so she wouldn't get lipstick on the dress, she pulled it over her head. Too late she remembered she had planned to put on a brassiere and panties.

*Didn't matter. Sexier this way.*

Dressed, she looked at herself in the full-length mirror screwed to the back of the closet door. Really looked. Days, weeks, years went by when she didn't. She'd fiddle with her makeup or her hair, buy cheap rings and arrange them in different ways on her fingers, file the acrylic nails or paint them, but the territory between lipstick and toes she didn't address except to drape it with ever-growing yards of fabric. Red fabric. By the light of a single-shaded lamp she'd thought it would be okay—red light, red dress: romantic.

The shock of what she saw sobered her unpleasantly.

*I don't fucking fit in the mirror.*

Maybe she was standing too close. Piles of clothes and shoes spilling out from the closet had held the door open for God knew how long, but she pushed it anyway. An inch or two was gained.

"I am not this fat. This is like a circus sideshow. Shit!"

With relief, she remembered the bourbon in her hand and took a healthy swallow from the cut-crystal tumbler. It was real crystal; she'd picked it up in a junk shop. Drinking out of a nice glass was okay. Swigging it out of the bottle was what alcoholics did. She was no alcoholic.

Another pull lowered the bourbon half an inch. Careful not to dislodge the unstable stack of unopened mail and socks from a scarf-draped phone table, she set the glass down. That mattered too. Alcoholics never set their drink down, just carried it with them all the time.

Shuffling backward, bulldozing dirty clothes, old newspapers and two empty Diet Pepsi cans into an eight-inch berm of refuse with her heels, she gained a couple more feet. Still the mirror showed only her face and neck. And red, red from one side of the frame to the other. No arms, hands, hips, just red and fucking red.

A goddamn, freak, sideshow, circus-fat Woman in Red.

In the nineteen eighties the sobriquet had seemed marvelously mysterious. Sick unto soul-death of the pasty lump she had been since the cradle—or since she could remember—she had grabbed onto the colorful handle as she had grabbed onto her colorful new city.

Mister Marchand had been nicer to her in those days. They'd gone to the shops on Decatur. The Quarter was rougher then; stuff was still cheap, and drugs and real sex shows could be had any time, day or night. He'd bought her everything she wanted. She'd point and he'd pay. They'd come away with armloads of bags containing red scarves, shoes, hats, dresses. The grand total had been one hundred seventy-eight bucks.

*Big spender, big fucking spender,* she thought as she stared into the Wal-Mart mirror on the back of her closet door. But it had been big to her then. It was the most she'd ever spent on clothes at one time in her life. Mostly, it was big because he was with her; because he'd done it to make her happy she was happy, happier than she'd ever been before or since. That day she became the Woman in Red.

The neck of the caftan was pooching out. With the flat of her hand she smacked it down. Not even tits. *I'm a fat freak with no tits,* she thought as she smashed the neckline down again. She'd put it on backwards and the label wouldn't lie right.

Hooking a finger under the loop of cloth, she gave it a yank to rip it out. The label held. She jerked harder. When it came free it tore the neck of the caftan halfway to her gut. White flesh rolled into the red in the mirror, limp deflated breasts over mounds of flab.

"Fuck you!" she screamed and backed away. "Not okay. Not okay." She crashed into the other room and began throwing things off one chair onto another, digging like a badger and chanting, "Fuck you, fuck me." At last her hand closed on what she sought. Clutching it to her bare chest, she staggered back to the bedroom, held out the can of flat black spray paint she'd gotten to refurbish her setup, depressed the nozzle, and crying, "Fuck yoooooooooou!" sprayed the mirror and the closet door until all that remained in the looking glass was her disembodied head floating on a sooty cloud. "'Bout damn time," she told the head. "'Bout damn fucking time."

A sharp knock on the door froze her in her tracks.

Her hands were splotched with black paint that had leaked from the nozzle, her dress torn; mascara ran down through the thick makeup. Tonight was important, really, really important. She had to look her best, she had to *be* her best, but she couldn't remember why.

Mr. Marchand.

*He was here.*

"No, no, no, no," she whimpered, looking around

as if there would be a new escape door, a place big enough for a circus sideshow fat woman in red to hide.

Knocking.

"Just a minute," she sang out. "I'm coming."

She could tell him that a man—a black man—broke in and raped her. Ripped her dress. Hit her. She could, she could . . . She couldn't find her drink, her glass of bourbon.

Bang. Bang. Bang.

This time the knocking shook the flimsy wall.

Ripped her dress. Hit her . . .

He'd never believe it. Maybe, if she did something nice for him, something special, he would overlook her dress and her face; if he said anything it would be that she had taken good care of him and he'd had a good time. That was better than the rape story. Nobody cared whether you were raped or not.

She'd give him a blow job.

Men liked that. And it was a nice thing, easy. Most were real quick so it didn't ruin the whole evening or anything. When business was slow, and Mr. Marchand didn't think to send her anything, she often gave little blow jobs to keep some money in her pocket.

"Coming," she sang with false good cheer. She grabbed the bourbon from the cupboard and took a healthy slug right from the bottle. If he didn't want a blow job, it wouldn't matter whether or not she was an alcoholic.

# 25

She wiped her mouth on the sleeve of the caftan in hopes of diluting the whiskey smell. Lipstick smeared across her cheek and chin.

"I am the Woman in Red," she said.

Pulling from the depths of a battered past the confidence and allure that name had once inspired, she clutched the torn caftan to her shoulder in what she hoped would come across as sexy dishabille, threw the dead-bolt, and opened the door.

"Why, Mister Marchand," she said coyly. Then, "You said . . ."

"Never mind what I said. What kind of woman answers the door looking like that? What happened to you?" He pushed by her and surveyed the trashed sitting room. "I'm doing the world a favor," he muttered.

"What did you say, honey?"

He was carrying a package, a big one, like the boxes holding a dozen long-stemmed roses she'd seen delivered by bellboys in old movies. There was no ribbon on this one, and it was bigger. She couldn't remember the last time she had been given a present. Fear that had her verging on tears was instantly ameliorated by a warm buzzing excitement.

"Honey, just let me change. This old dress tore when I was putting it on, but I didn't want to make a guest wait on the welcome mat." There was no welcome mat. Like much else it had turned to rags and drifted away. But it sounded nice to say it.

"Never mind that. Sit down. If you can find a place to sit." He looked around at the rubble of her life. Without waiting to see if she obeyed him, he swept a pile of junk from an old Naugahyde recliner.

He was wearing gloves.

With clarity as sudden as it was unwelcome, she saw her home through his eyes. Filthy. Unsanitary. So disgusting it could not be touched by bare skin for fear of contamination. Before she imploded with shame, the vision blurred. "I've been meaning to straighten up a bit," she said. "My knee isn't what it used to be—you remember when I fell and twisted it?"

Of course he wouldn't. Mostly she knew what she knew and lived with it. Tonight for some reason—maybe the gloves or the broken nail or the torn dress or the ruined makeup—she needed to believe he thought of her sometimes when he didn't need her, that he cared she'd been hurt. He didn't answer but kicked the crap on the floor out of the way so he could move a footstool.

He didn't remember; she could tell by the nothing on his face. Against all reason, it hurt her—not that he didn't remember. Who'd remember she'd been injured? It hurt her that he didn't pretend to remember. What would pretending have cost him?

"And I've let the place go a little," she finished lamely.

"It doesn't matter," he said kindly, the hostility of a moment before seemingly forgotten.

Relief flooded her. She was to be forgiven. "I won't be a minute." She again started toward the bedroom to change.

"Stay. I like it like that," he said, and there was a spark of something in his eyes. Interest. Or humor. Maybe he was laughing at her. He did that. She'd gotten used to it; it was just his way. Still, there were times it made her feel bad. Not that he thought she was a clown or a fool, but that he didn't care enough to hide it from her. This time though the spark was ambiguous. It really could be interest, the kind a man has in a woman.

It had been a long time since she'd seen any-thing in men's eyes but a passing smirk, if they noticed her at all. Usually, despite the red of dress and hair and lips, they didn't see her anymore. That spark in Mr. Marchand's eyes thrilled her. She let the caftan slip an inch to show the top of her breast. No more than that. Mr. Marchand would not be pleased by crude behavior.

"Why don't you pour yourself a drink?" he said. "Make yourself at home."

Again he looked around the ruin of her apart-ment. This time she did not suffer the instant of clarity. The offer of a drink made her realize how much she needed a little courage, a little comfort.

Careful not to seem too eager, to move too quickly, she followed the path to the cupboard. The bottle was still on top, the cap off, lost in the clutter on the floor. Shielding the bottle with her body so he wouldn't see it was already open, she found her tumbler and poured. "Can I get you a drink, honey?"

"No, thank you."

No, thank you. He was being a gentleman, a gentle man. This was going to be a good evening. *A date,* she remembered. Smiling, she took a drink before she turned around. She needed to get one sizable shot into her, then she could sip politely.

"Come sit," he ordered, a hint of sharpness returning.

Holding her drink in both hands so it wouldn't slop, she scurried back. It would be just like her to ruin everything by being stupid, trying his patience, saying the wrong thing. The eggshells she walked on were fragile and the breakage cost dear.

*Don't say the F word. Don't gulp your drink. Don't laugh too loud. Don't talk too much. Don't burp. Please, please, please don't let me fart, Lord,* she prayed as she made her way to the chair he'd so peremptorily cleared for her.

"Aren't you going to sit, honey?" she asked, as she lowered herself carefully into the chair. Like a lady, not plopping; lowering.

He smiled.

God, but she loved that smile.

Even through the bourbon, and the excitement, and the fear, she knew he wasn't smiling because the offer pleased him. He smiled because to sit in her home appalled him. Still, she could pretend, and so she did. "Let me tidy a chair for you," she offered and tried to rise. The chair and the booze conspired to suck her back down and she laughed.

"Oops-a-daisy," she said as she fell back, drink in hand, sloshing onto the chair arm. *Bad. She was acting drunk.* Contenting herself with the fact that she had not said the *F* word by accident, she smiled up at him.

He set the package down near her feet and pulled up an ottoman. Tilting it so the papers, shoes, and two purses she had forgotten she had slid off into the rest of the litter, he moved it so he could sit facing her. Before he sat down, he stared for a moment at the nubbled brown fabric scarred with cigarette burns and, in a flash of ESP, she knew he was thinking of getting his handkerchief out and spreading it over the top. That he didn't, she took as a compliment and smiled as he sat on the stool at her feet.

"It's so nice having you here," she said and meant it so much she nearly ruined everything by crying. "It's like family, you know."

"Like family," he said in a distant voice, a sound from a long way off, coming through years of darkness and cold.

For reasons she did not identify, she shivered.

"You brought something," she said brightly to make him come back from wherever his voice had gone.

"It's a present," he said. "I need you to do something special for me tonight."

Blow job, she hoped, but he didn't act like a man who wanted a sexual favor.

Methodically, he began unwrapping her present, talking as he did. She would rather have unwrapped it herself while he watched. That would have been more special, more intimate, but she didn't spoil the moment by pushing what she wanted on him. A present was enough.

*He was here, and sitting in her home, and giving her a present.* She said those words in her mind because she wanted to remind herself how happy she was.

The gift wasn't wrapped in white paper as she had first thought but plastic, two enormous sheets of it. Painters' drop cloths or clear shower curtains. As he unwound them, he took out roll after roll of packing tape, the superstrong kind with fibers all through it.

"Are we building something?" she asked. The tape and the plastic were giving her a bad feeling. Nobody wrapped gifts in plastic and tape you had to cut with a knife.

"Sort of," he replied. "A box for a friend of mine." He smiled more to himself than to her. The bad feeling didn't go away. She poured bourbon on it to quiet it down.

At last, the plastic and the tape had been set aside in a neat pile, and all that remained was the gift loosely wrapped in brown paper.

*No long-stem roses for her.* What it was she couldn't guess.

"Before I give this to you I want to tell you a story," he said and, looking her in the eyes, his gloved hands resting on his knees, he began: "Once upon a time there was an ugly duckling . . ."

"Does she turn into a beautiful swan?" Her hand flew to her mouth. She had interrupted him. He hated it when she interrupted him. Before she could say she was sorry, he went on.

"No. This is a true story. In real life, ugly ducklings, at least the ones that aren't savaged by dogs or eaten by cats, grow up to be big ugly ducks. Big fat ugly quackers," he said. Relieved he'd not gotten angry at her interruption, she scarcely noticed the hard edge his words took on.

"This ugly duckling was a nosey little bird, a spying little bird. She had very sharp eyes, and she saw things that she wasn't supposed to see."

The set of his mouth, the mocking way he was telling the story, cut through the alcohol, and she realized he was talking about the Woman in Red, about her. She knew this the way she knew things, the way the tarot had unlocked for her.

*She was the spying little bird.*

She tried to think of what she could have seen that she wasn't supposed to. He knew she'd been watching the office, but even so he hadn't done anything interesting. He'd gone over to Polly Whatsername on the bench that day. Anybody could have seen that. That was about the most interesting thing he'd done. Other than that, it was clients and business.

"What did she see?" she asked. Bourbon slurred her words and she was ashamed. He didn't get mad though.

"You know what she saw."

She didn't, but she was afraid if she said it he would think she was stupid or being contrary. Then he really would get mad, so she nodded.

"The prince—every story has to have a prince," he said, and there was genuine warmth when he looked into her eyes and smiled.

*I would die for an hour of his love.* The thought floated like a bubble on the bourbon and the fear. He was so beautiful.

"The prince paid the ugly spying duckling to keep what she had seen a secret. Oh, they never talked about it; a prince doesn't share things with fat ugly birds, but he paid. He paid so much that the ugly duckling came to owe him.

"One night the prince came to the duck's nest to collect the debt." At this point in the story, he reached down and meticulously loosened the masking tape holding the wrapper in place and folded the brown paper back.

"An axe," she said stupidly.

"Melodramatic, isn't it? A child's weapon, but I need historic continuity so an axe it has to be." He didn't move to pick it up or touch it but kept looking at her, smiling warmly.

She couldn't take her eyes off the blade, blunt on one end, sharp and shiny-sharp on the other.

"Yore gimmin me nax?"

What she had meant to ask was, *Are you giving me an axe?* Usually, she didn't get to the point her lips numbed and her words slurred until she was alone.

"Sort of. See all this plastic? I'm going to spread it out over the floor—assuming there is a floor under all this dross—and you're going to stand in the middle of it. Sit in the middle; I doubt you are in any shape to stand. That's okay. Bourbon is a good anesthetic. I don't wish to hurt you, so I will make the first blow count. If you don't move, you shouldn't even feel it."

The smile was still cozy and comforting on his face. Smile and words were at such odds, it took a moment for the meaning of the latter to sink in. "You are going to kill me." A jolt of adrenaline sobered her for a minute. "Why?" she wailed and tried to stand. He leaned forward, put a gloved hand on her chest, and pushed her back. Forgotten, the caftan gaped open, her left breast exposed. "Why?" she repeated, the wail degenerating into a confused whimper. "I love you."

"I know. It will be better if you don't think about

251

it as me killing you. Think about it as you giving me the thing I need right now. I'm not mad at you. This isn't punishment. I know you didn't mean to be a spying, prying little duck. That's the least part of it, really. It's something I need you to do so I can make right a wrong. It's the way you can show me you really do love me."

While he talked in a nice reasonable voice, he shook out the plastic sheets and spread them over the detritus of the room, careful to overlap them several feet. Together, they covered nearly the entire space.

Watching him, she did not know what to feel. He would kill her; she knew that. Part of her thought to get up and run for the door, but she knew she'd never make it. Screaming crossed her mind, but she didn't do it. The fear was there, so intense she tingled with it, but it wasn't the bowel-loosening fear she suffered when she crossed him.

"What do you have to live for anyway? Look at yourself. You are middle-aged and pathologically obese; you live in a sty that any self-respecting pig would be ashamed of. The people you know laugh at you. The people you don't know laugh at you. The greatest emotion you inspire in others is disgust. You're a drunk. Liver disease will probably kill you in the not-too-distant future. This is your chance to make your pathetic miserable life end with some spark of meaning. You don't want to keep on living do you? Not a drunken slut selling blow jobs for five dollars a pop? Yes, I know about your little side business. You have made yourself a whore, and a cheap one at that. Let me take you out of this mess."

He'd come back to her chair and now held out his hand to her. Tears were pouring down her face; she knew this because she felt the warm drops hitting her bare chest.

"Could you take off your glove?" she pleaded, her voice small and sweet, the way it had been when she was little, before she'd become a lump, then a lard, then a whore, and a cheap one at that. "Please? For just a second?"

If she could feel his flesh, hold his hand, it would be okay.

For a moment she thought he would refuse her but, in the end, he did care for her; he took his glove off and helped her to her feet. She staggered and would have fallen, but he steadied her with an arm around her waist.

*We could be dancing,* she thought. *Her hand in his, moving gracefully around the floor, candle-light turning the world to gold, and him smiling down at her, holding her as if she were the most precious thing on earth.*

When they stood in the middle of the plastic he'd spread, he looked around. "This should do it," he said matter-of-factly. "There will be some spatter, but I think we've got it covered. I'll do you with the blunt end of the axe and let you lay for a minute. If your blood isn't circulating it will be neater."

He wasn't talking to her; he was talking to himself, so there was no need for her to listen, no need at all. She concentrated on not plopping as he helped her to sit on the floor.

*Like a lady.*

"I'm giving you a present," she said and was proud that her words were clear.

"Yes, you are. A fine present. 'Tis a far, far better thing and so on." He took up a towel that had somehow found its way into the living room. "Think of this as a blindfold," he said as he dropped it over her head. "If I hit too hard, this should take care of any mess."

"Please, I want to see your face," she begged, but he made no move to take the towel off.

He wanted her to have the towel over her.

At first, she didn't think he was going to answer, and she waited for the blow that would end her life.

"Okay, sure," he said.

He cared about her.

She could feel him leaning close. His hands touched her head gently through the terrycloth. He folded the towel back so her face showed. The smell of his cologne brushed her senses. More than anything in life she wanted him to kiss her—not because she asked, but because she was necessary to him, because she was the Woman in Red and only she could give him whatever it was that meant so much to him, because he was the miracle around which she had formed her life.

He stood and surveyed her. "I think it will be fine. Leave it there, though." He fetched the axe and came back. "This isn't something I particularly enjoy. I'm not a lunatic for God's sake. It has to be done to make things right; there's no passion involved to speak of."

He lifted the axe, turned it so the blunt end was down.

The last thing the Woman in Red heard was, "I guess that's the difference between art and science."

## 26

Danny set down his menu and waved as his sister-in-law swept into the Bluebird Cafe and settled with offhand grace. Tension pulled at the skin around her eyes; she looked as if she hadn't slept.

But wasn't that how brides were supposed to look? Danny doubted she had begged a meeting in order to regale him with the glories of married life. Neither spoke until the waitress, efficient as always, had taken their order, tucked the ticket between the salt and pepper shaker, and hustled away.

Then, "Tell me," he said.

"I do love a direct man." Polly's usual twinkle was

dulled, the half-hearted flirting merely habitual.

"Very well. Marshall is . . ." Polly stopped and took a sip of the coffee the waitress had unobtrusively set on the table. "He is suffering and I cannot for the life of me figure out why. We had a wonderful time on our honeymoon in Venice. The girls adore him and he them. He and I haven't had so much as a squabble. But something happened nearly as soon as we returned. Marshall stays at work until past nine. When he comes home, he takes a Valium and goes to sleep—with his back to me more often than not. He's distracted. He isolates himself from us and he won't talk to me about it. Absurd as this sounds, I think he is frightened of something. Has he said anything to you?"

Danny chose not to answer. "On the phone you said something happened yesterday that made it worse."

As her coffee grew cold, she told Danny the bizarre tale of her tarot reading. Her description of the reader as a "shattering racket of reds" made him smile, but he did not underestimate the impact the event had on her.

"I told Marshall about the reading. Danny, I swear that man turned to stone right then and there. It was as if, like Lot's wife, he looked back and turned into a pillar of salt."

"I am not surprised he was upset . . ." he began in defense of his brother.

"Upset is not the half of it, sugar. He couldn't

eat. He could barely talk. He left the dinner table to rush upstairs. I found him standing in the upstairs bedroom staring down at the bed. He very nearly jumped out of his skin when I came in. You would think I had caught him in that bed with the entire Russian gymnastic team rather than woolgathering all alone. His face turned the color of old cigar ash, and he left. He was gone for over three hours.

"I was so worried . . ." Tears welled up in Polly's eyes. She covered this lapse of good manners with a shake of her head and touch of her napkin.

Danny appreciated it. "Any man might get a little sensitive if his wife told him she'd been to a tarot reader who told her that her husband was a fake, a liar and, what's more, she's going to kill him. It doesn't help matters any that you believe in that stuff," he added pointedly.

Over the rim of his coffee cup, he watched his brand-new sister-in-law. She had to be in her late forties—with Southern women it was hard to tell and she wasn't telling, at least not the truth—yet she was easily the most beautiful woman in the Bluebird Cafe. Not to mention the one with the fewest tattoos.

A lot of things about his brother's wife appealed to him: the taper of her fingers, the manicured nails, the way she tilted her head and didn't wind-mill her hands when she talked, that she walked as neat-footed as a cat. Beautiful women didn't disturb his peace the way they did that of other men.

He couldn't imagine going through the emotional storms Marsh was weathering for a woman. Or a man, for that matter. Once, when he was too young to know, but old enough to care deeply, he'd thought he was gay. Over time, he'd realized he wasn't. Having anyone in his life in that way would be too complicated. And dangerous. Life would have been a good deal easier if Marsh had shared that epiphany.

Thinking of his brother, he smiled and shook his head.

"I must say, I am having a difficult time seeing the humor in this," Polly said, a hint of lemon in the natural honey of her voice.

Realizing he was not responding appropriately, Danny apologized. "Sorry," he said sincerely. "I don't know why you open yourself up to those so-called fortune-tellers. Most have day jobs as hookers or drug dealers."

"You are right. I suppose I have a streak of super-stition in my makeup. No, that is not totally true. I *know* I have a streak of superstition. Try as I might, it bothers me when black cats cross my path or the girls run under ladders. I probably shouldn't have told Marshall about the reading but I thought he would laugh at it, and I dearly needed someone to laugh to get the taste of that awful woman out of my mouth. Sorry about the image that must con-jure up while you are trying to eat your lunch; it was an exceedingly unappetizing episode."

"Not a problem," he assured her. "A lot of people have a vein of the old dark magic: witches or angels, lucky bowling shirts. Mom was a court stenographer with a college education, but she'd believed in that sort of thing. Scaring the dickens out of her was a piece of cake. A little knocking, a few whispers, and she wouldn't go to sleep until Frank got home."

"Your father? You call him Frank?"

"We weren't all that close," Danny said dismissively. "Anyway, I was about to say that our folks died around this time of year. Psychologists say the subconscious doesn't let go of those dates, even when the conscious mind can't recall them. It hit us both hard, but I think Marsh got the worst of it. Mom made a pet of him. He was that kind of *Leave It to Beaver* kid." He stifled the impulse to look at his watch or reach for the bill.

Discussing his brother with Polly was putting him on edge. She spoke of Marsh as if wife and brother were equals. Women took on an irritating sense of proprietorship when they married, an unquestioned belief that, with the ring on their left hand, came a profound understanding of the man who'd put it there. A few weeks of marriage was not on a par with half a century of blood.

Polly might have marched into Marsh's id like the Russians into Warsaw, but she didn't know him like his own brother did. Danny was finding it grating to have to pretend she did.

"What did you make of the tarot reading?" he asked to change the subject. "Aside from the effect it had on Marsh, it must have jolted you considerably."

"Considerably," Polly agreed. "When I first came to New Orleans, for a brief time, I lived in that subculture. They are not without honor. There are customs and taboos, as there are in any culture. Those who are serious about their trade—or as serious as one can be when one's clients are wearing feathers and silly hats—would never tell anyone they are sick or dying. It's an unwritten creed." Polly lifted her coffee cup and took a sip.

"This creed was undoubtedly unwritten in stone because readers predicting great evils got their heads taken off by irate customers," she said looking as mischievous as Emma. "Which is what I should have done when this floozy, a-flap with scarves, told me I was going to *kill* my husband."

"It's hogwash."

"Yes, it is."

The waitress brought their food. A moment passed. Danny ate two French fries.

The Bluebird did them up fine, but then he'd never had a bad meal in New Orleans—maybe one or two in the weeks after the flood waters abated, but he'd been so glad to be out and fed, he'd not been critical.

"Pure balderdash," he said. "Absolute poppycock. So why let it bother you?"

Polly took a deep breath and gazed into space above and to the right. Danny'd read somewhere that people gazed in one direction to remember and another when they were trying to think of a lie. He couldn't remember which was which.

"I thought that reader was a mad woman," Polly said finally. "I wondered what side of the world she'd gotten out of bed on that inspired her to do something that mean. The wretched thing was clearly unbalanced."

She stopped speaking. Danny let the silence sit.

"That awful woman knew things about my life that I have not shared with anyone but Marshall," Polly admitted after a few moments. "There is no logical way this great red harpy could have known. Strange as it may be, she had to have seen them in the cards." Her hand, the one with the two-point-five-carat diamond, twitched. It was her nature to touch people. To her credit, early on she had picked up on the fact that Danny didn't like to be touched and honored his idiosyncrasy.

"That would be unsettling," he said with no trace of humor or sarcasm. "It would be hard not to take it seriously."

"Thank you," Polly said.

"Some of these people are clever," he said. "Professionals make a living doing mentalist shows in Vegas. You're sure you told no one but Marsh of these events from your past?"

"Believe me, I am sure."

"Are you sure Marsh told no one?"

"Of course."

In the way she firmed her lips and delicately flared her nostrils, Danny saw the dawning of suspicion. He watched her shake its icy tentacles from her mind with a toss of her head.

"You are right, of course," Polly said. "Could they genuinely see the future, they'd not be on the square but making their fortunes at the track." She took another sip of coffee, made a moue of distaste—it would have grown as cold as Danny's—and said carefully, "What concerns me is that this absurd woman's words somehow damaged Marshall. Since I told him, Mr. Marchand, *my* Mr. Marchand," she added in polite acknowledgement of Danny's existence, "walks this earth like he's haunting it rather than living on it."

"I'll talk to him," Danny promised. He'd planned on talking with Marsh about the bogus reading anyway. Marsh was beginning to fray a little at the edges.

"That would be wonderful." Relief and hope made her voice lush. "Marshall loves you very much. You are good for him."

"And he for me," Danny said curtly. It irked him that she would attempt to define a relationship she knew nothing about.

He took the check the waitress left. "I'd better get to work or they'll rob me blind. Today, it's meetings and on-the-ground checks."

"It's so romantic havin' a brother-in-law who's a drug dealer," Polly drawled and waved as he crossed toward the doors opening out onto Prytania Street.

*A drug dealer.* Danny was amused. In the eighties, when money grew on trees, he had invested in a pharmacy. With the one-size-fits-all mentality of Walgreen's, Rite Aid, CVS, and Wal-Mart, moneymen believed the individual pharmacy had gone the way of the dodo and good service.

He'd restructured the business into what was being hailed a "boutique pharmacy." Designed along the lines of an old apothecary shop— Marsh's idea, Marsh's design—his four-link chain of stores carried the usual pharmaceuticals as well as traditional folk herbs and medicines. Drugs, even legal drugs, were exceedingly profitable, but what brought the high-end clientele into Le Cure was quick, knowledgeable, and very personal service. Danny had not intended to do site visits today, but his meeting with Polly reminded him there were more reasons for being a drug dealer than money. If he didn't get Marsh relief before he became too tightly wound his brother could snap.

That wasn't something his wife and children would want to see.

*Scott Peterson. Wife and unborn baby. 2005. Why this one I don't know. I haven't written about this for a long time. Maybe because I can identify with Peterson. Not with what he did, but with his living a secret life, a life of lies, knowing what people liked about him was a lie. The truth was shameful. He was nothing without those lies. They were him. He'd told the lies so long, he may have felt that being exposed, having his fiction struck down, was tantamount to killing him. The "him" he'd constructed, the persona in which he was a man to be reckoned with, was going to be killed. In his twisted world he acted in self-defense. He started with a new woman who knew nothing about him and destroyed the woman he believed would rip away the Scott Peterson he wanted to be and expose the pathetic little man hiding beneath.*

*That Peterson did such a bad job of it is the best I can say of him. I believe the slaying of his wife and unborn child destroyed him from within, and because of that, he bungled it, was captured, and sentenced to death. I would hope my fiction would not demand such a price should it be threatened.*

## 27

Harsh sun highlighted fine lines in Polly's face, invisible even two weeks before—the velvet glove of autumn over the iron fist of summer. Glare forced her to narrow her eyes and the heat pressed down. She should have worn a hat.

*Any Southern woman with an ounce of good Christian vanity should wear a hat,* she thought absently.

Tilting her head back so tears would not spill over her lower lids, she pushed back on the bench deeper into shade of Jackson Square's live oaks and let the disquiet blossom into a frisson of true fear.

The things that terrorize are those you don't see coming.

The unexpected. "That which we must embrace," the tarot reader had said. Or endure. The sixth card in the Celtic Cross, that which is to come.

"That which we cannot find," Polly murmured aloud.

"You talkin' to me?"

A young, African American man had joined her on the bench. Sandwich held suspended halfway to his mouth, he looked at her with concern. The tears, though unshed, must have shown. Polly was sorry for that. Not that tears weren't a perfectly good expression of emotion—or means to an end—but to lose control was unseemly. And usually ineffective.

"I have been trying to find one of the tarot readers," she said. "A generously constructed woman: red hair, red dress, red nails, red lipstick."

"Sounds like the fire truck," the man noted and took a bite.

"Ye-ess," Polly said, making two syllables of the word. "A siren at any rate. She certainly got one's attention."

"I pretty much know the regulars." The sandwich had gone in three bites. He wadded up the paper and tossed it expertly into the trash barrel several yards away. Polly made no comment. He was sufficiently pleased with himself, she needn't add a thing. "Haven't seen her in a while." He stood to go. "Try the readers. They'd know better than me."

Though she had promised herself she wouldn't, Polly opened her handbag and took out a white unsealed envelope. She pulled out a card, pinching it fastidiously between the tip of her index finger and thumb, lest its inherent filth come off on her hands. The envelope wasn't there simply to protect the card from the elements, but the elements from the card. Or the inside of her bag, at any rate.

Slightly smaller than a standard postcard, it was not of a size the post office would usually deliver, but this was New Orleans and, despite Katrina, the city's tradition of aiding and abetting human idiosyncrasies survived.

Polly did not doubt where it came from. It was

from the Rider-Waite tarot deck, worn and darkened by handling with unclean hands, the edges frayed from use. Had Polly access to criminal forensic laboratories she would have bet the red seeress's DNA would be all over it. It was the ugliest of the cards, suggesting the true evil that inhabited the world. The Devil was a squat, potbellied satyr with ears that grew into hairy points and a skull sprouting rams' horns. The wings of a bat sprung from his shoulders; the talons of a bird of prey took the place of hooves. Chained at his feet were the naked figures of a man and a woman.

Symbolic rather than literal, the Devil had many meanings: bondage, addiction, greed, obsession, lies, betrayal. Unlike other cards in the tarot, none of the meanings were auspicious. Only the Devil's placement in the layout could ameliorate his dark presence.

Polly's card had had a special placement. She'd found it in her mailbox. On the back of it, printed across the faded, dirty, white-and-blue checks, was the Marchand address and a stamp. On the face, scrawled across the Devil's genitals in what looked like red nail lacquer, were the words, "Help me."

There was no return address.

Handling it as if it had been dusted with anthrax, Polly returned the card to its envelope. Fear and anger coalesced into hard tears in the corners of her eyes. *If this keeps up, I must begin to wear waterproof mascara*, she mocked herself.

She'd received the card several days before and had done nothing, told no one, shown it to no one, not even Marshall. He was acting so strangely, she had no desire to exacerbate matters by showing him the Devil in all his naked glory.

A sensible woman would have consigned it to the garbage, but it was contrary to her nature to ignore a plea for help from even the least savory of supplicants. There had been a time when she, as had Blanche Dubois, relied upon the kindness of strangers.

The card readers huddled under the meager shade of their ratty umbrellas talking desultorily among themselves. Only one of the six tables had a client. Tourists were not as likely to want to see their future in the stark light of day as they were on romantic evenings, when all things seemed possible.

Polly started at the corner of St. Ann's and the square. A man, grizzled and looking as if he'd slept in his clothes not just the previous night but for many nights over many years, listened to her description.

"For twenty bucks, I'll read your palm. It's all written there," he said cagily.

Polly moved on to the next umbrella where a rail-thin woman, her skin so damaged by years in the sun that it was impossible to determine her age, sat on a metal folding chair, a cooler beside her, an aging dachshund on her bony lap. A teal evening dress, half the spangles gone from the bodice, hung off her bones by spaghetti straps. One had broken and been patched with an oversized safety pin. Her long, narrow feet were encased in stiletto heels, the black rubbed off the sides and backs.

She looked as if, twenty years ago, she'd had one hell of a night on the town and, come morning, could not find her way home. The dog and the woman's genuine smile encouraged Polly. She sat in the other folding chair. Smarter by one rejection, and feeling compassion for the old dog and the dachshund on her lap, she took out a ten-dollar bill and laid it on the table.

"All I want is information," she said.

"That—and love—is all any woman needs," the reader said, catching up the bill and folding it neatly into a plastic purse. "For ten dollars I can give you both. What a deal, huh? My name is Emily." Her voice and her smile were so full of kindness that Polly laughed and felt better for it. She described the woman she sought and waited.

"Red," Emily said immediately. "The Woman in Red—that's what she likes to be called. Forty years and forty pounds ago it might have caught on. Now, well . . . She can't help it, bless her heart."

Polly smiled. In the South, one could say anything and, if it was followed by that incantation, the sayer was freed from the stigma of speaking ill of others.

"Do you know her real name?"

"Most of us can't even remember our own real names, let alone anybody else's, hon. Red has worked the square for years. She's here almost every day, but I haven't seen her for a week or so."

"Do you know where she lives?"

Emily gave an enigmatic smile.

"I'm not with law enforcement or anything of the kind," Polly blurted out and was mildly offended when Emily laughed, as if that were patently obvious. "Here." Polly pulled the envelope from her purse and took out the card. "I got this in the mail. I think it's from her. She may be in some kind of trouble."

Emily shifted the dog and leaned in to look. Like Polly, she seemed to have an innate aversion to touching it. "The Devil," she said.

"Yes."

"Kind of theatrical. What with cell phones, faxes, instant messaging and whatever, you'd think somebody in trouble would be able to do better than this."

The same thoughts had plagued Polly. The grubby card, the lack of a return address, the melodramatic words in red paint; it had more to it of a trick or trap than a genuine plea for assistance. A game designed to draw Polly into something she'd rather not be a part of.

"Do you have any idea what it is about?" Polly asked.

"Monkey business," Emily said succinctly. "And I don't even need the cards to foresee that. What kind, I can't say. Smacks of evil, though. Would you like me to read your cards and see?"

The offer was well meant, but Polly had had enough of the tarot for several lifetimes. "Thank you, but not today. Do you know where she lives?"

"Red is a loner, doesn't mix much with the rest of us. That's not unusual for the dilettantes, but it is for those of us who've worked the square for a while. We kind of need to hang together."

"Or we will most assuredly hang separately," Polly said.

"No shit," Emily said. "Greta," she called to a woman two tables down. "Do you know of anybody who might know where Red lives?"

As Emily and Greta discussed the possible whereabouts of their fellow practitioner of the dark arts, Polly found her eyes and mind straying to the cathedral, to the clean, white stone of the façade and the solid safety of the great double doors. St. Louis seemed to offer shelter and decency, a respite from the Devil in his hairy crouch, the muck of the world's weaknesses caked under his painted nails, crazy lies behind his oily smile. It interested her that a momentary belief in the Devil brought with it a momentary belief in the church.

"Greta thinks that Red's got a place in Center City, off Jackson on Loyola," Emily told her.

"Thank you," Polly said politely. "And thank you, Greta."

The part of the city where Red was reputed to live had been an unheralded slum before the hurricane. Now it was famous for its murders. The streets were broken and filled with potholes, the houses in various states of disrepair, some ruined by fire or collapsed by the wind. Cleanup in this part of town had not moved with the speed it had in wealthier neighborhoods.

At one time, the area had been middle-class, lined with charming homes and apartments. Only their bones remained, their souls cobbled up inside with duplexes, and quadraplexes, and cheap rooming houses. The residue of fast-food lunches and blasted buildings littered the gutters. Lawns were bare dirt.

Polly parked her Volvo in the shade of one of the live oaks—the last of the gentility living in this part of town—but left the ignition running for the air-conditioning. Not knowing quite what to do next, she studied the street where the Woman in Red was said to have her lair.

*Abode*, Polly corrected herself. It was hard not to think of the poor, raddled woman as a beast.

The decaying buildings told her nothing. She was not sure what she had expected. Perhaps to see the woman in all her fiery glory sailing down the street or, in a Valentine-red robe and fuzzy slippers, having a cigarette on her porch. The only visible life at the moment was a small girl squatting on a broken walkway having an earnest conversation with a dog who outweighed her by at least fifteen pounds.

Little girls saw much and were seldom averse to talking about it to anyone who would listen. Reluctantly, Polly left the cool of her car. The child was tiny—four or five maybe—and small for her age. The dog was large, black, and apparently devoted. Polly didn't guess at his age.

"Pardon me for interrupting your conversation," she said to the two of them. "But I am in need of assistance."

Both child and dog looked up at her.

"You lost?" asked the little girl. She stood and smoothed down the hot-pink tank top she wore over lime-green shorts with a pink frog appliquéd on the pocket. Barefoot, she padded down the walk to where Polly waited. Her little feet had to be hard as rocks. She didn't flinch at the burn of the superheated concrete. The dog, his head as high as his mistress's shoulder, walked beside her. The child's face was open and trusting. The dog's was not, and Polly was relieved. Children needed bodyguards.

"I am not, myself, lost, but thank you for asking. It is a friend of mine who is lost. She is very big and dresses all in red, even her hair and fingernails and lips. You looked like someone who notices things, and I hoped you'd seen her."

"Yes, ma'am. She don't like kids much. There's

a man comes to see her sometimes, but nobody else. He's not from around here. I went over there one time, and she yelled at me to get off her porch. I wasn't on her porch. Well, I was on her porch, but I was getting this thing, this round, throwy thing, like a flying saucer that Kaeisha had throw'd, and it had floated down there. And me and Newt was just going to get it, and she come out and yelled like we were going to steal things; but she don't got nothing to steal anyways. She's just a poor old white lady, Momma says, and to leave her be because she maybe got troubles we don't know nothing about."

"Your momma is a very smart lady," Polly said.

"Yup."

"Which porch did you and Newt chase the Frisbee onto?"

"Yeah, a Frisbee, that was the throwy thing. We chased it up there."

The girl pointed back the way Polly had come. Three houses down, on the corner, was a two-story pink quadraplex, porches below and balconies above, forming a wooden shadowbox front. Nothing on the building was straight. Shingles shagged off the roof's edges; the porch and balcony posts tilted drunkenly; the ridgeline sagged like the saddle-back of an old nag. Raw and sunburnt, pink paint peeled from eaves to foundation.

"The top one?"

"Yeah. Kaeisha's real strong, stronger than a boy.

She threw it up there, but she's a scaredy cat and, even though she's bigger than me, she said I should go get it because I've got Newt, and Newt won't go with her. He'll go with her, but only if I go with her; and so me and Newt got it ourselves, and we were about to throw it back down, and out comes the lady that lives there and starts yelling.

"She called me a bad name," the little girl added, more in shame than anger.

"Her momma must not have taught her good manners like your momma taught you."

"I guess."

"Thank you, you've been most helpful," Polly said and reached out to touch her hair. Newt bared his teeth. "Good boy," she said.

Stairs led up a dark passage sandwiched between the two downstairs units. The stairwell was unlit and stank of lives lived out in clouds of cigarette smoke and boiled sausage.

Having climbed to a narrow landing with a door on each side, Polly paused, straightened her collar and ran her tongue over her teeth to dislodge any unsightly foodstuffs or migrating lip color. Habits of a lifetime of benevolent seduction.

Then she rapped loudly. No one answered, but the door moved inward, and icy air poured out of the dark apartment. Blinds had been drawn and drapes pulled.

"Hello?" Polly called. "Is anybody home?" There was no answer. Probably the Woman in Red had moved out when whatever was troubling her caught up with her.

Polly pushed the door, and an unseen barrier gave way with a slithering noise. The scant light from the landing didn't penetrate the darkness. Reaching around the doorsill, she fumbled for a light switch, found it, and flipped it up.

"Lordy!" she whispered.

It was a garbage house. Polly remembered one in Prentiss, the children taken away by county services, a photo of the parents and their living room on the front page of the local paper. Carver, the father of Emma and Gracie—and all the atonement Polly thought she would ever need to guarantee her a place in heaven—had a mother like that. He spent nearly a month literally shoveling out her house. The Woman in Red's shotgun apartment was half the size of Polly's ex-mother-in-law's, but it would take more than a month to clear it.

It would take an act of God.

The heap that had fallen with the slither of many snakes when she'd forced the door was a three-foot stack of old magazines. Junk covered every square foot of the floor: newspapers, boxes, bags, books, half-empty pop bottles, dryer lint, garbage bags spilling food wrappers and toilet paper, clothes, and clothes, and clothes, pots for planters and cooking, buckets, shoes, hats, purses—dozens of purses, some still with the price tags tied to the handles— candy wrappers, television guides, overflowing ashtrays, pizza boxes. The detritus of the woman's life was deepest in the corners, creating slopes of man-made scree from the picture rail down.

The floor was buried in two, three, and four feet of garbage. A narrow path from the front door to the adjoining room had been stomped through the hills of junk. Off this path, there were places Polly could not have walked upright. Furniture had been buried. The end of a chair arm, covered in gray, nubbled fabric aerated by cigarette burns, thrust out from a corner slope, and what looked like rabbit ears poked out of a pile of clothes.

*TV aerial,* Polly thought. *Or car antenna.*

The image of an automobile lost in the crud on the second floor of the old house brought laughter up in her throat. Nerves, or absurdity, or pity would not let go of the laughter and, as she crossed the wasteland of a woman's life, she could not stop the gusts as she imagined ever more absurd things lost beneath this sea of trash.

The room at the end of the trodden path was faintly lit as if by a night-light. Polly stepped in through a door that had not been closed since July of 1991. At least that was the date on the *Glamour* magazine on top of the waist-high pile leaning against it.

It was the bedroom. One side of the double bed was relatively clear of debris, and the path leading to the bathroom showed hardwood in places. A small television sat on a dresser in a tangle of cosmetics, scarves, hair decorations, and undergarments. Open, overfilled drawers made a colorful stairway up from the floor. The room's only window was blocked by layers of curtaining, the sill gone to a slide of knickknacks and papers that continued unbroken to the seat of the chair beneath. A closet regurgitated cheap red clothes.

An oddity in this house of oddities was the full-length mirror on the closet door. The bottom two-thirds had been spray-painted black. The job had been done quickly; clouds of paint discolored the door behind the glass. When Polly looked at her reflection, all she could see of herself was her head. The image was surreal, threatening, as if, in some unknown future or universe, she had gone to the guillotine.

She quickly looked back to the only space that could still support life, the bed. Empty hamburger wrappers and paper cups were piled high enough to fall and begin spreading beneath, the tide rising around the woman's last island of space.

No wonder she had reeked of despair.

Across the room was a small bath with barely enough space for a tub with a shower curtain around it, a commode, and a small sink. The bathroom looked as if it had been force-fed beauty products until it had foundered. Claustrophobia and compassion began to suffocate Polly. She had the answer, not only to the Devil card with its plea for help but to the bizarre and terrifying reading.

The woman was mad.

The weight of the horded misery pressed on her rib cage, making it hard to breathe. Whatever help this Woman in Red needed, it would be more than Polly could give. Turning to leave, she saw that the tub, too, had been filled. A great plastic sheet had been bundled into it and strapped 'round and 'round with packing tape.

Suddenly certain what she would find, Polly pulled back the shower curtain in one quick ripping motion that tore half of it from its hooks.

The cloudy plastic cocooned something very large and very red. Oddly empty of feeling, Polly stared down at the bundled dead. Why would the Woman in Red have thought she could help, could have stopped this? Polly had nothing to do with this poor thing's life. No connection but the reading.

*You will kill your husband.*

At lunch with Danny Polly had told him the woman knew things that she had told no one but Marshall. Had Marshall shared them with this awful woman? A mind game? Gaslighting the new wife? Had he told her he was going to kill her, hence the Devil card in the mailbox?

Her house had burned down but Marshall had called to awaken her and been there before the fire department to rescue her. And take her and her children into his home.

Like he'd wanted.

No time for her to think, to get to know him better.

Once married, he'd become evasive, secretive, spending more time at work and with his brother than with her and the girls.

The emptiness in Polly began to fill with black ice. A sense of falling took hold of her and she knocked half a dozen oddments to the floor as she clutched the edge of the sink to remain standing.

Maybe the card had been sent so she would save this woman. More likely it had been sent so she would find the body. Why? In this hell hole of a place was there evidence hidden to frame her? Why would anyone frame an English professor for murder? To get custody of her children?

The ice began to break apart, slivers of cold knifing along her veins.

Atop the body was a piece of lined, three-hole-punch binder paper crumpled into a fist-sized wad. She watched her hand float out over the sea of red-stained plastic and pick the paper up the way a mechanical arm in an arcade game might pinch up a stuffed toy.

She flattened it against the wall. In the top left corner, written in pencil, was a single sentence.

*Why kids? Is killing them easier? More fun?*

The handwriting looked like her husband's.

Polly didn't call the police. She'd not been raised to trust them and, until she knew why she had been dragged to this apartment to find what she had been meant to find, she would tell no one.

Taking the note, touching nothing else, she left the way she had come. She closed the apartment door behind her and wiped her fingerprints from the knob.

## 28

Polly had rifled through two floors of her husband's things and found nothing suggestive of murder, nothing of betrayal, only a man with simple needs and too many prescription drugs in his bedside table. Turning out small envelopes of collar stays and bundled business cards she felt for the first time how little she knew of Marshall Marchand. They'd married in the fairy glamour of first love when nothing matters but the moment and the man.

If he had friends, there was no trace of them in his personal belongings. No family but Danny, no photographs of him as child.

Finally, she reached the cellar. Half a dozen boxes were stored on stacked wooden pallets. This high-water storage was set along the two-by-four studs bisecting the basement lengthwise.

One was out of alignment with the others, peeking from beneath a tarp as if it had been recently moved and hurriedly put away. Perhaps upstairs, in the sunlight instead of skittering like a cockroach around a dank basement, she might not have noticed it.

With the heightened awareness sleuthing engendered Polly knew this was what she'd been searching for—whatever that was—and she eyed it with loathing. Lifting a stick from the scrap lumber bin, she used the end of it to push the tarp off of the carton then, again using the stick, flipped the cardboard lid off as if the box contained water moccasins.

When she saw it was free of snakes and three-quarters full of papers thrown in willy-nilly the anxiety didn't lessen. Wishing she could walk away and accepting that she couldn't, she gave up her stick, carried the papers to better light by one of the windows, and looked at the uppermost page: handwritten, no date, no name. She read the first line.

"I spend most of the time wondering if it feels good to kill people. A rush like good weed or what? And little kids, are they more fun? Killing them feel different?" Nearly the same words on the page in Red's sepulcher. Had that been copied from this? Or a theme revisited?

Polly retrieved the page found at the tarot reader's from her pocket and laid the pieces of paper side by side. The writing was not identical but that proved nothing either way. One's own signature differs from signing to signing.

Polly flipped to the next. "I had the dream again last night. Blood all over me so fresh it's warm, and me, laughing like a lunatic."

And the next.

"Why an axe? Because you get more splatter? The only noise is screaming? It's macho?"

"I think about killing all the time—I mean *all* the time. Day and night. I guess once wasn't enough. Not like I'm jonesing to do it again, just thinking about it."

The pages were not numbered and in no apparent order. Some of the paper was college ruled, some wide ruled; some was graph paper. The random journaling of a deranged mind.

*A deranged mind expressing itself in her husband's handwriting.*

Nausea took root in her, a poisonous plant with fast-growing vines, so harsh and voracious it doubled her over. Vomit burned the top of her throat. Her heart pounded bruisingly against her ribs. She made it to an old, cushionless wicker chair, collapsed, and hung her head between her knees.

Blanking her mind, Polly reined in the organs of her body bent on flying out of her mouth. Breathing in and breathing out, she slowed her heart. Self-preservation had always been strong in her, but never had it been as strong as after Gracie was born. Alone, Polly could fail; she could be severely injured; she could even accept dying. With two of the most precious little girls in the world depending on her, she looked both ways before she crossed streets and took her vitamins.

Emma and Gracie would not be back from the

zoo until three-thirty. Marshall seldom got home before nine. Upstairs, she was guaranteed privacy and air-conditioning, but the idea of carting a box filled with sickness into the space where her daughters played was anathema. In life, there were poisons for which there was no antidote, filth no amount of Clorox could clean up. Mothers did not keep these things under the sink where children could get into them.

Polly compromised by bringing the box to the rear stairs where there was enough light to read. Sitting on the first tiny landing beneath the window where the narrow stairwell made its first twist, the file carton between her feet, she stared through the dirty glass into the backyard. Flowers were in full autumn glory. The garden's lushness, shadow filled with color, usually soothed her. Now, she saw only steamy fecund overgrowth, dead flies on the windowsill, a spider waiting in its web to suck the life out of her neighbors.

With a repressed shudder, she turned her attention back to the carton and lifted a pile of newspaper and magazine clippings and computer printouts onto her lap.

"The Boston Boy Fiend," "Bad Seed Kills Toddlers," "Murder for Kicks," "Jury Unconvinced in Phillips' Case," "Raines Indicted for Family Slaughter," "BTK Killer Confesses," "Speck 'at Home' in Prison."

The stories chronicled children killing children,

children killing parents or neighbors, wives killing husbands, mothers killing their babies, brothers killing sisters, Bundy and Speck and Gacy and Dahmer killing everybody.

"The Boston Boy Fiend" was a mimeograph—something she'd not seen for years—of an article written in 1874. "The Boston Boy Fiend has struck again, and the great tragedy is that this little girl did not have to die. After this beast in boy's clothing confessed and was convicted of killing four-year-old Horace Mullen and sexually torturing seven others, he was released early by a reform school board that chose to ignore the court's warnings. He has now been convicted of the brutal death of a ten-year-old neighbor girl."

In fading blue ink, next to "sexually torturing seven . . ." was scribbled in Marshall's idiosyncratic hand, "Why didn't I do this?" and "Incest or pedophilia, take your pick."

Nausea, temporarily quiescent, raged back. Eyes closed, Polly rode it out until the danger of vomiting or running screaming from the house abated, then pushed on.

"Bad Seed Kills Toddlers." Another mimeograph. "1968 England" was penciled at the top of the page. "Eleven-year-old Mary Flora Bell, 'Fanny' of 'Fanny and Faggot,' as they styled themselves, was today convicted of two counts of manslaughter for the slayings of two toddlers, one gone missing and believed to have perished of an accident three months previously, and the second, found four weeks later, dead of strangulation, the body mutilated."

"Two toddlers" was underlined. In the margin Marshall had written, "Two? Shoot, and I thought I was the record holder." Then, "Why little kids? Because they're so easy?"

"Murder for Kicks" was clipped from a newspaper. No date, but the paper had discolored with age. "According to the testimony, Cindy Collins, age fifteen, and Shirley Wolf, age fourteen, were trying doors in their apartment building. They'd planned to get keys and steal a car, they said. An elderly woman let them in. Shirley Wolf confessed to pulling the woman's head back by the hair and stabbing her to death. An autopsy report said the victim had been stabbed twenty-eight times. Both Wolf and Collins told the court that they thought the murder was 'a kick'."

Scrawled at the bottom of the page was, "Stab an old dame for the fun of it. Kill for fun. That ought to stick in your mind."

The sun moved down the sky. Heat and glare poured through the window. Sweat stuck Polly's hair to her forehead and cheeks, glued her clothes to her skin. Flies battered against the window glass, a desperate buzzing that ran along her nerves like electricity.

The next article was headlined, "The Real Amityville Horror."

288

An image of her home crawling with bloated flies flared up, so real she cried out. In true nightmare fashion, she couldn't move; her legs would not lift her. She could no more escape that stairwell than could the flies.

She lifted out the rest of the newsprint and set it down beside her, unread. Beneath were scraps of pages, halves, or thirds, or quarters—not torn but cut clean with a razorblade or scissors. None had number sequences. Or if they had, they were cut off. A handful contained only a line or two of text.

". . . the cat was dead, our old Ginger cat, and when I looked, her guts were all over my hands . . . I drown them . . . anybody tries to stop you, you just shoot them . . . I went from room to room and they were all full of blood; I started to laugh . . . When the other guys heard what I'd done, they looked . . . If I ever get a chance to do it again . . . fucked from the start . . . I had a knife in my hand, and I was chasing . . . mass murder. I can see myself doing that . . . biting chunks of flesh out . . . murders. Sure . . ."

The scraps ran on in that vein unceasingly. Their deep-rooted sickness twined in through Polly's eyes to her mind and she hated that she was a member of a race capable of such cruelty.

Further down, some pages were whole. Judging by paper type and ink color—or in some cases pencil—they were written on different days, maybe in different years. Sentence construction and uneven letter size suggested a young writer.

A young Marshall Marchand.

"Monster" and "child" were not antithetical to Polly. *Lord of the Flies. The Bad Seed.*

She picked up what looked to be the earliest writing, the oldest paper, the penciled letters awkward: "John List. Killed wife, mother, and three kids. 1971. Sure. I can see killing like this. This List guy had God on his side. That makes it work for him. He wants out of this family thing. He's pussy-whipped, and his mother's a nag, and he doesn't have the balls to leave . . ."

The next was in faded ballpoint:

"They just did what they wanted. Took what they wanted. Then died in a blaze of glory. That looks pretty good from where I sit." And again ink: "Shooting the family starts to look pretty good. Sane even. Until you get to the kids. Maybe he figures they aren't quite people; with eight of them they wouldn't seem like an endangered species exactly, just a housecleaning issue."

There was more but Polly put the papers and articles back into the carton and replaced the lid. *Pandora repenting too late.*

The writing was sick-making, violent, boastful, gloating, heartless, the profile of a man without a soul, a ghoul who gloried in causing harm. They were horrific. But Polly was not as shattered as she thought she should be. Having read critically countless thousands of passages, she couldn't but see the contradictions in this—she sought a word—collection? Grouping? Opus?

The voice in the writing had been directed at the reader—no, at an internal judge. Perhaps they had been written during a period of severe abuse and meant to be read by an abuser or a therapist or aloud in a group therapy situation.

The span of time over which they were written suggested an outside influence, someone who required the pieces. The earlier words smacked of the braggadocio of a vicious killer preening, comparing himself to his godforsaken heroes, but they were childish in style and content. The comments written in subsequent years were oddly detached, as if jotted by an actor preparing to play a role, making notes, a character study of evil.

Or by a monster seeking to find where, in a monstrous universe, he fit. Seeking . . .

"Seeking to kill little kids," she interrupted her thought aloud. "Wake up and smell the corpses, Pollyanna," she snapped.

This wasn't a Frankenstein monster of literature to be parsed and analyzed; this was her husband boasting that he "thought he was the record holder," her beloved Mr. Marchand asking, "Why little kids? Because they're easy?" The man who came to bed with her each night, wondering why he hadn't sexually tortured seven children.

Tears began, then burned away. Sobs started,

then froze in her throat. Her hands came up to cover her face, then fell helplessly onto her thighs. Anger flashed. By its lurid light she could see the fear at the back of her mind.

Like drops of quicksilver held on the palm, emotions slid away when she tried to touch them.

"This is real," Polly said, and her voice was as tiny and sweet as Emma's.

But not as innocent.

The absurdly delicate and graceful gold wristwatch Marshall had given her suggested it was close on two o'clock. The watch was beautiful and, like a true femme fatale, did not need to be exactly on time. The girls would be back in ninety minutes. Gracie was old enough that Polly could leave the two of them unattended for a little while, but she did not want them left alone.

*What if Marshall came home?*

She nearly gagged on the thought. Sweat was sticky on her skin. Flies lit on her arms and buzzed close to her eyes. Her legs were stiff. Her back ached as she forced herself up from the narrow step as if she'd been hunkered there a day instead of an hour. Still unwilling to allow the carton into the house, she left it in the utility area at the top of the stairs with the dryer lint and dirty laundry.

She showered, dressed in fresh clothes, and applied lipstick. In the kitchen, she scribbled a note for Marshall. "The girls and I will be staying with Martha." That done, she called Gracie's cell phone. "Honeybunch, can you get Mrs. Fortunas to take you and Emma to Aunt Martha's instead of home? No, no, baby. Everything's alright. I'll explain later. Thank you, sugar."

She gathered up the carton and headed down the basement stairs.

Danny was waiting at the bottom step.

"I thought that might be you," he said with a smile.

The box in Polly's hands grew as heavy as if she carried a decapitated head.

"What've you got there?" he asked mildly.

"What are you doing here?" she demanded. The startled look on his face reminded her that the box contained only bits of paper, that she was a respectable woman passing through her own cellar.

He held out his hands for the file carton. "Do you need any help with that?" he asked politely.

The box jerked.

Danny laughed. "Did you get Gracie that kitten after all?"

"Kitten?" Polly said stupidly. Then it came to her, the kitten Gracie wanted for her twelfth birthday. "No kitten," she said. "Just some papers Marshall wanted me to bring by the office."

Reflexively, she glanced at the folded-back tarpaulin where she had taken the box from the pile. Danny followed her glance and she saw a flicker of emotion in his face, a rigidity that moved from his lips to his cheeks; a smile aborted or a sour thought too close to the surface.

*He knows,* Polly thought. *The telltale heart. Edgar Allen Poe was a genius.*

"I'm going out again in a minute," Danny said. "I'd be glad to drop them by and save you a trip." Again he reached for the carton. For a second, Polly wondered if he were toying with her.

## 29

The first bottle was empty; the second was headed in that direction. Emma and Gracie had long since been tucked into bed. Polly and Martha sat in the living room of Martha's tiny turn-of-the-century house. Each detail of the place was exquisitely Martha. Fifty-three of her eighty-four years had been spent in this house. Bit by bit, it and the garden had been made over in her image: eclectic, smart, witty, and conveying a deep sense of contentment.

"I still think these sound like dreams," Martha said. Her voice was cracked and high, like that of a boy whose voice is just changing. "I mean, listen; these are dream images." Martha picked up several of the strips of paper piled beside her lounger and leaned into the circle of light from the table lamp.

"Think dreams: 'I went from room to room and they were full of blood.' You don't say that about seeing bloody people. These are pictures from the subconscious: 'full of blood.' " She read another. " 'I had chopped this little girl in half, but there wasn't any blood on my hands or my clothes.' . . . I think Marshall was writing down his dreams."

Polly had come with the intention of telling Martha the papers were from one of her graduate students about whom she was worried. They'd not gotten the cork out of the first cabernet before she told her the truth. The only detail she had omitted was that wretched tarot reader who, like Marat, lay dead in the bath. Martha would insist on calling the police. As a child, Polly had been infused with the sense the police were useless; the New Orleans PD after Katrina had done nothing to dispel that idea. When she had the facts, when she would only be ruining the lives of the guilty and not the innocent, then she would call the cops.

"This one's classic," Martha said. " 'The cat was dead, our old Ginger cat, and when I looked, her guts were all over my hands.'

" 'When I looked,' it says. If you have cat guts running though your fingers, you know it. You don't look and be surprised. This is a dream." She shook the strips for emphasis.

Polly agreed with her but she had been fiercely arguing against the dream theory because she so desperately wanted it to be true.

"You may be right," Polly admitted.

"I am right. Here's another perfect example: 'I kept hacking at this huge cop, and nothing was happening. He was taking the hits and smiling like I was hitting him with a feather, and I kept yelling . . . ' Dream! Tell me that's not a dream."

"How about the rest of the pages and the newspaper clippings? They are not dreams," Polly said. She sipped her red wine and held it in her mouth for a moment before swallowing.

Martha thumped her recliner down from its relaxed position and stared at the papers scattered all over the rug. When she was alight with ideas, with her bright colors and extra pounds, she put Polly in mind of a disco ball.

Scowling at the questionable materials, Martha pursed her lips. "This boy was abused. Major abuse. Somewhere along the line, he did something—or maybe just wanted to—and he decided he was a monster and not fit to live. From what we've been left to see . . ."

Martha was still talking, but Polly's mind had taken flight. "Yes," she said loudly, interrupting the other woman's flow. "Yes. Listen to what you've said. That's it. You said, 'What we've been *left* to see.' This, the bits, the pieces, no names or dates to distract or inform, to *check,* this was made for us—me, I'd guess—to find and see. We weren't allowed to see the whole. It's been snipped, and trimmed, and tailored.

"Why do you tailor anything?" Polly demanded.

"To make it fit," Martha answered.

"Yes. These pages were edited to tell a story. If the writer had simply dumped them in a box, why not dump it all? I cannot think what could have been left out that would be more damaging than what was left in. Therefore, things that were removed, were removed not to paint a prettier picture . . ."

"But to paint a darker picture," Martha finished.

"Yes!" Polly laughed her little-girl-gone-wicked laugh. "Oh, my, yes."

They sat staring at one another as a cat might stare in the mirror, smiles filtering through schools of thought. Martha took a sip of her wine. Polly looked at the papers strewn over the floor. By Martha's witnessing what she had found, discussing and studying them, the sinister magic Polly had granted the pages was dispelled.

Polly had not happened upon a can of worms. A can of wormlike objects had been placed for her to find; it made all the difference in the world.

"It makes no difference," Martha said.

"It does," Polly cried, and realizing she sounded childish, she obeyed when Martha gestured for silence.

"It doesn't." Martha waved her hand over the mess. "Even if these have been arranged to make Marshall look as bad as possible, Marshall still did write this stuff. It's his handwriting in the margins of the articles. Who else but he would edit it and put it where you'd see it? Why? Does he want to get caught, found out? Does he need you to see him in as bad a light as he sees himself ? Regardless of his reasons, this is too volatile to gloss over. Marshall is in trouble. That means you, Gracie, Emma, even Danny are in trouble."

Against Martha's good counsel and with her promise to look after the girls, Polly didn't stay the night but left a little after twelve-thirty a.m. Driving down Carrolton Avenue, feeling the effects of the wine and the fact that the dead of night in New Orleans was deader than it had been pre-Katrina, she had no idea why she'd left.

Did she plan to slide into bed next to Marshall, curl up on his shoulder, her right thigh thrown across his legs, as she had done nearly every night since they had been married, and simply ignore the murders real, imagined, literary, and historical?

"What did you do today, my love?"

"Nothing much. Got groceries. By the way, darling, did you happen to kill anyone before you went to the office?"

Laughter frothed up, surprising Polly.

"I do so love that man," she whispered. Through her mind tramped pictures of herself in the guise of countless battered women, torn and bleeding, teeth knocked loose, standing in front of tribunals of family and police, bleating, "But I *love* him!"

*This was different.*

Maybe they are all different.

Marshall had left the gate open for her. Since three feet of water and a magnolia tree had happened to it, it hadn't worked properly. Still, she didn't pull in behind the building. The parking area in the back garden was beneath the bedroom windows of both units. She did not want to awaken anyone yet. For a few minutes, she sat in the car, not knowing whether to stay or go, where to go if she went, what to say if she stayed.

Unsure of what she was doing—what she would do—she let herself quietly in the side door of the basement and locked it behind her. Cities were never seriously dark. The streetlights did not penetrate the frosted windows more than a few feet. Their glow served only to deepen the shadows. On a moonless night, the woods around Prentiss, Mississippi, had been as dark as the bottom of a mine. There had been plenty of nights Polly had run to that darkness because it would hide her until morning, when monsters turned back into people for twelve hours.

After the heat of the outdoors, the cellar felt cool. Feeling half a ghost, Polly glided to the back of the space on Danny's side where dirt replaced concrete, where the boxes were piled, and sat down in the old wicker chair. Blanketed by night and reassured by aloneness, she leaned her head back and closed her eyes. In the comforting darkness she had intended to formulate a plan, make a timeline, give herself in some way at least the illusion of control. Wine and weariness overcame her and she drifted seamlessly from waking to sleeping.

A sound brought her back, as alert and as clear as if she'd never dozed. The one functioning fluorescent on the far side of the cellar had been turned on. Through the upright two-by-fours and the fringe of rakes, shovels, picks, and other tools hanging from nails along the center beam, she saw her husband. Had he chosen to look, he could have seen her as well, but she didn't think he would. He believed himself to be alone.

The ghost feeling strengthened and, with it, came a sense of power. Undoubtedly, the sensation that kept cat burglars burgling cats. Marshall had brought something down from the apartment. Walking toward her in his parallel universe, he took the object to the battered workbench. It looked like a broom or perhaps a new fluorescent bulb to replace the one that had burned out. Then he laid it on the bench and she saw it for what it was: an axe.

Her husband had had an axe in their apartment, in their home, and now, in the middle of the night when he thought she was away, he was bringing it down to the cellar. Her scalp crawled, hairs stiffening, skin shrinking around the roots.

This was the boy who bragged of killing toddlers and cats all grown up.

Polly watched with the burgeoning terror of a woman being pushed inexorably toward the lip of a high sheer drop as Marshall removed the lid from a can of paint thinner, soaked a rag, and carefully wiped the head of the axe clean. When he was done, he threw the rag to the floor and tossed a match on it. Sudden bright flame lit up Polly and her chair as surely as if she were in a spotlight center stage. Marshall never looked up. The flash of fire was gone almost as quickly as it had come, leaving the air smelling of chemicals and burnt cotton. With the slow methodical movement of a sleepwalker, he stomped out what was left of the cinders, fetched the push broom, swept the ashes into a dustpan, and emptied them into the trash.

Gacy and his crawlspace full of the corpses of rotting children rose in front of Polly, as real as if she'd been there and not merely seen it on television. She could smell the decaying flesh.

With precise, careful movements, Marshall hung the axe on the central beam, then crossed to the rear stairs. He didn't climb them but sat on the bottom step, elbows on his knees, his face in his hands, and wept. Silent as the ghost she'd become, Polly rose to her feet, drifted across the concrete, out Danny's back door and into the garden. Soundlessly she slipped through the gate and got in her car.

Whether or not Marshall noticed, she did not know. She couldn't bear to look back.

# 30

Polly had become one of the city's vampires, slinking about in the night, thinking of blood. That had to be what had stained the axe Marshall had so melodramatically carried into the basement. Why else clean the blade with turpentine, then burn the cleaning cloth?

The Woman in Red's blood? Had she been killed because she had warned Polly? Because he had shared Polly's history with her. Or had he shared her history with the reader so she would warn her? Or did he do it for reasons only psychotics understand and never succeed in communicating to the sane?

She leaned her head against the Volvo's leather headrest and closed her eyes. Not seeing was worse than seeing. Eyes closed, the pictures in her mind took on heightened sharpness. In what seemed like a moment—the time since that horrible pathetic woman had foretold Marshall's murder at her hands—the delightful life of a middle-aged English professor, in love for the first time, had become the stuff of B movies.

"Typecasting," Polly murmured. Her mother had been fourteen and living in a trailer when Polly came into the world. Trailer trash.

"Why, my dears, I come from the Trash of

Prentiss, Mississippi," she said to an imaginary social elite. "My mother was trailer trash and my daddy, why, he was from white trash."

Polly had taken what gifts she'd been given—from her mother the ability to endure, from her grandmother the ability to work, and, undoubtedly from some traveling Fuller Brush man, a good mind—and used them to get off that trash heap where life was cheap and dirty, broken washing machines lived in the front yard and old cars were put out to pasture in the weeds under the kitchen window.

Tonight, she felt as if, snakelike, time had coiled around on itself and she was once again a little girl caught up in a life comprised of cigarette butts, crumpled beer cans, and rotting rubber tires. Perhaps she was born into trailer trash for this very night—the gods' way of preparing her for "that which must be overcome."

She fastened her seatbelt and turned the Volvo's ignition key.

She did not park on La Salle in front of the run-down fourplex but around the corner on a side street that was less trafficked and darker. As she locked her car, she questioned the wisdom of the transparent subterfuge.

What would she do if the car was stolen or broken into? Call the police? A life of crime was not as easy as one might think.

The door to the stairwell hung open, inviting her into absolute blackness, the maw of a leviathan with particularly unappetizing breath. Tom cats, either the four-legged or the two-legged variety, had been marking their territory with pungent regularity.

"The more it reeks, the less likely muggers and murderers are lurking within, said Pollyanna brightly," Polly whispered.

Moving quickly in hopes of reaching the top of the stairs before she had to breathe, she entered the inky recess. On the narrow landing outside the door to the tarot reader's apartment, she stopped. The climb was short but her heart was pounding as if she'd jogged to the top of the Empire State Building.

A push and the door opened. Feeling slightly foolish and terribly brave, Polly eeled in, closed the door behind her, and switched on the light. There was little danger it would give her presence away. The windows were covered with yellowed blinds and draped with everything from towels and sheets to a flowered bed skirt. The place was more lair than home. In the sense not that Red was an animal but that this was where she hid from the world. Quelling the knowledge that, in the bathroom, the body of a slain woman lay cocooned in plastic, Polly surveyed the bizarre landscape. She was put in mind of Dickens's *Little Dorrit*—the dust man, picking through mountain ranges of

London's garbage year after year, looking for a lost treasure.

Lest it be swallowed up in the morass, she set her handbag on an overturned basket by the door and started in on the nearest heap like an archaeologist digging through the refuse of a lost civilization.

Within an hour she had moved three yards into the room. Where there had been hopeless disarray, there remained hopeless disarray, but none of it had gone unexamined. Stooping, crawling, sifting, Polly looked at each item—be it a dirty coffee mug or a slip of paper—then tossed it behind her. Because she didn't know what she sought, she couldn't afford to overlook anything.

Fatigue quickly wore out any sense of disquiet she suffered from sharing the apartment with the— one might assume—unquiet ghost of the murdered woman. Without consciously choosing to, Polly began talking with the Woman in Red, discussing her discoveries as she came upon them: "You like *Arlo & Janice*; I'm surprised you didn't have a cat. Do you have a cat hidden in this mess? Here kitty, kitty. Red! Sorry, sugar, but I have just ruined one of your lipsticks. It's all over the bottom of my shoe. I don't suppose the cleaning lady will notice my tracks. My lord, girl, what were you going to do with all these purses? There is not enough money left in New Orleans to fill the wallets. You never used them did you? Look, this one still has the tag. You poor dear. It must have felt good to buy yourself a treat and a dream. A bargain at nine-ninety-nine. Lighters, and lighters, and match-books! It's a wonder you weren't arrested for arson. *AARP!* And a subscription! There must be forty magazines here. Sugar, I would not be caught *dead* with one of these in the house. Sorry, darling, you *were* caught dead. I read *AARP* secretly at the doctor's office, like a little boy peeking at a *Playboy* magazine under Dad's mattress. My dear you are braver and less vain than I."

By three a.m., Polly had worked her way to the wall between the main room and the bedroom and bath. Her eyelids grated against her sclera, and her throat was raw from dust.

The corpse lying in the tub weighed more heavily on her mind now. So long deluged in the residue of the dead woman's life, she had come to feel compassion for her and, finally, a kind of affection.

Sorting through her rag-tag belongings Polly learned that the Woman in Red loved Nancy Drew, Ethan Hawke, and a pro wrestler named the Mondo King. She loved shoes and scarves. A cigar box lined with blue velvet held treasured trinkets—from a lover, Polly presumed. The items in the box represented the only order in the apartment. A boy's high school ring; a silver heart—not real silver, but silvery metal—on a tarnished chain, the kind won at fairs or bought in souvenir shops, with a *V* engraved on it in fancy script; three rosebuds, shriveled until they were more brown than yellow, long pins through the tape-wrapped stems; a pair of bead earrings; and a button were displayed in careful rows as if Red looked at them often, or once had. For Polly, this box was the saddest of a dumpsterful of sad items. Red's inamorato had given so little of himself his gifts could be kept in a six-by-eight box, the whole not worth the cost of a pack of cigarettes.

Though the apartment was glutted with things, the cigar box was the only thing Polly found that was truly personal.

Polly was not given to the accumulation of worldly goods, but, had anyone gone through her house, they would have seen pictures of children and friends, letters from students, invitations accepted and declined, calendars marked with upcoming events, hand-drawn birthday cards, inscribed books, awards, diplomas, notes on bulletin boards—a short history of Polly Marchand in three dimensions. In Red's plethora of objects nothing that spoke of her heart had surfaced, only evidence of compulsion, addiction, and depression. But for the cigar box, there was no indication that anyone had touched her life—or that she had touched the life of another.

"Keeps to herself," Emily, the tarot reader, had said.

*Filling the emptiness,* Polly thought, looking at the mess of goods with which Red had surrounded herself.

Beneath the bed, where the Woman in Red had made her last stand, still using the furniture, still turning on the light, reading her magazines and smoking her cigarettes, Polly found the second personal item: a photo album embossed with over-sized leatherette daisies in the psychedelic colors of the sixties, the kind a teenaged girl might have been given. In keeping with her usual style, Red had not put her memorabilia under the plastic page covers but jammed it in every which way.

Sitting tailor-fashion on the floor—whatever effluvia was there would surely be less toxic than that on the dingy bedsheets—Polly put the album in her lap and turned the garish cover. Between the first page and the cardboard were snapshots. They'd been taken by an old Polaroid instamatic and the colors had faded. Several were stuck together from being mashed against one another so long. There was a photograph of a man and woman standing on the steps of a brick house. A bicycle was overturned by the bottom step. A pretty little girl of eight or nine sat beside it smiling for the camera. Two other pictures of the family group featured the mom, the little girl, and a shy-looking teenager. The face had been scratched off the pic-tures of the older girl.

"That's you, isn't it?" Polly said to the ghost who kept her company. "You poor thing. Terrible to erase yourself like that. I would dearly love to wring the necks of whoever made you hate yourself."

Polly set the pictures aside and turned the page. Again, photographs had been shoved in but not arranged. These appeared to be the "art" shots every young girl feels compelled to take when given her first camera. One shot had been taken through what looked to be a knothole. Three were of the house, the camera held at funky angles. The rest were long shots of a boy, the angle suggesting they'd been taken from an upstairs window. The indifference of the subject to the camera suggested they'd been taken in stealth. The distance was so great Polly couldn't tell if the boy was happy, sad, handsome, or plain. He was white and in his teens; he could be any boy anywhere. In the faded Polaroids he mowed grass, fixed the tire of a bike, went in and came out of a two-story brick house. The photographer had taken twenty-four shots of him, a single roll of film.

Polly wondered if this unsuspecting model and the high school ring in the cigar box were related. Clearly, the Woman in Red had suffered a passion for him at one time, but Polly couldn't see this boy giving his ring to the shy girl who'd scratched out her face.

*Maybe she stole it.*

"I'm sorry, sugar. That was uncharitable. I know you did not steal that boy's ring," she apologized to her invisible companion whose corporal self continued to rot in the tub in the next room.

Polly set these snapshots with the others. When

she turned the next page of the album, yellowed newspaper came out in a crumpled wad.

"What is it with old newspaper clippings tonight? I swear I have not looked at this much newsprint since Gracie went through her parakeet phase," Polly said, smoothing them out on her thigh. The newsprint would stain the linen, but after the first hour, she had decided to get the slacks cleaned and donate them to Goodwill. Between then and now, she'd decided to burn them instead.

"There must be forty articles!" Polly exclaimed. "I am not going to read them all, sugar. I don't care how long you've been collecting them."

"Raines," she read aloud.

In the file box in the basement there had been a mention of the Raines trial.

"Damn."

Without warning, the lights went out. Darkness struck like a blow. Shuttered, blinded and draped, midnight in the apartment was absolute. Disoriented, Polly grunted, a tired helpless sound comprised of exhaustion and surprise.

Darkness and silence—the air conditioner was no longer running.

"The power has gone out," she said into the stillness.

Then she heard someone moving in the living room.

Polly had been immersed in the tarot reader's

sordid universe for so long her first thought was of the ghost of the Woman in Red. "Is it you?" she whispered before she could stop herself. A sharp intake of breath answered her. Ghosts had no need to breathe.

Noise from the other room died with her words. The man—surely a man—had stopped moving. Polly stopped breathing to listen. She hadn't heard him come in. This was no opportunistic thief; he had been here before. Only someone with experience could negotiate from landing to living room in silence and without light.

Polly thought the day's adventures would have drained her adrenal glands, but her heart pounded with such force blood rushing past her ears drowned all other sounds. In the utter, mind-breaking darkness she felt her senses reach out, ears straining, eyes widening, nostrils flaring, every system seeking information she might use to survive.

There was no question in her mind that survival was the issue. The Woman in Red's killer was in the apartment. Violence permeated the air, a negative charge that raised the hairs on her arms. Raised in violence, Polly had never forgotten the edgy vibration in the void that preceded it.

Between one breath and the next, she understood what was meant by the cliché of one's life flashing before one's eyes. She had imagined it would be like a slide show on fast-forward, images of the good times one after another.

It was not like that. The whole of her life, who she was, what she had done—everything exploded at the same moment. A supernova of memory: people she'd fought against, those whom she had fought for, those whom she loved, and hated, and lost, and found. The life she had been handed and the life that she had made. Her girls at every age. The dirt of her childhood and the dirt of her garden. Evils she had run from and those she had embraced. The husband she'd left and the husband she loved. Axes and exes, birthday parties and pets, flat tires and spelling bees, labor, groceries, Emily Dickinson, shoes that pinched, tonsillitis. All of it was there.

Then it was gone. Polly slammed back into total darkness of mind and body. But not spirit. The images ignited a fury for life. She would *not* end up as another bit of trash on the floor of a garbage house. By the age of four, Polly was accustomed to escaping drunken men and mad women. On bad nights, she would come awake thinking she'd heard raging footsteps above her hiding place beneath the trailer.

She'd been so small then, she could wriggle through cat doors and wood piles, lie flat in high grass. Here, she had only darkness and silence. If the man in the other room had a flashlight, she was a dead woman. Seeing was to his advantage, and she wondered why he'd turned off the power.

*He didn't want to be recognized.*

Because she knew him.

For a snick of time, the thought that it was Marshall robbed her of her desire to remain among the living. But her life was too rich to destroy in a snick.

"You will kill him," she heard Red hiss. "You will kill your husband."

*Gracie and Emma, holding hands and laughing.*

*So be it,* Polly thought.

Moving smoothly, each hand placed, each foot shifted with care and in silence, Polly stood up from the floor. Her limbs were not stiff, her back not sore. Adrenaline had seen to that.

"Unh!" came from the living room. Like her, the man was trying to move without sound.

He'd turned off the lights because he knew the paths through the house. But, over the hours, Polly had rearranged the garbage. Suddenly, she remembered how she had reconfigured the map of the mountains of junk, envisioning not just a vague image of where things were but a complete catalog of everything she had touched, where she had tossed it and how hard.

Total recall.

*An English professor's equivalent to lifting a tractor off a child,* she thought and wondered why her brain still loved whimsy, why she was not paralyzed with terror.

Maybe because now she had something—someone—real to fight. At that thought her fierceness lost some of its punch. Physical strength was not an attribute she cultivated. Her fights had been of the intellectual variety. She'd gotten old enough to have an intellect by hiding and escaping.

These thoughts exploded in the same gestalt manner her life story had—seen and grasped in an instant. The man in the next room gave up on silence and blundered toward the bedroom. A lamp fell. With perfect detail, Polly saw where she had pushed it behind her on the path, the shade crooked, the wire wrapped around its base. Next, he would step on empty bourbon bottles.

He yelped and fell heavily. Polly took two steps back and melted into the closet. The soft wall of clothes, hanging and falling, heaped and sliding, molded to her back. The fabric beneath her feet absorbed the sound of her passage. The polyester wall pressed around her, snaked over her head, curled around her arms and hands, then enveloped her completely.

A scratching sound and a light flared from beyond the doorway.

The man had found one of the hundreds of books of matches Red had scattered among the magazines and cigarette butts. Polly pulled a scarf over her face, let it drop over her eyes. Whether it was so she would not be seen or so she could put off the shock of seeing the killer, she wasn't sure. Through the thin fabric she could make out only shapes and light and dark.

The match expired. There was a sound of slithering papers and a muffled curse.

The AARP magazines.

Polly had tossed them over her shoulder one at a time after shaking each, in the event a note or picture had been thrust between the pages. They made a glossy slick where the path neared the doorway between the living and bed rooms.

Startlingly red light cut through the sheer fabric over her eyes and moved like a star into the bedroom's firmament. It bobbed and danced, then, with a squawk, was shaken out.

The killer did not speak. No "I know you're here," or "Where are you?" or "It will do you no good to try and escape"—all good killer things to say. He did not speak even to curse when the matches burned his fingers or as he fell over one of Polly's inadvertent traps.

He didn't want her to recognize his voice.

Instinctually, Polly knew it was not because he intended to leave her alive. It was because he did not wish her to see him for what he was.

Another match was struck. This one came at her face like a fireball.

He'd seen her. He was going to set the closet on fire.

Before she could move, the match flamed out and welcome darkness veiled her. Footsteps moved away, shuffling as he waded through the ankle-deep castoffs on the bedroom floor. Through gauze, Polly watched a tall figure shrink as he squatted with his back to her. Three more matches were struck as he studied the picture album by the bed.

The situation was not going to improve for Polly. Soon, she would be found. He knew she'd been here, was here. He was probably the one who'd lured her here with the card, followed her when she returned after leaving the cellar.

Screw your courage to the sticking place, she told herself and, sucking in a lungful of air, yelling in her mind as she had once yelled before leaping into icy creeks, *Here goes nuthin'!* she exploded from the closet trailing clothes and screaming like a banshee. Her face masked by the scarf, blouses, skirts, and shoes scattering before her, she charged the crouching man. Polly plowed into him, shoving and stumbling. He went over, the match went out. The yards of fabric that had been so welcome when she hid tangled around her ankles and she crashed against the bed stand.

A hand clamped iron-hard on her left thigh.

Polly wrenched free and felt her way like a blind woman through the doorway to the living room, Red's laundry like ghostly hands trying to drag her back. A softness coiled around her feet and she fell to her knees. Fingers raked her ankle, then wrapped around it, digging hard into her Achilles tendon. Pain dragged a cry from her.

Her attacker grunted with exertion.

And pleasure.

Scrabbling on sliding magazines, Polly was losing ground. The man's fingers were wire cables, his strength enough to drag her backwards. Far stronger than she, he could have hammered her kidneys with balled fists; he could have thrown himself upon her and snapped her neck or slammed her head into the floor. He did none of these things; slowly, as if he savored the process, he was pulling her into himself, swallowing her as a snake would swallow a mouse. Garbage piled up under Polly's chin, drowning her. Scrabbling on the glossy magazines, her hands found no purchase. When Gracie was a baby, too little to walk, she would crawl across the satin bedspread. Polly would catch her tiny, pink feet, pull her back into her arms, and kiss her, then away she would crawl again, laughing. Not Emma. Emma would roll over and kick out in anger.

Polly rolled onto her back, twisting her captured foot painfully. Using the foot that was free, she kicked with the desperation of the trapped. Animal sounds, grunts and shrieks and roars, poured from her. The killer held on, his faced pressed against her leg. She could feel the wet heat of his breath through her trousers. His mouth was working up behind her knee to her inner thigh, as if he would chew into her. Polly struck out again and again and felt her foot glance off his back, his shoulders. Finally her heel struck bone, smashing part of his head or face. Her captured leg broke from his hands. She kicked again, then scooted backwards like a crab. Before she got to the door she must have turned and stood, but she remembered none of it. By luck or instinct, her hand found her purse on the overturned basket. Grabbing it, she hurtled down the steps and out into the street. Maybe she was chased; maybe she wasn't. Her escape made so much racket, she couldn't tell.

Outside, streetlights seemed preternaturally bright and endlessly reassuring. She ran toward her car.

Hands shaking so badly she could scarcely get the key into the ignition, she started the car and drove across Jackson Avenue, then into a smaller street. At each corner, she turned. As she crossed Louisiana Avenue, she watched the rearview mirror. After all the evasive maneuvers, she realized she was praying the murderer had followed, praying she would see a black SUV or a sleek sedan tailing her.

Anything but a cherry red, mint-condition, 1949 pickup truck.

*Charles Whitman. Texas Clock Tower. I can see myself doing that. Not right now (no gun, ha ha). Charlie is this marine, right? So, he likes guns and has them. Maybe he's got this wife that needs stuff and maybe she's even nice and all but she NEEDS stuff and she's always at him. And maybe at school he's got these teachers yammering at him to get stuff. Maybe old Charlie got to thinking everybody was eating him, biting chunks of his flesh out, and he was running out of flesh. Pretty soon he gets to feeling the whole world is made of biters, so he gets his rifle out and decides to take a few biters with him when he goes. Yeah, I could see doing that.*

# 32

Marshall had not cried in so long his body did not know how. Sobs sawed out in anguished groans. Hot and niggardly tears crept from the corners of his eyes. His shoulders and arms jerked as if he fought to free himself from the clutches of sharp-nailed fingers.

The fit lasted only minutes. Tears were not cleansing; there was no relief, only an ache in his gut where muscles had clenched in a vain attempt to vomit out the unvomitable.

*Breathe, you psycho fuck*, he ordered himself and drew in warm air, thick as night, exhaled noisily and again took a lungful of the static air. A semblance of sanity returned with the oxygen. He looked up at the basement's center beam.

The axe hung where he'd put it not five minutes before. It had not migrated up the three flights of stairs to secrete itself under the bed like an ogre in a children's story. It had not flown out of the darkness like a sentient thing, a bat spiraling upward in the night to prey on the innocent. That was a comfort of sorts.

The cellar was dark enough the newly cleaned metal gleamed only in Marshall's mind's eye. Still he reached up and flicked off the overhead lights. True or not, TV crime shows had him convinced that scrubbing with turpentine would not be enough. A crime scene investigator would spray the axe with a magic substance and it would glow blue where blood had seeped into the wood, clotted in the crevices between handle and head.

*There is no crime scene*, he told himself.

A key grated in the outside door. Polly had come home.

"No!" he cried as the door swung inward.

Danny screamed, high, wild.

"Sorry, man. It's just me, Marshall."

"Damn it!" Danny yelled.

"Sorry," Marshall said.

"The door's unlocked in the middle of the night. What the hell . . . What are you doing here?" he demanded.

Had Marshall not known his brother never took any drug but aspirin, and that sparingly, he would have thought he was high on something with an edge. "I live here," Marshall said. "Take it easy. Sorry I startled you."

Danny closed the door, shutting out most of the light. For a second, Marshall felt threatened. Instinctively, he stood up.

Threat vanished—that or he had imagined it.

"Sorry myself, brother," Danny said. "I shouldn't have gone off like that. Scared me is all. Door's not locked, you yelling from the dark. I jumped so high, I'm surprised I didn't bash my brains out on the ceiling." Danny turned the lights back on and looked at Marshall.

"What are you doing in the basement in the dark anyway? Where's Polly? The kids? You don't look so good, Marsh."

"Polly and the girls are staying at Martha's," Marshall said wearily and, the effort of standing suddenly too great, sat on the step again.

Danny sat next to him. The closeness was comforting. His brother glanced toward the center beam that bisected the cellar.

"It's there. I just put it there."

"I wasn't looking for the axe," Danny said. The lie was kind but transparent.

"It wasn't there last night," Marshall said. "It was upstairs. Under the bed for Christ's sake. Like before."

"And you don't . . ."

"No. I don't remember a thing. I'm a fucking werewolf. At night I turn into a predator and wander the streets thirsting for blood. God damn." He rubbed his face, as if he could scrub the image from his mind.

"You're too hard on yourself, Marsh. Nobody's been hurt."

"There was blood on the axe, Danny."

Danny said nothing. Marshall didn't appreciate it. He needed the reassurance of excuses made up by somebody other than himself.

"You're sure it was blood?" Danny said finally.

"Pretty sure. There was a lot of it, smeared over the blade, the butt, down the handle."

"Like before."

"Yeah. I brought it back down, cleaned it with paint thinner, then burned the rag. A criminal mind, no doubt."

"Maybe it wasn't human blood," Danny offered.

"That makes it better? Sneaking around the neighborhood hacking dogs to death? There's no way out, Danny. Psychotherapy is crap, and the psycho pharmaceutical companies haven't come up with a drug for the likes of me. I can't keep screwing around with half-assed theories. It's too dangerous. Polly, Gracie, Emma . . ."

After a minute, Danny asked, "What does that leave?"

"Suicide." Marshall laughed.

"Don't say that!" The fear in Danny's voice was sharp. "Ever. You're with me for the long haul brother. You and me. You don't get to cut out early." He put his arm around Marshall's shoulders. "We'll get through this. I will see to it that we get through this. Have you been taking the Valium before bed? One of the worst things you can do is let yourself get overtired."

"Pretty much. They knock me for a loop."

"They're fairly mild. You're just so keyed up, it feels like they knock you out. Your body needs to rest. Wait here."

Danny stood and looked down. "Will you promise . . ."

"I'm not going to off myself with the table saw

while you run upstairs," Marshall said. Danny smiled crookedly.

The sound of his brother's footsteps climbed into the air behind his head where the stairs corkscrewed up. Marshall loved this building. The rooms were full of light. There'd been so many windows and doors—front, back, balcony, and cellar doors—they'd made them all open with a single key so they wouldn't be carrying key rings the size of janitors'.

Danny's steps descended again, the *thip, thip, thip* of soft-soled shoes spiraling back down. For some reason it made Marshall think of Edward Gorey's *The Doubtful Guest*.

"Here." Danny poured half a dozen small white pills into Marshall's palm.

"What is it?"

"Valium. The same old thing in a new bottle. The drug reps give me so many samples, I could relax half the Third World. I can run back up and get the literature if you want."

"Never mind. Thanks."

"Take two—three won't hurt you. Get some sleep."

"Sure," Marshall said. Danny squeezed his shoulder.

"Go to bed. That's what I'm going to do. Good night, brother." Danny's footsteps corkscrewed upward. Marshall heard his kitchen door click shut.

He stared at the tablets.

*You get, you share.*

The thought made him smile.

Even in the bad times, there were good times. By virtue of their rarity, they were experienced more keenly, remembered more fondly. Maybe that was why men remembered their wars with such relish. Maybe that's why he'd never had the tattoo removed.

He pushed up the sleeve on his left arm and looked at the old marks. Crude green slashes, once sharp but now blurred and faded with age, formed the numbers one and three and the fraction one-half. A classic prison tat. He'd been anesthetized with cheap bourbon one of the "girls" had gotten from a guard in trade for a blow job. The tattoo artist had been as drunk as the rest of them. Marshall remembered the sting, and the blood, and the laughter.

"Thirteen and a half," Draco had said. "One judge, twelve jurors, half a chance."

Marshall pushed the sleeve back down and looked again at the pills. He'd sworn off illegal drugs a long time ago. He didn't trust doctors and he hated "mental health professionals" of any stripe. Now he was a prescription junkie, hunkered over in a basement with a fistful of unidentified pills, joking about suicide.

How the hell had that happened?

Tippity.

After he'd nearly frozen Elaine's dog, the nightmares had come back—not as bad as when he was a kid but bad enough—and Danny had given him something to help him sleep. Danny got them as samples that came in small brown envelopes.

Marshall had taken them for a year or so after the Tippity debacle, then quit. When he married Polly, Danny worried he'd go into whatever the hell it was he went into when "emotionally charged"—Danny's term for love—and suggested he start again. "Keep the monsters at bay," Danny'd said.

Though Marshall hated to admit it, after so long alone, he didn't sleep well with someone else in the bed. And he'd been more scared of the monsters than he'd wanted to admit. So he took the pills.

"Same old thing in a new package," Danny'd said.

Same old Butcher Boy of Rochester in a new package?

## 33

Thirteen and a half.

The tattoo brought back memories Marshall hadn't allowed out of his subconscious for twenty-five years at least. Not even the good memories; for Marshall, it had never been possible to pick and choose. The floodgates were open or they weren't. Tonight had opened them with such suddenness, the images carried him like a leaf on a tide rushing back. The past rose around him, as the waters had risen when the levees broke, and he watched with the same sense of helpless, frightened wonder.

Draco. Dr. Kowalski. That stupid Swede, Helman or Herman. Dr. Olson. Phil. Phil Maris, his math teacher, the guy who taught him to build in his mind, the guy he'd dropped acid with. They guy who'd abandoned him then saved him.

Marshall was not merely remembering; people from his past were with him. He could smell the perennial cigarette stink of Draco's hair. Phil smiled, and Marshall was a proud teenager. Then Kowalski leaned back in his chair.

Marshall snapped out of the living memory and into his cellar.

God, he had hated Kowalski. Most of Ward C hated Kowalski. Dozens of punk criminals, including one mass murderer and two knife wielders, and yet nobody had killed the psychiatrist. What a waste of talent. After the acid trip gone awry he'd never seen the bastard again. The joke in the ward was that since he'd tried to kill Kowalski, that proved that he was innocent.

*Tried* was the key word. Draco started it, saying if he couldn't off that spineless fuck, he was obviously a washout as a stone-cold killer, and somebody else must have done his family.

He had never seen Phil Maris again either. The morning he got out of the infirmary, his brain still scummed with LSD, the warden announced that Phil had taken a better job in St. Cloud. It was midterm; Phil hadn't said anything about any job, and he hadn't said good-bye to anybody.

The "better job" was as much bullshit as Kowalski's "better job" had been.

For a while he looked for letters, waited on visitors' day, but there'd been no contact. The warden refused to give him Phil's new address so he could write. He'd tried to talk to Rich about it, but Rich had taken a dislike to the algebra teacher.

When he asked the staff about Phil they got cagey, like people used to get when a girl got pregnant in high school. "She transferred," they'd say, or "she's visiting her aunt in another state." Then they'd look at each other in that certain way.

Phil had fucked up somehow and gotten thrown out. Not fired; if that had been the case, there wouldn't have been the slitty-eyed smirks and knowing looks.

A year or so later, he'd heard that Phil really was teaching high school in St. Cloud, so maybe it wasn't total bullshit.

After the initial weirdness of Phil's disappearance wore off, he'd let it drop. In juvie, weird was a way of life. Questioning it was not only a waste of time but could get a kid in trouble. Looking back, Marshall wondered why the staff had done the "little pitchers have big ears" routine after Phil left. If he'd been canned for dropping acid, they'd have said so, used it as an object lesson against the evils of drugs.

And Dylan hadn't been a "little pitcher." At fifteen, he was five-ten, one hundred sixty pounds, and a convicted murderer. What could be so bad they wouldn't want to sully his underage ears with it? If they thought they were protecting his innocence, they'd been three corpses too late.

Then out of the blue, two years later, Phil gets him out of DuWalt. He didn't see Phil and Phil never contacted him. It had been done behind the scenes. Since Dylan hadn't been into looking gift horses in the mouth at that juncture, he'd let it slide. Marshall had let it slide as well. Working hard to put "Dylan, boy monster" behind him, he'd been relieved to move out of Minnesota, change his name.

Be a "real live boy" for a change.

Marshall laughed. The sound rang hollow in the hot damp of the cellar.

Dylan Raines was never going to be a real live boy. One day, the poor little bugger was going to remember the murders, and Marshall's house of cards, complete with a cardboard marriage and borrowed family, was going to come crashing down.

With a rush of yearning startling in its intensity, Marshall wanted to see Phil again, show him how he'd turned out, and thank him for teaching him to build with his mind. He wanted to do it before the house fell. The need was so strong, it lifted him half off the step, as if he was going to run to the phone or the train station and look up his old teacher.

Surely, with the electronic ears and eyes everywhere, trails left by each purchase, every plane ticket, telephone calls, he could track him down. Phil Maris wasn't that much older. He was only . . .

"Nearly seventy," Marshall said aloud. He sank back down onto the step. The man might be dead; might not remember a murderous child who'd loved him forty years ago.

Without Phil, and his brain puzzles, and the garden they'd started together that last night, Dylan would have stayed Butcher Boy.

"Thank you," Marshall said to the dark ceiling. "Wherever you ended up. If you hadn't gotten me out, I'd undoubtedly have more tattoos and fewer teeth."

The day of his release from DuWalt unfolded in Marshall's mind. The man from the department of corrections, Mr. Leonard, had turned out to be alright. He'd helped with college, moving, and, though it went against his stolid Midwestern way of life, even the name change Danny had wanted.

Overweight, late forties back then, Mr. Leonard was probably dead by now. Marshall missed him as well. Dylan missed him not at all.

Maybe because Mr. Leonard hadn't liked Phil either. At the time, Dylan made a half-hearted effort to get Phil's phone number so he could express what passed for gratitude in those days. Mr. Leonard refused. He said, "You've got no need to go contacting him. He owes you this much and more." Dylan didn't waste time trying to figure it out. Soul-searching—his or anybody else's—was a pastime he never dared mess with. He was free and shaking the Minnesota snow from his boots.

Decades later, Marshall was wondering why Mr. Leonard disliked Phil so much. Leonard had seemed like a good guy, straightforward. Dylan's release might have been won by Phil, but it was orchestrated by the Minnesota Department of Corrections. It mattered to Leonard. Why would he hate the man who had been instrumental in making it happen? And what on earth could Phil Maris owe Dylan for?

Dylan believed, while his brain was scrambled, he'd said something about them dropping acid together and that's what got Phil booted out of DuWalt. Nobody ever said anything about it; so, after a while, Dylan had relaxed on that count. Besides, a lot of the guards did a hell of a lot worse than drop acid with their little charges and they never got reported. They just disappeared.

*Child molestation.*

"Holy shit," Marshall murmured.

Phil wasn't fired for dropping acid. He was fired because he'd dropped his pants. Marshall felt the betrayal as if it were yesterday, and he was still eleven years old. Phil was doing the boys. He started to cry again, rusting machinery grinding painfully. Abruptly, he stopped. Anger flared too hot for tears. Lightning-fast he smashed his fist into the wall between the studs.

"Crap," he yelled. "That has got to be crap." Phil never touched Marshall—Dylan. He didn't do anything out of line, not once, not a look, not a smirk, nothing for four years. Phil never messed with any of the other guys either, not that Marshall knew of. And he would know. Everybody would know. The algebra teacher didn't get talked about, and in lockup, there was nothing much to do but talk. Guards never snickered or sneered when he came by. There was nothing.

Phil wasn't buggering his students.

"Why do you care now, for Christ's sake?" Marshall asked himself. But he did care. A lifetime later, and he cared a lot. Phil was a hero in a world where there were too few heroes and more than enough villains to go around. He'd loved Phil. He'd told him so after the acid trip that had landed him in the infirmary.

No, he'd told Danny. Was that why Phil had gotten thrown out of juvie? Because a doped up kid said he loved him, and somebody figured it was more than just spiritual?

Marshall shook his head and then lowered it into his hands, his elbows braced on his knees to take the great weight of his thoughts. "Damn it."

His life was coming apart, his wife was leaving him, and this was the time he'd chosen to lurk in the basement worrying about Phil Maris, who was most likely dead, or retired, or had rejoined the Peace Corps and gone to some disease-ridden hole to help more boys.

Pebbles pressed into his cheek. The pills. Danny's pills. *Something to help you sleep.*

Marshall reached up and flipped on the stairwell light. His brother had said they were Valium. Marshall threw a couple of them into his mouth to swallow dry but a strangeness made him spit them back into his palm.

There was a wrongness about them. A wrongness about a lot of things. His on-again, off-again memory that worked fine between murders and attempted murders of small dogs; an axe that he didn't remember using forty years ago but suddenly took to carrying up and downstairs in his sleep; Phil getting canned the day after Kowalski's acid experiment; Mr. Leonard saying, "He owes you."

Marshall desperately needed to put the pieces together, but what he had weren't solid enough to be referred to as pieces. Drifts of fog. Whispers in the dark. A long time ago Marshall had learned never to seek out the dark corners of his mind, never to listen to unauthorized murmurs. At eleven, he'd taken his dad's old wood-chopping axe and butchered his mother, father, and his little sister,

Lena. Then he killed Ginger, the family cat. All those years that quack Kowalski had been trying to get him to remember, Dylan had been trying to make sure that he didn't. Not remembering was the only reason he didn't have to be fed with a spoon or peeled off the ceiling every morning.

Dylan didn't want to remember, and Marshall refused to look at those years. Both man and boy knew remembering would be the end of it. Nobody sane could stay sane having that knowledge in their bones.

This was the first time since the night Dr. K. and Phil had been thrown out of DuWalt that he had thought about the bad old days. Or about how the bad old days had come along into the good old days, robbing him of Elaine and, now, of Polly, Emma, and Gracie, just as he had robbed himself, Rich, and the world of his mother, and dad, and little Lena.

Polly and her goddamn tarot cards.

A wrongness there as well. Marshall might be an insane mass murderer, but he wasn't crazy enough to think a raddled old woman, subsisting on tourist donations, was privy to the secrets of the universe. Or his wife's mind. It was a trick. A con's trick. It had to be. Somehow the reader had gotten hold of memories Polly thought were a secret. She must have told someone.

"No!" Marshall said abruptly.

She had told someone. She'd told him.

# 34

The habit of doing as his brother told him was strong, and Marshall took himself upstairs. He stopped beside the bed, where he'd taken to standing in recent days, doing his Superman routine, trying to look through the mattress with his X-ray vision to see if he had unwittingly secreted an edged weapon beneath. Tonight, he wasn't looking for the axe. He was fixated on the pills Danny had given him.

Any other night, he would have swallowed a couple without much thought, looking forward to a good night's sleep. Tonight, he found he had to know what the pills were. Exactly what they were. What they did. Who made them. What the side effects were.

So much was out of whack. Not so much that it showed up readily, not so much that people dialed 911 or checked into Betty Ford, but wrong—a note played sharp, a ping in the engine. When he got this feeling on a job site, he'd stare and pace, sometimes sleep at the construction site, waiting for the dishonest color or anachronistic pattern to reveal itself.

His wife and brother came and went in the dead of night like actors in a French farce.

An axe appeared and disappeared.

A scribbled note on the counter.

A tarot reading that told secrets and made threats.

There was nothing he could do about flitting axes, nothing he could say that wouldn't frighten Polly further from him. But he could identify the medications he put down his throat night after night.

In less than a minute, Marshall descended the backstairs to his brother's kitchen door. "Danny," he called. "It's me. Open up." A light showed under the sill, but there was no response. "Hey!" He knocked and tried the knob. The door was locked.

A quick trip to the cellar for a spare key, and he let himself in. Music played softly—a sonata of some sort. Despite Danny's efforts, Marshall managed to remain fairly ignorant in the field of performing arts.

"Dan? Danny?"

The bed was made, the towels in the bath dry and neat.

"Where the hell . . ."

Danny'd said he was going to bed. Marshall pulled apart the slats in the blind and looked into the garden. His brother's car was gone, the gate left open. Unless Danny'd left by the front door, Marshall would have seen him. Regardless of how Danny departed, Marshall should have at least heard the car leave.

He must have pushed the car out—easy enough

with the gentle slope and concrete pad—and left the gate open. Why? Didn't want to wake his brother? Danny wasn't that considerate. Where had he gone at three in the morning—or four, or whatever the hell time it was?

To get lithium for his psychotic brother?

*Psych ward. Cootie central.* Marshall suppressed a shiver. It had been bad enough when he was a kid. Now, it would probably kill him. Shrugging off the thought as he had shrugged off legions of bat-black thoughts, he went to Danny's office.

Marshall switched on the lamp. Magic beans, he thought, as he spilled the pills onto the smooth metal surface of the desk. Their shape was distinctive, but there was no lettering stamped on them. They might be too generic to trace. He found the *Physicians' Desk Reference* in the bookcase, opened it on the desk, and searched by color, size, and shape. The pills were not generic.

They were Ambien.

"Take two, three, if you think you need it. Valium," Danny had said.

Marshall knew little about prescription drugs—he left that to his brother—but Ambien had been in the news. One of the side effects was amnesia. If the person taking it did not go to sleep, he was likely to do any number of things that he wouldn't remember in the morning.

Was that what he'd done? Taken the drug, played with axes, refrigerated Chihuahuas, and God knew what else, then gone back to bed and woken without any memory of it?

Why would Danny give him a drug that caused the very thing they'd both worked so hard to avoid? Why tell him the drug was a mild form of Valium?

The foundations of Marshall's life were as sick as New Orleans after sitting so long in poison waters. Buildings were tilted. Doors would no longer close. Windows no longer stayed open. Cracks appeared.

Wading carefully through treacherous waters, he opened his brother's filing cabinet. With all his wealth and taste for fine things, Danny lived a monkish life. What he had was of the best quality, but he needed little and kept what he had in rigid order. Unsure of what he sought, Marshall thumbed quickly through household bills, warranties, computer manuals, and the leases for the rental properties Danny owned.

Four, Marshall knew of; he'd done the design work on two and found Danny a crew to reroof a third. The fifth lease, filed under the letter *V* was new to him. An apartment building in the slums of Center City. Because it was different, because it was secret, Marshall pulled the file from the drawer. One of the apartments was let to V. Werner.

Vondra Werner. Rich had sex with her when he was thirteen; that's what he was doing while his little brother orphaned him. Vondra had been obsessed with Rich, still begging him to let her drive him to

DuWalt three years after he got his driver's license.

Vondra was in New Orleans, and Danny had given her an apartment. Secretly. Marshall glanced at the contract. Secretly and rent free. Vondra Werner was Danny's—what? Paramour? As far as Marshall knew, Danny didn't have lovers—not women, not men. Evidently, Danny didn't tell him everything. Not like he told Danny everything.

The rental agreement listed her profession as "Tarot Reader, Jackson Square."

Polly's tarot reader?

Marshall put the lease back in the file. A sense of inevitability locked on his brain. Marshall would know. Kowalski had been right; the truth was locked in his skull. He left the office for the bedroom. Danny was too private a person to keep personal items in his public spaces.

The master bedroom was the width of the building, thirty-three feet wide and twenty-two deep. The bed, raised on a shining black dais like an altar to sleep, was at the far end from the door. Exercise equipment, coupled with Danny's taste for chrome and steel, leant the room a futuristic look. Marshall had found the bureau for the room. It was shaped like a classic Chippendale, but the entire surface was mirrored.

He opened the top drawer.

An oval box, sterling silver with tortoiseshell inlay and spindly piano-shaped legs, nestled among the tie clips and collar stays. Crying out,

Marshall gathered it up gently, as if it were a living thing, and carried it over to the bed.

The box had belonged to their mother. She kept it on her dressing table. Since the police dragged him from the house, it was the first and only relic Marshall had seen from his old life. He'd refused anything from the house. He kept no pictures, and he never asked what Danny did with the place or its furnishings. Danny had inherited a chunk of money, as well as the house, when their folks died. Marshall had never asked what the numbers were. Given he'd hacked them to death, it seemed cold to ask about the payoff.

Marshall wanted nothing from his childhood; he was afraid of the memories that would be evoked. Sitting on Danny's bed, he was stunned at how good it felt, cradling his mother's jewelry box. There were memories in it, he knew, but his mother's shade would not let them cut too deeply. Polly had taught him that; mothers forgave their children. Even the monsters.

The silver box closed with a tiny catch on the left—he marveled that he remembered. He flicked the lock with a fingernail and opened it. On the brown velvet lining lay the simple gold cross his mother had worn every day of her life. She was wearing it the night she was killed. Marshall had seen it fall from her robe when she leaned down to kiss him goodnight.

Beside it, much tinier, was another cross on a

chain. It wasn't real gold, and the chain was sturdier. To Lena, it had been perfect because it was just like Momma's. Once it had been fastened around her neck, she refused to have it taken off. It had been a wonder she never lost or broke it. Marshall smiled at the memory of his little sister, then abruptly stopped, waiting for the memory of how she died to overlay it.

The picture in his mind of a round-cheeked two-year-old, blonde hair in wispy curls, her precious gold cross pulled up on its chain and stuck in her mouth, wavered but held. "Hey, Lena," he whispered. He'd never dared remember her, except fleetingly and as an addendum to something else.

Marshall pinched up a copper disk the size of a nickel. On the back was engraved: "Ginger Raines. 1341 Epcott."

The cat's tag. Ginger had a red leatherette collar, he recalled, with a tag on it. Not knowing what it was doing in his mother's box, he put it back and lifted out their dad's wedding ring. On the inside was inscribed, "Frank, my hero." A private joke they hadn't lived long enough to share with their children. Laying the ring in the center of his palm, Marshall looked at it in the unilateral light of Danny's bed lamp. Their father had been proud of the scratches in the soft gold. "A wedding ring is for life," he'd tell his sons. "No need to take it off. Like love, time only makes it more beautiful." Marshall had forgotten that. He had forgotten much of his life. Eleven years. Like it was a book he read once and never thought of again.

The last item in the jewelry box was a pair of silver-toned hockey sticks, a pin Dylan's fourth-grade team had won. Between ages seven and ten, he'd had a passion for hockey. The Fighting Marmots—a name as inexplicable as it was hard to chant—had taken first at state. He was way too cool to wear the pin, but he'd liked to look at it when Rich wasn't around to rag him.

Never a sentimentalist—his life had not been the kind Hallmark wrote cards about—Marshall was taken aback at how much he wanted to hold on to these keepsakes.

It was foolish to believe their owners lived on through them. Foolish to believe. To feel it was a different thing.

Again he lifted out his mother's cross, supporting it by the slender broken chain.

It must have been taken from her body before the burial and given to Rich. Marshall thought about that, as he watched the golden cross turning hypnotically.

Mr. Kroger, their dad's partner, had made all the arrangements. Rich told him that the first time he'd visited him in DuWalt. There was no funeral—Mr. Kroger had the bodies interred as soon as the autopsies were completed—but they were going to have a memorial service when the news people quit dogging everybody concerned.

Marshall tried to picture their dad's rough-voiced partner. He'd seemed like such a big man and so old, but he couldn't have been more than forty-five. He'd liked Dylan, and used to growl at him, and act like he ate children. It would sound sinister to tell but it wasn't. It was fun.

The forensic pathologist must have removed the wedding ring and the necklace. Marshall couldn't picture Mr. Kroger prying his dad's wedding ring off. No one would pry off a man's wedding ring before burying him next to his wife. At least no man from Minnesota. The same went for the gold crosses. The undertaker, the pathologist, the preacher, Mr. Kroger, all would have sent them to God with their bearers.

Closing his hand on the shards of his boyhood, Marshall felt the points of the cross and the hockey sticks pushing into the flesh of palm and fingers. This was all that remained of who he had been before he was Butcher Boy.

The round smoothness of his father's wedding ring clicked against the gold of Marshall's own wedding band, and he wondered why his mother's ring hadn't been in the jewelry box as well.

With that thought, the warm and fuzzy memories blasted out of his mind.

One ring had been taken and one left on its finger. Because Dylan had his mother's cross for a souvenir and didn't need anything else.

Dylan had taken the jewelry from the corpses

after he killed them, and Rich had kept it for him. Kept it from the cops, more likely.

*Who the fuck do you think you are, Psycho Boy? The Beaver? Dennis the Menace? Some cute little boy, prone to mischief? You fucking butchered everybody.*

"I was eleven years old, for God's sake," Marshall whispered. "I was a little boy."

The necklaces, Lena's and his mother's, would have been drowned in their blood. Marshall was shaking his head, trying to see himself digging through matted hair and brains to steal away the last glitter of their lives.

"No," he cried out and opened his hand: the crosses, the ring, the hockey pin, the brass tag.

There was nothing there of Rich's. Dylan's pin was there, in the box with the things taken from that night. Dylan. Mom. Dad. Lena. Even Ginger the cat.

Rich wasn't there. If Dylan took them, why would he keep a memento of himself and not of his brother, another of his intended victims?

## 35

The emergency gas can Danny carried up the narrow stairs didn't have more than a gallon in it, and the fuel was several years old, but from what he'd seen of the rat's nest upstairs, it should suffice.

Danny was fairly sure Polly had no idea who'd attacked her, but she had to suspect it was

Marshall. There was enough evidence Marsh could end up in prison—grown-up prison—for the rest of his life. Kicking the door open, he picked his way through the dark rooms using the flashlight he'd taken from the trunk when he'd retrieved the gasoline. The narrow beam played across the unmade bed, the littered floor, Vondra's scrapbook.

He wondered if Marshall was featured in it, if the trial or Rochester were mentioned. There was no time to look. He followed his light into the bathroom and directed the beam into the tub.

"God, but you're disgusting," he said as he stared down at the plastic-and-blood-wrapped woman. "You ever see *The Blob*, Vondra? You could have played the title role." Grabbing the shower curtain with both hands, he braced himself against the side of the old claw-foot tub and heaved. The plastic tore away, and the corpse flopped back the few inches he'd managed to raise it.

Peeling away the curtain, he looked for something to grab onto that wouldn't give. The creepy drape she'd put on was already torn half-off the body. Holding his breath, he fished out a fat hand. Red acrylic nails clattered against the side of the tub, and he jumped.

With a grunt, he pulled the body over the rim of the tub and staggered back as the wad of limbs and curtain slapped to the floor. Distorted like those of a drowned woman, Vondra's dead eyes peered at him through a film of plastic.

Debris was plowed aside as he dragged her to the bed and propped her against it. It would have to do; he wasn't going to throw his back out trying to lift her onto the mattress. Sparingly, he sloshed gasoline on the bedding. There were enough cigarette boxes and matches around for it to look like she'd fallen asleep with a lit cigarette.

Maybe the investigators would look past the obvious; maybe they wouldn't. Since Katrina, the building had had no insurance. There would be no monetary gain to the owner. New Orleans was filled with derelict buildings. There wasn't a lot of interest in those the insurance companies didn't have to fork out cash for. It was a risk he'd have to take.

"A scrapbook!" he said as he struck a match from one of the thousands of matchbooks lying about. "Photos, newspaper articles. I think your killer is off the hook; I think you died of stupidity," he said. He tossed the match, heard it fizzle out, and struck another.

Fumes. It was the fumes that lit, not the gasoline itself. Danny took a few steps back from the bed, waited a minute for the fumes to build up, then struck another match and tossed it onto the pyre. A thin, blue tongue licked out, liked what it tasted, and flowed rapidly over the cloth and paper.

"Bingo," he said and watched the rapidly growing fire for a second or two.

He needed the place to ignite quickly and

cleanly. He needed to call Polly and warn her before Marshall found her.

The fire grew more voracious and began devouring the trash, half filling the bedroom. "Four million dollars in the bank, and I'm a cleaning lady," he said. Trailing gasoline, he left the apartment.

Away from the building, where responding fire or policemen wouldn't see him and wonder what he was doing in a bad neighborhood so late, Danny got into his car, a swift and classic BMW convertible. For a moment he sat behind the wheel listening to the grinding of the gears in his head before he realized he was grinding his teeth. He stopped the scrape of metal thoughts and tooth enamel and took his cell phone from his pocket.

For a moment, he toyed with the idea of calling Marsh, inviting him to the party.

He deserved to be there. Had he not gotten so full of himself over this marriage and family thing Vondra would still be alive, and Polly and her kids would be safe. Polly Deschamps, not Polly Marchand.

There were only two Marchands, brothers.

He and Dylan had found the names on a crypt in a cemetery in Metairie. They'd just arrived in New Orleans. It was early spring—the dead of winter in Minnesota. Azaleas were blazing, kept from spontaneous ignition only by the intense cool green of new grass. Aboveground burials, the stuff of movies and old black-and-white photographs, lured them in from the highway.

The place was deserted but for a groundskeeper or two. Live oaks hushed the noise from I-10. They wandered in perfect harmony along the lanes, admiring the mausoleums. It was as close to peace as Richard had ever known. It was bliss. Just the two of them, safe in the city of the dead.

A mausoleum, small but exquisite in detail and design, stood between two monoliths; beside them it looked like a dollhouse. There were only two names on the tiny door, infants who had died at birth: Marshall Dillon Marchand, born and died December 1, 1872, and Daniel Richard Marchand, born and died December 1, 1872.

Identical twins.

It had been a sign and they embraced it. From that day on, they had been the Marchand brothers of New Orleans, and they had prospered. When it was just the two of them, life worked.

That Marsh had the occasional dalliance didn't worry Danny overmuch. It was his brother's tendency to obsess—an addiction to a cloying sort of relationship—that was dangerous.

Elaine would never know it, but Danny had saved her life. Even her rat-sized dog had survived. The incident smashed Marsh's notions of recreating the same sort of sick family situation they'd had as kids.

Until Polly.

Danny hoped to keep Polly, Gracie, and Emma alive, but Marsh was becoming volatile. The business with the axe should have been enough to wake him up, but he was resisting the inevitable with a tenacity he'd not shown with Elaine.

He punched in his sister-in-law's cell phone number.

"Polly, it's Danny," he said when she answered. "Where are you?"

She was at Fontainebleau and Broad.

"Don't go home," he told her. "Marshall's gone berserk. I'm afraid I'm going to have to call the police, but I want to talk with you first. Maybe between the two of us we can get him to calm down. Can you meet me . . ." Danny rapidly scanned the map of the city that he carried in his head. The cemetery where he and Dylan had become identical twins—the Marchand brothers—would be a fitting place but it would be closed at this hour.

Marsh said the kids were with Martha. If Danny remembered correctly, Dr. Martha Durham lived up near City Park somewhere. "Meet me in City Park," he said. "There's a big live oak in front of the Christian Boys' School. Meet me there."

"My God, Danny . . ." she said, then no more, her words trailing away like a forgotten dream.

"Can you do it? We can meet someplace else if you'd like."

"No. It's . . . City Park . . . I can do it." She sounded exhausted and scared. No wonder, Danny thought. It was odd that she didn't mention being assaulted.

Probably she didn't want to accuse her beloved Mr. Marchand.

"I may be a few minutes," he said. "Lock your car doors and wait for me. If you see Marsh's truck, get out of there. Quickly. It'll be okay," he promised. "We'll get through this."

Danny hit "end" on the cell phone, punched in 411, and asked for the number of Martha Durham.

Then he asked for the address.

## 36

Danny kept the blinds closed regardless of the time of day. Marshall had gone to great pains to make the old sash windows functional, as he did with every building he restored, but he needn't have bothered with Danny's unit. His brother believed the out-of-doors should be kept out of doors.

For reasons he was unsure of—except that darkness covered more sins—he switched the lights off before he sat on Danny's bed. He no longer wanted to see the relics of the lives in his hand but held them tightly; they gave him courage. For the first time in his life he tried, consciously and whole-heartedly, to remember the night of the killings. The night he became Butcher Boy and, along with his family, his childhood was slaughtered.

Mack the Giant had ripped him from sleep—or

the dead sleep of unconsciousness. He'd been groggy from the concussion and the medicine his mom had given him. His head felt as if would break open and spill his brains out if he moved. The cop had jerked him hard. Marshall remembered the pain and the fear. He'd thought they were all going to be murdered.

The guy, the huge cop, had dragged him down the hall and forced him to look at Lena. Then he knew they were all going to be killed, that the carnage had already started. He remembered fighting then, as hard as he could, to get away from the man in the policeman's costume. Dylan thought it was a costume. Real police didn't come and kill people for no reason.

Marshall tried to go beyond what he could remember, to see the time before the police had come: himself alone, crazy, a boy, pulling the gold chain from around his baby sister's neck.

There wouldn't have been any pulling. Her neck was severed lengthwise, a blow that had split her nearly in two from her crown to below her tiny bird-boned shoulders. The chain would have been cut. He tried to picture himself, that boy, Dylan, setting the axe down and fishing the gold cross out of the gore.

The only boy he could see was the terrified child fighting to get away from the man he thought had killed his sister. He couldn't remember being Butcher Boy.

"Psycho fuck." Mack had called him that.

Traumatic amnesia. Psychotic break.

When he'd seen little Lena, Marshall remembered Mack's hand closing harder on the back of his neck. In the darkness of Danny's room, he felt it happening again. The cop stepped over Lena, jerking him along behind. Terrified his feet would touch his sister's blood, he'd grabbed the cop's leg. Mack backhanded him.

Later, at the trial, the cop said he thought Dylan was going for his gun.

His mother had fallen in the doorway of the master bedroom. She was face down, her long brown hair thrown forward. The amount of blood and its bright, comic book color shocked him.

To get the cross from around her neck he would have had to fumble though the sopping mess, dig out the chain, and yank until it broke.

Trying to picture Dylan—himself—doing that, all he saw were the butterflies, how beautiful they'd been above Kowalski's office, how they'd died.

*The kiss, the last good memory.*

Dylan hadn't seen his father. At least not that Marshall remembered. So much of his life had been haunted by that phrase, "not that he remembered." He'd come to accept that the origins of Butcher Boy were the only thing worth remembering and worth forgetting. The rest of the memories of his young life had been locked behind that paradox.

Once the monster had been laid over that little kid, Dylan, nobody ever thought about him again. Marshall hadn't thought of him again. Butcher Boy in DuWalt had not thought of him. In every way that mattered, Dylan had been murdered that night as surely as his mom, dad, and Lena were.

"God, I miss you." Marshall heard himself cry the words. "I loved you." Saying the words felt strange. He didn't know if what he tasted in the back of his throat was the foulest form of hypocrisy or freedom. Before DuWalt, maybe as early as the trial, he had forbidden himself to feel love for his family, to feel anything. The jewelry had brought it all back.

"I loved you," he said again. Forty years of accumulated emotion hit him, and he began to dissolve, ice breaking away, glacial silences turning to liquid and pouring through the barren scoured places.

"Momma and Daddy, I loved you. Your boy Dylan loved you."

Dylan, the real, live boy, the boy before that night, came back to life, and Marshall saw him, was him. Freckled in summer, hair blond from the sun.

*Laughing.*

It surprised him to remember how much he had laughed when he was a kid. How much fun it had been being a kid in Minnesota in the sixties. Maybe the last gasp of the Norman Rockwell times before drugs, and twenty-four-hour news, and school shootings changed small-town America.

He had friends; there'd been a gang of kids, their lives centered on sports: Little League in summer, hockey in winter. Between seasons, there were forts made from haystacks and riding the elevators when they could sneak into the downtown buildings and get away with it.

Riding bikes.

Marshall laughed aloud.

They had ridden thousands of miles. They rode all summer to each others' houses, and the river, and the lake. They rode in the winter when the ice pulled the wheels out from under them. Boys on bikes were free.

Ricky, and David, and Charlie, and Al—God but they'd had fun.

Little boys who loved their moms and dads, their friends, their bicycles, John Wayne, and the Green Lantern, little boys like that surely didn't turn psycho overnight.

Rich, though he wasn't much older, wouldn't have much to do with them except to give them a bad time.

*A rotten time.*

Rich had reinvented himself after Dylan's trial. Marshall had forgotten that too. Dylan had been so glad somebody still loved him he'd have been willing to overlook just about anything. Rich had been his lifeline in DuWalt .

That brother—the DuWalt brother—had not always existed, Marshall realized. As Butcher Boy had hidden Dylan, Richard—the new improved DuWalt Richard—had hidden Rich.

"A rotten time" was an understatement.

Rich had tortured the hell out of them. He was so good at it he almost never got caught. Half the time, Ricky, Charlie—none of them—knew he was doing it until it was too late, and they were screwed.

Rich had a hole where there should have been snips and snails and puppy dog tails. He didn't care about things the way other kids did. He didn't cry when he was hurt. When someone else got hurt, he'd laugh or, more commonly, study them like a scientist with a rat. If there was an accident, he'd call for help a little late or not at all. He'd know the cat was locked in the garage, or that the gate was open and Lena could wander out into the street, and he wouldn't tell anyone.

Charlie's mom didn't like him playing with Rich, and Ricky's wouldn't let him stay for sleepovers if Rich was going to be there. They didn't even want their kids in the same house with him.

How could he have forgotten that? How could he have forgotten eleven years of his life?

Because Rich became the big brother Dylan needed. Rich became the best part of Dylan's confused, insane world. He came to see him, went to bat for him at DuWalt. Dylan—Marshall—had forgotten his brother had ever been any other way. Maybe the loss of his family changed Rich on some fundamental level.

Three murders and Rich is a nice guy?

A damned thin silver lining.

Marshall remembered that Rich—the pre-DuWalt Rich—could be funny, even fun, but when the littler kids hung out with him, things had a way of going sour.

Other than the usual punches in the arm or noogies, Rich didn't hurt them. It was just that, when Rich was around, they got hurt. Charlie was nearly killed when Rich dared him to dive off the railroad bridge when the water was low. Charlie was Rich's easiest patsy because he was always out to prove what a tough guy he was.

*Nine, and we're tough guys.*

Ricky had a thing about snakes, a phobia, Marshall knew now. Then it was just Ricky being a sissy. Rich waited until they were crossing a log that had fallen over a ravine, then he'd tossed Charlie a water snake he'd been carrying in his pocket.

"Catch!" Marshall could hear him yell. A gleeful, boyish prank. Except that Charlie had fallen twenty-three feet and busted his right ankle and sprained his shoulder.

Rich facilitated, Marshall realized. Clumsy kids were led on tricky climbs. Sensitive kids were told scary stories. Fat kids were stuffed, bullies egged on, shy kids humiliated, evil kids taken to new heights.

Rich was shameless. Every now and then he'd get caught in lies or petty cruelties. If the punishment was severe, he was resentful; if it was mild, he was contemptuous. He was never sorry. He'd go through the motions if it was to his benefit, but he mocked them behind his folks' backs. He never regretted what he did.

Marshall vaguely remembered starting to sense that Rich's behavior wasn't quite normal, but then his parents and little sister died, and he'd gone into DuWalt, where Rich was the norm for big brothers, and fathers, and uncles.

Then the new Rich, Richard, appeared.

Why had his brother changed so suddenly? Had a triple murder finally made Dylan interesting enough to bother with?

When Charlie and Ricky had been hurt, it was Dylan who'd finally run for help. Rich had just watched them crying and struggling. Charlie might have drowned outright if Dylan hadn't jumped in after him. He'd lost two toenails on a rock that time.

Was Rich—Richard—watching him in De Walt?

Rich had been one mean son of a bitch when he was little. Reality shifted, and Marshall knew, *knew*, he'd been a good kid, a nice kid, a real boy.

*Maybe Dylan didn't do it.*

Maybe he didn't do it.

Marshall wanted to laugh, but there was no air.

He'd had that fantasy often enough. Like in *The Fugitive*—they'd find the one-armed man who killed his family.

"Get a grip," he whispered to himself. "You are most assuredly losing it. Jesus. Breathe." A thousand and more mornings, he'd opened his eyes, and the first thing he'd done was check his hands to see if they were clean of his crimes.

Little boys with clean hands didn't wake up with DNA evidence all over them. But back then there'd been no DNA evidence. No way to test whose blood it was.

Maybe it had only been Rich's from the cut on his leg, none from Dad, or Mom, or Lena. "Bullshit," Marshall said.

He'd been the only whole person left in the house. His pajamas were stained red. Rich had the cut leg and the eyewitness account; Rich had Vondra for an alibi. Dylan had the axe, Mack the Giant, the public outrage.

*Slam.*

*Dunk.*

*Thirteen and a half.*

# 37

Polly nosed the Volvo into the azaleas surrounding the pullout in City Park. Danny had told her to stay in the car with the doors locked but she couldn't. For hours she had been embalmed in the air-conditioned exhalations of a lifetime's cigarette smoke, the invisible effluvia of twisted dreams settling out of the stale air onto her hair and skin. She had to move and breathe.

It wasn't long until dawn but the temperature was in the seventies. Polly drew the scented air into her lungs and rubbed the damp, like a balm, into her neck. Forgetting for a blessed moment the trials of the night, she unbuttoned the top two buttons of her blouse and let the soothing reality of the natural world drift under the wilted fabric. Mosquitoes left her alone. Whatever had settled out of the atmosphere in the Woman in Red's apartment made Polly unpalatable to even the greediest.

A quarter of an hour dragged by and Danny did not come. Unwilling to get back into the car, she paced. The gravel crunching beneath her feet was jarringly loud, stilling the twitters and scuffles of the small creatures who love darkness.

Her right ankle and her calves ached. Her nails were ragged and torn. The clothing that had started out so fresh was filthy. A man who might have been her husband had attacked her in the house of a dead woman. Her brother-in-law told her not to go home because her husband had gone insane.

Suddenly Polly was too tired to stand.

Fifteen yards from the Volvo lay a fallen oak. A limb as big around as the trunk of many adult trees ran in a gentle rollercoaster along the ground.

Polly sat on it, feet dangling like a child's. Often,

when she was out of doors and alone after sunset, she felt like a child. When she was a girl, darkness was her friend, her cloak of invisibility when ogres walked the Earth.

Trouble would start, and she would go out the small trap door in the back bedroom that let into a luggage compartment under the trailer house. From there, she would run across the open space—the "lawn" her mother called it, where the weeds were kept mowed some of the time—and hide in a hollow at the roots of a fallen tree. Her hiding place was framed on three sides by the rotting trunk of the hardwood.

In the Mississippi woods, there must have been fire ants and red bugs, mosquitoes and ticks, but Polly didn't remember being bitten. She remembered feeling safe, invisible and invulnerable. She was close enough to the trailer she could hear the shouting but it sounded far away, in some other little girl's reality. That's what the past twenty hours felt like. Those terrible things had happened, but they had happened to someone else a long time ago. For the moment, she was safe, invisible in the arms of a night tree.

Note by note, the Pinteresque concert of the night returned: a peeper, then ten, a night bird, the whispered timpani of claws in the undergrowth.

Time passing at its inimitable petty pace.

Hypnotized by the warmth and the living quiet, she let her thoughts float up from the deep.

Marshall had "gone berserk," Danny said.

Berserk? Berserker rage? Chopping through walls with the axe? Crockery off the balcony? Raping and pillaging from a Viking's longboat?

"Berserk," Danny'd said.

Polly saw her husband cleaning a bloodstained axe. She had found a murdered woman, a woman who knew secrets Polly had shared only with him.

When Marshall sat on the step in the cellar and wept, she wanted to hold him, stand beside him regardless of what he had gotten himself into.

Love did that. Wives did that. Mothers didn't.

*Berserk.*

Marshall Marchand was the antithesis of berserk. Polly could not picture him turning vicious and running amok. He was considerate in the true sense of the word. Everything he did was considered, measured beforehand.

*Still waters?*

Anything was possible.

Danny was the greater mystery. Gracie felt it, too. Though Gracie liked her uncle, more than once Polly had caught her watching him the way a cat might keep tabs on a strange dog in the yard. Not so Emma. Emma would crawl up on Lucifer's lap and tug on his horns.

Her cell phone rang, and she was jerked into visibility and vulnerability. It was Marshall; his name came up on the screen. Polly pushed the green button. "Hello?" she said uncertainly.

"Polly, is that you? You sound funny. Where are you?"

"Marshall?"

"Yes. I need to talk to you. Where are you? Jesus, is it a long story! Are you at Martha's?" He laughed. Polly didn't like the sound of it.

"Marshall, I have had a long strange day. You are making no sense.

"Do you know anyone called 'the Woman in Red'?" she demanded. "She lives in a garbage dump on Loyola."

"Loyola. V. Werner. Vondra." He sounded vague. *V. A fancy script V on a silver heart in the treasure box. V, Vondra.*

"Where have you been tonight?" Polly was surprised she wasn't shouting. She was staggeringly rational. "Have you been out? You're calling me from your cell phone. Where are you?"

"I've been out. Not out. Away from the phone. Please, Polly, come home. Where are you?"

"I am about to meet with your brother. He said you had gone berserk."

Headlights broke the peace of the night, a sports car coming up the road.

"Danny's here."

"Don't talk to him. This is important. Come home. Talk to me. Don't even meet with him. Please."

The headlights of her brother-in-law's car went out. Ambient glow from the streetlights lit the passenger seat.

"I have to," she said. "He has Emma and Gracie with him." She turned the cell phone off.

Emma was sitting on Gracie's lap.

*No seatbelts*, Polly thought, as if that was the greatest danger of the night.

Dark and sleek, the car idled in the glow of the streetlight. From inside came the soft strains of cool jazz. The girls were in their pajamas. Polly stepped into the light and ran across the gravel toward where they waited.

Danny unfolded himself from the driver's side. "You girls stay in the car," Polly heard him say. "I'll leave it running so you'll have air-conditioning. Don't worry; I'll just be a minute."

"Polly," he said with evident relief. He stopped her and took her hands. She felt as if she were made of wood. His touch scarcely penetrated. "Marshall knew where the girls were staying, so I thought it best to pick them up. I'm sorry for the cloak and dagger, but things have gotten out of hand."

He smiled his old crooked smile, and Polly suffered a confused relief. He was sane. Or appeared to be. In a night of insanity, even the appearance of rationality was reassuring.

"What is going on?" she asked, her voice hollow in her ears.

"My God, what happened to you?"

Polly looked down at her filthy, torn clothing. A hand strayed to her hair. The ends were sticking out like straw from a haystack. "Somebody attacked me. I think . . ." She couldn't tell him what she thought. Saying it would make it real.

Danny looked at her long and hard. The faint light was behind him, and she could read nothing in his dark eyes.

"Marshall isn't Marshall," he said gently.

*"Your husband is not who you think he is,"* the tarot had said.

"Our parents did not die in an automobile accident. Marshall—his real name is Dylan Raines. Mine is Richard, Richard Raines."

*The Raines trial. Butcher Boy.*

"Dylan was a troubled kid. He spent seven years in a juvenile detention center in Minnesota. When he got out, I brought him down here. I changed our names so he would have a chance at a new life."

Polly nodded. Numbness had worked from her hands up over her heart to her throat, and her head bobbed as foolishly as a doll on a dashboard.

"Are you up to talking to him, do you think?" Danny asked kindly. "I thought if we all—what do they call it?—had an intervention, we might be able to calm him down, convince him to get some help."

Danny still held her hands. Polly pulled her fingers from his. Her arms fell lifelessly to her sides.

"What about the girls?" She was whispering. "What about the girls?" she repeated. This time her voice was too loud. Messages from her brain were not reaching her organs with speed or clarity.

"I thought they could ride with you. I'll follow you. Are you up to this? You don't have to. I might be able to handle it by myself," he said, but he didn't sound as if he believed it.

"Yes," was the best she could manage. "Richard," she said.

"Yes."

"There's a dead woman . . . I was in her apartment . . ." Polly didn't know how to finish the sentence.

"Vondra Werner," Richard told her. "I know, Marsh told me. She was a friend of mine. Dylan—Marshall—hated her. She testified against him."

"Marshall attacked me?"

"Yes. I'm sorry." Danny waited for her to say something, but Polly found she had nothing to say. Reality had become too bizarre for language to encompass.

"If we're going to do this thing, we should get started," he said kindly.

"Yes." Her eyes returned to the car. Emma and Gracie were chattering to each other. "The girls shouldn't be with us."

"I don't think it would be a good idea to take them back to Martha's. We can tuck them into my bed downstairs. Marshall won't even know they're there. Hide in plain sight," he said, maybe hoping to get a smile.

"Okay," Polly said woodenly. Exhaustion was falling heavily on the backs of her eyes. The injuries from the attack settled in to a bone-deep ache. The same ache surrounded her heart, squeezing so tightly she could feel each heartbeat.

Buckling her daughters into the back seat of the Volvo, she had to steady herself on the door. Her husband was not who she thought he was.

Red had said, "You will kill your husband."

Was that, too, foreordained?

Keys in hand, she walked around to the driver's side of the Volvo. Danny stopped her. "Here," he said and took the keys from her nerveless fingers. "You look too beat to drive. We can come back and get my car another time."

Without waiting for her to agree, he opened the driver's door and got in. The ignition turned, and the motor hummed to life. Afraid he would drive off without her, Polly ran to the passenger door and scrambled in.

"I would have waited," he said.

"I was perfectly alright to drive," she replied with more hostility than she could account for.

Twisting around, she checked on Emma and Gracie. They had curled up on the wide backseat, like yin and yang, foreheads touching, knees drawn up, little feet twined together.

"The poor little things are worn out," Polly said.

"Both asleep?"

"Dead to the world," Polly replied, then wished she'd used a different phrase. This was not a night one should tempt the gods.

"That's for the best," Danny said. "I didn't want to talk in front of them, but I'm sure you have a lot of questions."

Polly thought about that for what seemed an excessively long time. In truth, she had nothing she wanted him to answer. She needed answers, but she would ask them of Marshall. Danny did not come to this meeting with clean hands. If Marshall's life was a lie, so was his brother's.

Lights shone from the third-floor bedroom. The downstairs unit was dark. "He must have fallen asleep with the lights on," Danny said, more to himself than to Polly. The sentence jarred, but Polly wasn't sure why. Before she could think, Danny was out of the car opening the rear door.

"You take Emma," he said. "I'll take Gracie. She's getting a little heavy even for me."

"They are not babies," Polly said more sharply than she intended. "They are too old to be carried around like sleepy toddlers." Why she wished to make her daughters seem more mature and independent, she didn't know.

"Never too old to be carried," Danny said, scooping Gracie into his arms. She was awake— Polly could tell in the way mothers can always tell— but pretending not to be in order to get a ride up the stairs. Emma was truly asleep. Her noodley form draped over Polly's shoulder as she gathered up her bare legs. Emma was growing coltish, long-legged.

She would be taller than Gracie.

The incredible sweetness of her child, nestled into the crook of her neck, struck Polly through the numbness that had overtaken her. There was an edge to this child-love that was so sensual, right and good, a true connecting.

She should have left them with Martha, away from whatever was coming.

She had them with Martha; Danny had taken them, taken them without asking her permission, though she was a cell phone call away.

"Wait," she cried as he started for the door into the cellar. Suddenly, she could not bear to have him carry Gracie into the black beneath the duplex. Terror that she would never see her daughter again gripped her and she yelled, "Wait, goddamn you!"

Danny stopped and looked back. "Of course I'll wait. Are you okay?"

"Thank you," she said as politely as she could. She didn't answer his question. It was absurd.

Why on earth would anyone expect her to be okay?

## 38

Light came sudden and hard into Marshall's eyes. Lost in the past, he hadn't heard anyone coming.

"Marsh!" His brother's voice was harsh with the shock of seeing him there. "You're supposed to be asleep."

Old memories and hard light cleared from Marshall's eyes, and he saw Danny with his daughter nightgowned and draped in his arms like Faye Wray. Gracie's eyes were open and her face blank. She was trying to figure out what the adult world was up to. With the sixth sense of a child, she knew not to demand answers in her usual, forthright manner.

Marshall's fingers closed over the remnants of his childhood still held in his palm.

"Get down, Gracie," he said in a neutral tone. "Uncle Danny can't carry such a big girl for too long."

Polly, Emma clutched to her side, stood at Danny's shoulder. Stainless steel lamps loomed behind them, reminiscent of a dentist-chair nightmare.

"Polly, take the girls upstairs and put them to bed," Marshall said. It was not a command; it was a plea.

"Don't do it, Polly," Danny said. "God knows what he's got upstairs. Stay with me. Otherwise, I can't keep you safe."

He sounded so certain, so sure of himself, for a moment Marshall was Dylan again, and Dylan believed himself capable of any horror.

Gracie struggled. Danny set her on her feet but kept her close to him, one arm locked across her chest protectively. "Polly, I think it's time you met your husband. The girls, too. It will help them with the transition," Danny said.

"Dylan Raines," Marshall said to his wife. "I'm Dylan Francis Raines of Rochester, Minnesota." The words tasted like a lie. He'd not been Dylan Raines for too many years. "And I'm Marshall Marchand, the man you married." He was sounding schizophrenic. He could see alarm growing in Polly's eyes. He didn't dare look at Emma or Gracie.

"Tell her how you murdered our parents and our little sister." Danny said this with a sadness that hummed along Marshall's bones.

When Danny spoke again his voice was pitched for the ears of children. "He didn't do it to be mean but because he went into mental illness for a while. I'm not telling you this to scare you," he said and kissed Gracie on the top of her head, "but because my brother is sick again. He's been losing time— doing things that he forgets he did. When that happens, people get hurt. The people closest to him get hurt."

The clear, mossy green of his wife's eyes was icing over.

Polly believed Danny. *Dylan believed Rich.*

Remembrance of who he'd been as a boy, how things were, was slipping away.

Marshall opened his hand and held it out. His brother looked at the pieces from their mother's jewelry box without recognition, and Butcher Boy slid up close beside Marshall's spine, a sword into its scabbard.

Danny opened his mouth to speak, then closed it abruptly. He'd realized what Marshall held. In that single, unguarded moment, Marshall read his own innocence in Rich's face. Not in Danny's, or even Richard's, but Rich's—the old face from when he was a boy, before he learned to hide the pleasure he took in torturing the younger kids, in manufacturing accidents.

Rich saw the tiny gold crosses, the wedding ring and the hockey pin and, for a heartbeat, a smug, sly smile flicked across his lips like the tongue of a snake. In that instant, he looked into Marshall's eyes and gloated.

"What are those?" Polly asked, breaking the moment.

"They are trophies," Marshall answered evenly. He couldn't take his eyes off of his brother, and he could not block the thoughts that flowed like lava, hot and inexorable, through his mind. Half a century of thoughts.

"They are trophies," Danny repeated. "Dylan took them off the bodies of our family. I found them clutched in his hand, just like they are now. I took them so the police wouldn't find them. Do they bring back memories, brother?"

Marshall started to stand up. The fear on his wife's face stopped him. She could not see the pride in Danny's stance or the satisfaction in the set of his lips.

"Don't believe him, Polly," Marshall said, but he

had little hope. If Danny—Rich—had bothered to hide his delight in what he had done to Dylan's life, Marshall might have believed him too.

"Polly, please take the girls upstairs. Let Danny and me talk."

"Stay," Danny ordered. Pressure was building behind Danny's mask. Marshall felt it in his own skull, a sharp bite of need. Polly bristled at Danny's tone. Marshall hoped she would rebel and leave the room with her daughters.

Danny's arm tightened around Gracie. "Polly, did Marsh tell you what happened—almost happened—to his fiancée? He tried to kill a pet dog she had. Why do you think he didn't want Gracie to have a kitten?"

Marshall watched his elder daughter's face close against him. Talk of old murders had not affected her. That was too much like the movies. Killing a little animal was within her child's grasp of consummate evil.

"He drugged the girl with doctored wine and put her dog in the freezer to die," Danny said.

The wine, the peace offering from Danny. That's how he had done it without waking them. Marshall was not even allowed the small triumph of knowing he'd figured it out. Danny just told him.

Danny wanted him to know. Danny wanted credit.

"Hidden your light under a bushel too long, brother?" Marshall asked.

Danny smiled. It might have read true to someone who didn't know him. To Marshall, it stank of mockery. He'd seen it when Rich lectured Charlie about water safety when they'd visited him in the hospital, when he swore to Ricky's parents that he had no idea their son was afraid of snakes.

When he told Dylan how sorry he was that Phil Maris got booted.

"Polly, why did you come back tonight? Why did you bring Emma and Gracie home?" Marshall demanded suddenly.

"Danny got the girls . . ." Polly started to speak. Then her voice trailed off.

"Why did you bring my wife and daughters here tonight?" Marshall asked his brother. This time he did stand, but the way Danny's forearm pressed against Gracie's windpipe kept him from closing the distance between them. "You figured I was knocked out on Ambien. Why would you bring them here when I was out?"

"I was afraid for them, Dyl, afraid you intended to do what you'd done before, clean house, kill everybody but your brother." He smiled his old crooked smile and carefully, gently placed one hand on Gracie's hair. It could have been a caress, but Marshall knew it wasn't.

Danny was going to snap her neck.

## 39

"I've had enough of this," Polly snapped. "Come on girls; let's let Uncle Danny and Marshall work things out between them."

Marshall watched helplessly as she turned and walked toward the bedroom door. "Polly . . ." he began, but what could he say? It's not what you think it is? Better she should leave. He prayed his brother would let Gracie go.

Danny, a half smile on his face, his hand still on Gracie's hair, looked at him over her head.

"Come on, Gracie," Polly said. Emma tugged her mother to a halt. "Not now, honey." Again Emma tugged, and Polly leaned down to catch a whispered confidence.

I'm scared. Daddy's crazy. Was that what his elfin daughter was saying?

Polly lifted her head and looked at Danny standing with his back to her, Gracie in his arms, and then at Marshall standing by the bed. A world of emotion passed through her face. Marshall could read none of it. The look of determination when it was done was unmistakable.

"Danny, darlin', I know you and Marshall have some talking to do," her voice was petal soft and so beseeching Marshall hurt hearing it. "But would you be so kind as to help me get the girls tucked in? What with one thing and another, we would feel more secure if you didn't leave us alone right now." The last words were said in a voice that turned Marshall to water, a voice he doubted many men could stand against.

Danny could, but he didn't. It was the opportunity he'd been waiting for.

"Sure thing. I'd rather you weren't alone. It's just not safe." He winked at Marshall and backed toward the door, Gracie moving awkwardly with him. Before he turned and followed Polly out through the kitchen, he smiled at Marshall, and stroked Gracie's hair. "You wait here," he said.

Marshall knew precisely what he meant.

Then they were gone; he heard the door to the backstairs close behind them.

He could call 911, but if the police came, sirens blazing, Danny would surely kill Polly and the girls. If he followed his brother, he would snap Gracie's neck without a second thought. If he did nothing . . .

If he did nothing, it would happen all over again.

Twitches wracked his body, a seizure of conflicting orders. Shaking, he took one step, then another. From overhead, he heard a faint thump—his kitchen door shutting. Footsteps whispered on the backstairs.

Was Danny coming back, Gracie's slender neck in the vise of arm and hand, listening to see if he followed?

Marshall moved again, softly this time, careful to make no sound on the hardwood floor. In the kitchen, he stopped and listened. Silence was not reassuring. The uneasy twitching of his hands worsened. Marshall was more frightened than he'd been since his parents were killed. He'd grown unaccustomed to physical fear. One of the perks of being a stone-cold killer was that one didn't worry much about other predators. He wasn't afraid for himself, but fear for his family was a solid thing, an entity, pumping so much adrenaline into his body he couldn't stay still.

A crash sounded overhead, and he was out the kitchen door and halfway up the stairs. A noise from below, from the cellar, turned him around. Black and panting, a troll's shape rushed upward.

"Danny," he said, and his brother stopped. The stairwell was dark but for the light from the street coming through the garden window. It was enough to see; Danny had the axe in his hands. Faint light glistened on the planes of his cheeks and across his flat brow. It flashed dully on his teeth as he smiled. Not his matinee idol smile. This smile was detached from his humanity, a cold mockery of amusement, of the weaknesses and failings of others.

"Put it down," Marshall said. His voice shook as badly as his hands.

"It's necessary, brother. You made it necessary. I'm just here to clean up after you. Like always. It's me and you, the Marchand brothers. I told you not to fuck that up. Now you've done it. You've killed them again."

*The Marchand brothers, identical twins, dead at birth*. Marshall took a step down toward Danny.

"No sense in it, brother," Danny warned him. "It's over. It's done. They're already dead. Easy pickings, so soft and sweet. I just got the axe for the finishing touches, history repeating itself. Juries love that. But I won't call the cops, not if you don't force me to."

All Marshall heard was, "They're dead." With the howl of an injured animal, he hurled himself at his brother. The blade of the axe cut into his cheek. He felt the force but not the pain. Before Danny could strike again, Marshall had the handle, his hands between his brother's on the shaft. The stairwell was narrow and twisted; Marshall's shoulders smashed into the walls as they struggled. Danny's face, still lit from the window, was as smooth and calm as if they played at cat's cradle.

Blood poured from Marshall's cheek, onto the back of his hand, leaking onto the axe handle, making the wood slick. His brain burned. His body was a machine gone amok. Another cry burst from him, and he heaved upward with all his strength. Surprise registered on Danny's face as his hands slipped from the newly slickened handle, and he began to fall backwards. Shadows took him, as he slammed onto the lower landing where the steps turned again into the cellar.

Sudden and complete silence filled the space. Then came a whisper, no more than a breath of sound.

"Dylan?"

Axe still in hand, Marshall slowly descended the stairs.

"Rich?" Time folded in on itself. Mack the Giant was but a few minutes away. Rich was crumpled at the bottom of the flight of stairs, his head propped up against the wall at the corner. Light from the window didn't penetrate far enough that Marshall could read his face.

"Help me, Dyl."

Marshall crouched down beside his brother, the space so tight his butt hit one wall and the head of the axe the opposite. "Are you hurt?" It wasn't Marshall asking, it was Dylan. Marshall heard the concern in his voice and hated it.

Dylan loved his brother.

"I broke something. You made me a fucking cripple." Danny started to laugh and the sound seared the last of Dylan from Marshall's soul.

Marshall rose and ran up the stairs toward his apartment, the staccato laughs following him in a poisonous swarm.

## 40

Marshall took the stairs three at a time and slammed into the door to his and Polly's kitchen. Danny had locked it. Marshall swung the axe and heard the frame splinter. A kick, and he was in. Lights were on in the kitchen and dining rooms. Both were empty.

He ran for the stairs and, for once, climbed them without feeling the clamp of Mack's hand on the back of his neck, his rasping insults at every step.

The upstairs hall was empty. His office door stood ajar. The master bedroom door was shut. Adrenaline drained out of him as fast as it had shot through his veins.

Like then, like Dylan, he did not want to see what lay in the bedroom. Visions of black-and-white photographs of his dad in the double bed, his face cloven in two, crowded Marshall's vision, shifted, became Polly's face. Lena appeared, her tiny body destroyed. Lena drifted, became Emma.

Sirens.

The police had arrived. Marshall was holding a bloody axe, the only one standing after the bloodbath. Danny—Rich—lay wounded at the foot of the stairs.

*Like before. Just like before.*

He was still standing there when two young policemen came upstairs, guns drawn.

"Put down the axe! Put down the axe! Put down the axe!" they shouted at him. Marshall turned toward them.

"Put it down," one of them screamed and pulled the trigger.

The sharp report of gunfire released Marshall's fingers. As the bullet smashed into the wall six feet from his head, the axe fell from his hands.

"It's down! It's down! He's dropped it, for Christ's sake!" one cop shouted at the other. Both were kids, both looked scared.

"It's okay," Marshall heard himself say. "You'll need to look in the bedroom. You can handcuff me if it will make you feel better."

His compliance reassured them, allowed them to move from scared to angry.

"You're damn right we'll cuff you. You're goddamn right," the shooter growled as he walked crabwise up, his pistol still held on Marshall.

"Could you radio for an ambulance? My brother's hurt, he's on the backstairs. I think I broke his back."

"Proud motherfucker, aren't you?"

Son of Mack the Giant.

Cuffed and pushed face down on the hall floor, Marshall turned his head to watch them open the bedroom door. It was good to be manacled. Prison would be good, too. No, not good, Marshall thought. Not good or bad. Nothing, really. Just one long unbroken nothing. Without Polly, life was his prison.

He wished they had put him where he wouldn't be able to see in. Because he could. He had to.

"God damn," the cop huffed as the door refused to budge. Son of Mack pulled out his sidearm again, readying to shoot the lock like they did in police shows.

"Oh, stop, would you stop with the gun?" the

other policeman said. "It's not locked. Something's wedged against it."

Both of them put their shoulders into it, and the door opened a foot or so. Another shove and whatever was blocking the way toppled with a crash that reverberated through the floorboards and quivered in Marshall's bones. The door swung wide. The policemen stood to the sides, guns drawn, backs to the wall. Marshall could see in.

Polly was there. And Emma and Gracie. The girls were on the king-sized bed and looked no bigger than fairies. Polly, her face white as wax and hard as granite, was at the foot, standing, facing the door. She had a cell phone in one hand and a carving knife in the other.

Ready to die for her children.

But she hadn't, and Marshall began to cry with relief. In the past weeks, he'd cried more than he had since he'd been little. These tears came easily from joy; they neither blinded him nor choked but flowed warm and comforting.

Polly and the girls were alive. The nothing he'd looked toward would always be peopled. Wherever he served his time, even if he got the death penalty, in his mind he would see them. He would never be alone. Marshall closed his eyes so he would not have to see his wife's hatred, the fear in his children's faces. That way he could remember only that which would allow him to live.

"Put it down. Drop the knife," he heard a cop yell, and there was a clatter.

Marshall's brain shut down, and he welcomed unconsciousness.

# 41

It was spring, and it was raining. Marshall felt the first warm drop hit his face. He didn't know where he was, and he didn't want to know. Here in this place where it rained so gently was where he wanted to stay. Another reality, the one outside this cocoon, pushed at the back of his wakening mind, but he ignored it.

Then he felt a hand on his shoulder and knew he was about to be dragged back. "No," he murmured. "Let me go."

"Shh. Shh. It's going to be okay now." Polly's voice gave Marshall the courage to open his eyes. She sat beside him, brushing the hair from his forehead. "You're in the hospital," she said. "We are all okay, and so are you." He tried to lift his hand to touch her face but hadn't the strength. He closed his eyes because he could no longer keep them open.

"You believed me," Marshall said softly. After a lifetime of living Richard's lies, he didn't know what he believed. "Talk to me," he whispered. "So I'll know you are really here."

Polly's genteel drawl drifted through whatever drugs they'd given him. "No darlin', I didn't believe you. I am truly sorry, but I did not know what to believe. Emma saved us. She saw the lipstick."

"Lipstick," he repeated. The word made no sense, but the sound of his wife's voice was a balm, and he wanted to hear it forever. "Tell me." His voice was mostly air, but she heard him, and he knew she was leaning close. The smell of her hair touched him even through the stink of hospital sterility.

"Yes, lipstick. The story is too long to tell without a glass of wine and a comfortable chair. Suffice to say, I was attacked—not hurt, my love— but I didn't know my assailant. It was at Vondra's apartment, and there was a great deal of red lipstick lying about. Emma saw a streak of red down the back of Danny's shirt, then I knew it was him at Vondra's.

"Emma saw it when the five of us were in Danny's bedroom. We were all caught in that terrible tableau." Polly laughed. "I felt like I was on stage in the last act of *Hamlet*. Once I realized Danny was dangerous, I thought if I could get him to move, to let Gracie come upstairs . . . I thought if he didn't think I knew . . . I don't know exactly what I thought." She finished by kissing him, lightly and sweetly.

"You are a wonder. A night like you must have had, and you still made Danny believe you." Marshall opened his eyes again. The sight of his wife melted away the haze of drugs and horror.

"Darlin', the day I cannot fool one more man one

more time, you may put me out on an ice floe for the polar bears."

She moved away. Marshall felt the cold come between them.

"I came across a carton of papers in the basement. They were notes and article justifying the most awful killings."

"You found them," Marshall said hollowly.

"With a little help from your brother. They were in your handwriting."

"Homework," Marshall said and years of poring over the butchery of the human race, of writing justifications for unjustifiable actions threatened his fragile hope.

Polly waited.

"At least at first it was homework; then, I guess it became habit. When I was at DuWalt . . ."

Polly looked confused. Marshall realized with a pang how much of his life he'd kept secret from her, how much of himself he had kept secret from everyone. The need to tell her everything, every small challenge and terror and delight, share with her the boy who'd been so scared, the boy who'd seen the butterflies and held tightly to his mother's kiss, the teenager who had so little hope he'd let the other boys ink 13½ on his forearm so he couldn't ever forget he had but half a chance in life—less, no chance at all—hit him so hard he laughed. Without warning, the laughter turned to tears. When she knew, she might no longer love him.

"Do I need to slap you, sugar?" Polly asked solicitously.

"No," he said as the tears morphed back into laughter at the touch of her voice on his mind. "I'm not hysterical. At least not too hysterical. DuWalt was where I grew up, a juvenile detention center in Minnesota. I was sent there when I was eleven years old. A year younger than Gracie.

"It's a long, long story," Marshall said, suddenly weary of his past.

"I have read *Coriolanus* seven times and *Bleak House* twice."

God, but he loved her.

"When I was eleven my family was killed: Mom, Dad, Lena—my baby sister—even the cat. They didn't die in a car accident. They were murdered. I was convicted of killing them."

"You were a little boy!" Polly exclaimed in disbelief.

"Yes. The papers dubbed me 'Butcher Boy.' I was the youngest person ever convicted of murder in Minnesota." Marshall couldn't bear to look at his wife's face, but he couldn't look away either. He was waiting for the moment of horror that closed people off from Butcher Boy as surely as if they slammed an iron cell door and shot the bolt. Polly's face showed nothing but concern, and he realized that she was as certain of the end of this story as she was of the last scene in *Coriolanus*. She knew he didn't do it;

she was just waiting to hear how the act played out.

"I love you," he said.

"I know, sugar."

"The tattoo, thirteen and a half, that you've asked about? I got it in DuWalt. I was there for seven years. The staff psychiatrist, a bastard named Kowalski, set me to writing 'homework assignments.' He'd bring me the newspaper clipping of some horrific murder and insist I put myself in the killer's head, think their thoughts, feel their disease on my brain, then tell him the reason I would have done killings like that. I guess he thought if he got me to go down that path enough times 'I'd remember killing my family. Maybe he only wanted me to say I did. The guy wanted to wring a best seller out of me one way or another."

"Now there was a Butcher Boy all grown up," Polly said with disgust. "Why did he have to torture a little boy to get his book?"

"Because I didn't remember doing it; I didn't remember killing my family. I'd had a cold, and Mom gave me medicine, and I slept like the dead. God," he said as the word echoed in his brain.

"It's okay, baby." Polly touched his cheek and the pain of memory lessened.

"The bastard wanted to be the one who made me remember—or made me admit I remembered. So, the homework. By the time he'd gotten on this kick, I'd been in DuWalt just long enough to get punky. Most of the stuff I wrote was just in-your-face rebellion. Since they'd dubbed me Butcher Boy, I'd be Butcher Boy. But those clippings were vicious, brutal things."

"I know. I read them."

Before Marshall recovered from that, Polly said, "I, too, have a long, long story, and I suspect Brother Danny wrote the script from start to finish. Your homework assignments were put in the cellar so I would find them."

Marshall nodded. He knew he should ask for her story, should listen to her. Polly had been hurt so badly by his past. The need to tell overcame the need to listen, and he went on: "The more I read those damn things—those lists of people butchering people—and tried to get into the skins of the killers, the sicker I felt. I knew I'd done it. Enough people tell a kid he did a thing, and he believes he did it. The shrinks came up with half a dozen reasons I didn't remember, and I believed them. Why wouldn't I? I'm eleven, and they're the authorities as far as I knew.

"So I knew I'd killed my mom, my dad, Lena—knew it but I never felt it. Do you know what I mean? I never felt like a killer, like some psycho. I still felt kind of like the kid who played ice hockey, the boy with the fishing pole. God, it was strange. I didn't know it was strange then. It was like air and stone walls, just there. Most of my life I've walked around thinking I was a time bomb that was going to explode and kill everyone around me.

"Tippity—the dog I told you about—she didn't jump in the freezer. She was taped up and thrown in. I figured I'd done it. The night was a blank, just like when I was a kid. I figured getting close to Elaine triggered it somehow." Saying the words aloud, Marshall realized he'd not "figured" that. Danny had told him that, and Danny had brought them a bottle of champagne that had knocked two adults out. It was drugged. Danny. The drug dealer of Le Cure.

"He was doing it," he rasped, his throat dry. "Danny was doing it. Danny was giving me drugs and moving things. My brother. My brother." Marshall felt his face turning inside out.

Polly's cool fingers and murmured endearments brought him back to himself.

"Just like he did it before?"

"Yes." Marshall stared at the shadows he and Polly cast on the white wall of the hospital room. He was seeing two boys, Dylan and Richard. "He must have been born with something broken inside of him. It's no easier for me to see him doing it than it was to see myself doing it.

"He was going to do it again. To you and the girls." The cold in his soul was deep. "I don't want to hate him," he said quietly.

For a while, they sat without speaking. Marshall's breathing evened out. His thoughts slid from frantic to torpid. Polly held his hand.

"You asked if I believed you," Polly said.

Marshall grew very still. He wanted, needed her

to believe in him—to believe in him when he was unbelievable.

"It was not merely the lipstick on your brother's shirt—though that had a comforting concreteness about it. It was partly that I did not believe Danny. I wish I could say I believed you, but, except to the writers of sonnets, love does not show one the way. When one has children, one cannot have faith where they are endangered. There are some mistakes a mother could not live with. Had I been twenty or even thirty, I might have been able to love blindly, unconditionally. No more. There are two conditions: Emma and Gracie.

"A part of me believed that I was not fooled by you. Part of me knows anyone can be fooled." She ran her fingertips down his cheek. His sadness trailed after her touch. "I am sorry, my darling. I cannot even apologize for not believing in you utterly and without question; that kind of love—faith—must be learned young. My early childhood instruction was centered around how to keep little girls alive."

Marshall let that soak in. The knowledge that she had entertained the thought he was a beast and a killer did not hurt him as much as he'd thought it would. He had not believed in himself. He'd believed in Danny.

"That's best," he said finally. "Civilized behavior is built on conditions. I love both your conditions." "They don't seem to be too traumatized," Polly said. "I hope to keep it that way."

"There will be newspaper articles about this, about the old murders, about who I am, and what Richard did, and what Danny did," Marshall warned. "The case was national news at the time. It might be hard to shield them through that."

"Surely the rebuilding of New Orleans is sufficiently ubiquitous in the press that they will not have space for an old story," Polly said with a smile. "We can hope most of our neighbors will be too occupied with their own dramas to read them."

"I'll read them," Marshall said. "I'll read them and try to figure out why, what makes a killer desire the kill, what made my brother take my family's lives and, then, in every way he could, take mine. Homework. I've done it for so long, trying to find myself."

"Well, my darling, you can quit looking. Gracie, and Emma, and I have found you."

## 42

Richard Raines was sentenced to life without parole. Because his injury had left him unable to use the lower half of his body until the swelling around his spinal cord went down—if it went down—he was put in the maximum-security hospital ward of the U.S. penitentiary in Pollock, Louisiana.

Twice a month, Marshall made the drive to Pollock to visit his brother.

Danny showed every indication that he enjoyed

these exchanges. The allotted hour was spent telling Marshall what had been done to his life. Danny used the time to talk about how he had used and used up Vondra, set her as a watchdog on Marshall's office, related Polly's secrets to her, and set her up as Polly's tarot reader; he described in detail how he'd told the warden Phil Maris was a pedophile and had raped Dylan, how he'd killed Phil, Sara, and several others. Some murders he made up just for the pleasure he felt in hurting the brother to whom he had given everything and who had abandoned him.

Marshall listened but, except for learning Phil had been killed, he was unaffected. At the telling—and retelling—of each horrific incident, he was reassured of his own innocence, his own sanity. And that of his wife. The tarot reader had been primed by Danny to wait for Polly, so the dissolution of Marshall's marriage could be set in motion.

Even after he no longer needed this assurance, he still made the drive. He did it because Rich had done it for Dylan, because Dylan loved his brother. And he did it because Danny was confined to a wheelchair, and Danny's lack of control—of himself and, most sharply felt, of others—was torture for him. Marshall drove out to see Danny this way because Marshall hated Danny.

Dylan Raines's name was cleared, but Marshall chose to keep Marchand.

It sounded better with the name Pollyanna.

Richard Raines. Killed mother, father, sister and the family cat.

"We get to the upstairs hall, and Pat finds a light switch. You're not going to want to print this next part, but by God this is how it was. In the middle of the rug—one of those long narrow hall rugs—was a baby, a little girl no more than two, and she had been cut in half. I about puked, and Pat looked like he was going to.

"We hear movement downstairs and think maybe it's the killer. Or somebody hurt. Pat goes first.

"In the back bedroom, there's two boys. At first, we thought both of them had been murdered. The older boy nearly had his leg cut off and had bled so much he was the color of a sheet of paper. The other boy was still in his bed, but at first we didn't even know it was a kid, you know? It just looked like a bucket of red paint poured over some blankets.

"Turns out this kid—the one in the bed—has got nothing wrong with him; he's just sleeping like a baby. Or that's what we thought at the time. The ambulance rolls up so there's paramedics stomping all over everything trying to save the kid with the chopped up leg when this little bast**rd wakes up from his beauty sleep. He sees his brother being carried out more dead than alive, and he starts laughing like a hyena."

# EPILOGUE

Homework? It's bullshit; you know that don't you? God knows I read enough of Dylan's homework. My baby brother is like the rest of you sheep. Pathetic. I'll tell you why I did it—why we do it. Because the sheep won't.

There is not a man in the world—and I mean a man; women are sheep's sheep—that doesn't want to be me, to do what I do. You all want to feel the kill, feel blood run on your hands. The asshole at the office, the fuck who cuts you off in traffic, the mealy-mouthed waitress spilling hot coffee in your crotch—you would love to watch those miserable little lives wink out.

Man was not evolved to love his neighbor. He evolved to kill his neighbor, and rape his neighbor's wife, and take his neighbor's property.

You want to know why I kept Vondra around? Because she lied for me on the stand, and I was grateful? Don't kid yourself. Vondra was useful. She watched Marsh's office for me. Did the tarot thing. I kept her around because she reminded me why I am who I am. Why I do what I do. The world needs people like me to rid it of people like Vondra, people like you.

Jack the Ripper. He did London a favor. Cleaned poxy whores off the streets. Dahmer got rid of fags half the Christian Right wanted dead; they wanted to do it, but they didn't have the balls. Dahmer was out of his fucking mind, but he did it. We are the world's garbagemen. Pest control.

I cleaned house that night. Got rid of the weak-kneed jackasses trying to run my life. Mom doted on her baby Dylan. I scared the shit out of her. She'd look at me, and I'd see this cold fear, where with baby brother it was all hearts and flowers. Frank—Dad—decided I might fit in better at this school for boys. Discipline. Structure. Challenge. Religious orientation. Spiritual guidance. Code words for "lock the kid up and brainwash him."

I wasn't warm and fuzzy like little Dylan. Frank looked at me, and it was the old wolf looking at the young wolf; he knew I'd take him as soon as I was strong enough. Except he wasn't a wolf. He'd let the teachers, and preachers, and other bullshit artists castrate him. So he wanted to castrate me.

That night was the night I was born again in the blood, as the Bible beaters say. Dylan was knocked out on cough syrup, the old fashioned kind with codeine; Lena was down. I'd been planning it since I was seven. Six. We are born to kill the way the wolf puppy is born to kill its meat. For a while it's all play—growling and pouncing—and then, one day, a primal urge kicks in, and the puppy tears the throat out of a squirrel, then a rabbit, then a fawn, then, when it's grown, deer and moose.

You dickless wonders, you sheep, let that instinct be beaten out of you. But you miss it. God, do you miss it. You glut yourselves on movies about killers, books about killers. You worship the killers because you want to kill. You need to. But you just watch.

I lived my life the way I was born to, not in the pen with my woolly, bleating brothers.

The plan was to kill Frank and Mom while they slept. I nearly freaked when Mom woke up and started gobbling like a turkey, then sprinted off, Frank's blood dripping off her. Then, she's running like a crazy woman down the upstairs hall, her night-gown flapping, and her hands flailing. That was worth the price of admission. I got to laughing so hard, it took me nearly five minutes to shut her up.

Lena was nothing.

The cat was just for fun.

I'm coming up from the cellar, there's blood on me, and all of a sudden the light goes on at the Werner's next door, and there's Vondra gaping at me like a landed fish. At the time, I figured she knew what was going on, but now I doubt it. Anyway, I fucked her to shut her up. I could have killed her then, but it worked out better keeping her around.

The only major screwup was my leg. I thought I'd killed myself. That turned out in my favor, too. The buffoons on the police force were so blown away, they couldn't bring themselves to look at anything too close. Dylan was there, he had the axe and the blood, and they fell all over themselves to hang him.

I'd planned on killing Dylan when I did the rest

of the family. He was a huge pain in the ass. And there was the money issue. Mom and Frank's estate would be divided. We were well enough off I could have made do with half, but it would have been a waste to give it to Dylan. What would he use it for? Braces for his kids?

I could have pinned the deaths on Dylan dead or alive—same story, only this time I hit my brother too hard, and brother dies in his jammies—but after I hit him, I thought I'd broken his neck without killing him. I figured he'd be a quadriplegic, or at the least a paraplegic. I would have enjoyed finding out how the kid everybody thought was God's gift to the world would deal with peeing into a tube for the rest of his life.

I'm the one ended up pissing in a tube. You fucking sheep can bleat your little sheep laughs, but it doesn't change anything. I owned Dylan for forty years. We were twins. We were closer than twins. Dylan was me.

That was the thing; I made him me.

## Center Point Publishing

600 Brooks Road ● PO Box 1
Thorndike ME 04986-0001 USA


**(207) 568-3717**


**US & Canada:**
**1 800 929-9108**
www.centerpointlargeprint.com